THE NOCTURNE ABYSS

DAKOTA WILDE

CONNECT WITH DAKOTA

If you love this book, be sure to join my facebook group , Dakota Wilde's Hellions.

You can also stay up to date on future books by signing up for my newsletter here, or by giving me a follow on Instagram!

If you find a typo, please feel free to email hadespublishingco@gmail.com

Please check the content warnings before reading at www.dakotawildeauthor.com

MASKS & THEIR POWERS

1. The Stag- Power to Animate Bones
2. The Crown- Power to Create Light
3. The Floral- Power to Create Flowers
4. The Onyx- Power to Control Shadows
5. The Bird- Power of Flight
6. The Gear- Power to Manipulate Metal
7. The Triplet- Power to Duplicate
8. The Medusa- Power to turn things to Stone
9. The Pyro- Power of Fire
10. The Timepiece- Power to stop time
11. The Spider- Power to create webs
12. The Enforcer- Power of strength
13. The Manipulator- Power to influence emotions
14. The Ghost- Power of invisibility
15. The Mender- Power to heal
16. The Siren- Power to control liquid

*To those who found their light in the darkness, may you burn so
bright that no one will ever be able to take that part of you again.*

CHAPTER 1
ODESSA

A knock on the door was all it took to completely dismantle my life. The Summons arrived on a Tuesday at half past three. I'd just poured myself a shot of espresso when the mail monkey knocked four times on our purple painted door. Now, most people wouldn't be alarmed by a simple knock on the door, but today was no ordinary day. Today was the annual summons from Nocturne Abyss, the deadly game created by the God of Death, that once invited to play there was no refusal. And a knock on the door could only mean one thing— someone in this house was being required by law to play the game of the gods.

Knots twisted in my stomach as I walked nervously to open the door. Sweat gathered in my palms as I turned the handle of the door— heart beating wildly inside of my chest. Maybe it was a mistake? They'd gotten the wrong house number and were looking for directions.

But as the door opened wider, I saw that I wasn't mistaken.

There was a small grey haired mail monkey decked out in its finest red and white uniform, with a small hat to match. The typical garb of official delivery members. It was waiting with a scroll in its small furry hands. The parchment was tied with a red ribbon around it that was gently blowing in the wind as if it belonged in someone's hair and not wrapped around the offensive offering.

"Good day, miss," the monkey stated in a cheery tone.

"Good day," I croaked out, sounding as if someone was squeezing my voice box. The paper found its way into my hands, and I nearly dropped it as if I were being handed a ticking bomb. The mail monkey smiled at my misfortune, tipped its hat, and scurried down the lane— I assumed to go and ruin someone else's day.

Once inside, I stared at the paper, running my fingers over it, wondering who it could be for. My brother was conscripted into the army and set to head off to training in a few weeks' time, so it couldn't be for him. My parents were far too old being over the age of thirty, so that only left me and my sister, Marley.

"Who was at the door, Pigeon?" My father called out from his workshop. My parents called me Pigeon because they said as a baby, I used to squawk like one when I cried. They loved to tell the story about how they had to keep the windows closed, otherwise I would call whole flocks over into the house. And the name stuck ever since. Everyone else called me Odessa, or Des for short.

"Mail monkey," I replied, feeling dazed with worry at the document in my hands. It felt heavy and rough about the edges.

"At this time of day, but it's—" He walked out into the

living room and stopped talking the moment he saw what was clutched in my hands. His apron still hung around his waist with smudges of clay stuck to it and his nearly gray hair was tied back with a black leather ribbon to keep stray pieces off his sweaty face. As one of the most esteemed potters in Paris, his workload was always full. He never complained though, because it kept food on the table and a roof over our heads.

"Let me see that," he said, grabbing the parchment from my hands. I let him take it, too terrified to look at the contents. Though, a heavy sense of dread was hanging about my shoulders like a coat warning me that I already knew the answer to my unasked question.

The red ribbon holding it together was discarded, wafting onto the floor appearing as if it were a slash of blood staining the white tile, feeling like a bad omen of what was to come.

My father read over the summons, face white with terror and lips moving as he skimmed over the words to himself more than once.

"What does it say?" The suspense was killing me, and I had to know what was making him look the way he was.

When he finally lifted his gaze to me, I knew without a word being uttered that my fate had been sealed. Still, I took the parchment for myself and looked upon the black ink scrawled across the paper, confirming what I already knew— that the trajectory of my life was forever altered in that moment. I was officially summoned to play at The Nocturne Abyss. I heard myself reading aloud from the paper, as if my mouth hadn't caught up to my brain just yet and needed to audibly speak the words in order for me to fully believe my bad luck.

"Odessa Devereaux, you are cordially required to attend

The Nocturne Abyss. ~~Beware~~ that not all who play will make it out alive. You are to be escorted from your home tomorrow morning. Be ready to receive the god's guards or face the consequences. All family members who are able bodied are required to accompany you for the parade. You may bring one piece of luggage for clothing and toiletries. No more than one bag is allowed. Weapons are not permitted and will be subject to your immediate dismissal from the games. It is an honor to be chosen as one of the summoned. You will not be allowed to transfer your summons to any person or animal. Once the summons has been received, you are considered an official contestant and must act accordingly. Best of luck." As I read the words, a dark winged figure appeared at the top in a ring of fire, eating up every inch of the scroll while I read line by line, until all that was left was my calling card. My confirmation. An Ace of Hearts sitting in the palm of my hand with the date of the competition etched into the upper right corner and my name scrolled in gold ink across the black background. I had one day. One day to gather my things and say goodbye to my family before I was escorted, whether I wanted to go or not, down into the catacombs where the games were held.

"Des? What's going on?" my sister Marley asked, having been upstairs. I didn't even hear her come in.

"I got summoned." The disbelief was evident in my tone. Though, logically, I knew there was always a chance, but in the way that you knew you could get struck by lightning or win the lottery. It was a distant possibility. The odds were one in a million, and yet fate had called me by name.

"What an honor!" she squealed. While I was the more timid one, always playing by the rules, Marley lived for adventure. A part of me thought they had chosen the wrong sister. Marley would probably win the entire tournament with her eyes closed and an arm tied behind her back. "What mask do you think you'll pick?"

"That depends when my name is called, Mar. You know how it works. First come, first serve."

"Right, but it's good to strategize just in case you're the first one called with your choice of masks at your fingertips. Just think, you could be walking away a winner this time next week. Imagine, all that money! Imagine having a power!" Her large brown eyes that matched mine, shimmered with the hopeful possibility I wish I could muster, but all I could feel was dread. The death toll Nocturne took each year was enough to make even the most cunning and agile warriors wary of the games. But Marley was always dreaming of bigger and better things, no matter the cost.

"Have you told Maman yet?" she asked.

"No, we just received it," father said, sounding every bit as crestfallen as I felt inside. He stood there, hands on his hips looking lost in his own house. With my brother, Jean, about to go off to training, and mama's health quickly declining, this news had come at the worst possible time. I didn't know if I was more upset for myself, or for my family that I'd be leaving them behind. Perhaps forever.

"Well, get ready for the waterworks. Let's go over what you're going to pack later, because we can't have you showing up looking a wreck. Oh, this is just so exciting. I'm a little jealous, I'm not going to lie," Marley said, practically skipping out into the kitchen to grab herself a snack. She was acting as if I'd been asked out by a cute guy and had to pick out a sexy outfit and completely oblivious to how dad and I were feeling. But that's typical Marley. If it didn't affect her directly, she didn't pay much attention. While I loved her dearly, she could also get on my nerves.

She arrived back in the living room with a bag of chips in her hands, chomping loudly on the cheddar flavored snack. "If you die, I get your room though, okay?"

"Marley, leave it okay? I'm going upstairs to tell Mama," I snapped. The words 'if you die' spun around my brain on an endless loop. My thoughts were a vortex, tipping between panic and numbness. The appearance of the summons changed everything. While I'd been planning for my graduation in just a month's time and a wedding next summer, I hadn't accounted for this. I was so close to achieving all my dreams and now, my future was uncertain. Even if I won, I wouldn't be allowed back to finish the remaining month. Magicks, haven't ever mixed with us at university. They kept themselves locked away in the First Arrondissement, while the rest of us were divided in the lower Arrondissements.

Going to break the news to my maman felt as if I were watching myself climb the stairs from above. With new eyes, I took in my surroundings that I'd been accustomed to seeing every day. I went past the many photographs of our family that lined the damask wallpaper, a mosaic of our happiest moments. How blissful we used to be before my maman's illnesses. My fingers lingered on the wall, feeling the aged paper beneath my skin. This house was where I grew up. Where I ran to when I had a good or bad day. I knew it would always welcome me. But now? It felt like this house was my past. A memory that was slipping through the cracks of time.

My parent's room was down the hall on the second floor, the furthest door on the right, tucked away from where my brother's and my sister's rooms were located. My room was on the third floor with a slanted ceiling and small balcony that afforded me a view of the city. If you strained your neck, you could just make out the top of the Eiffel Tower. And while our home was not large by any means, the walk to deliver the news to my mother seemed to take ages. My feet feeling full of lead with every step.

"Pigeon is that you?" Maman's frail voice called out from behind her door.

My stomach twisted into knots knowing that I was about to break her fragile heart. And after all the illnesses she'd fought off, I worried that the news would kill her.

I peeked my head into the door and found her laying on her side, wearing day old pajamas while tucked into her bed. Her brown hair tangled in a messy braid, tucked to the side of her head. There were several gray hairs that framed her oval-shaped face, accentuating the dull, sallow tone her skin had taken on. I remembered a time when she wasn't this way. When she was full of life and her smiles came easy. Her body was strong once, and her presence one of vivacity. Now a smile seemed to make her weary.

"My darling. Who was at the door?"

I winced. She sounded tired today. More tired than usual.

Cautiously, I ambled over to her and sat at the edge of the bed. Though it was clear she hadn't showered, she still managed to smell of lavender. A comforting scent that always made me think of her.

"I have some news, Maman," I said, taking her thin hand in

mine. A dark shadow was permanently etched under her eyes. In this lighting, her skin had a translucent sheen to it, and her once bright green eyes now looked partially sunken in as if someone had pressed their thumbs to her eye sockets. Her illnesses had wrecked her body and there was nothing conventional medicine could do. The doctors said only a magical cure would be able to make a difference in her condition, giving her only six more months to live, if that. While my father made decent money, we couldn't afford the cost of a healer from the 1st arrondissement where those who were lucky enough to possess magick resided. Plus, many who acquired that power were forced to the battlefields to use their magick to heal what they could of the soldiers who fought to protect our city from being invaded. While the gods were powerful, they spent a lot of their time squabbling amongst each other, resulting in nothing getting done, and our people suffering because of it.

My mother's brittle bones squeezed around my hand and their gaunt like feel jarred me back to the present. Gods, when did she become so thin? Was she like this yesterday and I just was too busy to notice? By chance if I were to somehow make it through the games with my life, would it even be in time? Perhaps winning the game was our only chance at saving her.

My tongue felt thick in my mouth as I attempted to form the words. "I was summoned today."

Her face contorted into one of heartbreak like I knew it would. Those green eyes of hers shimmered with tears dripping fat, wet splotches onto the cream-colored pillowcase below. While my sister Marley was constantly annoyed at our Mama's emotions being so close to the surface, I found it endearing.

Maman was the kind to feel things deeply and was never afraid to express exactly how she felt.

My thumb ran along her paper-thin cheek, chasing away the tears that have gathered there. "It's okay. I'm— I'm going to be fine."

"Odessa, I need you to hear me. I know that you like to keep to yourself. You tend to try and keep the peace, always doing what's asked of you. You're a sweet, kindhearted girl. And I love you. But I need you to promise me something."

"Anything."

"I need you to be ruthless, my darling girl. Be ruthless and unapologetic in how you need to survive. Come back to us, no matter what it takes. You have a strength inside that I don't think you're aware of, but it's there, waiting for you to grab hold of it," she began to cough fitfully, a slight rattle banging about in her lungs as she did. Was this going to be the last time I ever saw my mother? I couldn't accept that.

"Promise me that you'll fight."

How could I refuse her? "I promise, Mama."

"Good. Come here and let me hold you." And I let her. I curled up against her small body as if I were a child once more. To be honest, in that moment I needed her comfort. Maybe that was selfish of me, but I don't think you ever truly grow out of needing your mother. I might have been all of two and twenty years, but the fear of what's to come had me feeling vulnerable and small.

She fell asleep quickly, but I stayed listening to her shallow breaths, bargaining with the gods to give me more time with her. To walk out of Nocturne as a champion. I had to. I had to return, or my family would be losing us both soon, and I don't think they'd be able to survive that.

CHAPTER 2
ODESSA

"Theo, you're not listening. I don't have a choice." My fiancé of two years sat across from me looking angrier than I'd ever seen him, and I'd known him my whole life. His dark brown eyes were rimmed red with tears and there was a new hole in the wall of my parent's living room that left its mark on his knuckle. "I can't just run away. They would track me down and kill me for deserting. Then they'd slaughter my family. That's how it works. I'm not risking my family for a miniscule chance at freedom."

"Better them than you. You won't survive this, Dessy. You're too mild mannered and timid. Which I love about you, but it doesn't serve your best interests when trying to survive in Nocturne. You know the stories as well as I do about what goes on down there. Do you really think you could kill another person?"

His words were all ones I'd thought myself but hearing him doubt me like this felt wrong. Like a slap across the face, making my stomach sour and my anger rise. I could never do something to put my own family in danger, even if there were a way out and I could escape. Their lives meant more to me than my own. He should know that about me by now. Deserting was a sure way to have the gods condemn us all. Even Theo. They'd go for anyone close to me.

"I think people never know what they're capable of until they're faced with no other option."

"Don't be naive, Odessa. That sounds like a lie you're telling yourself to make yourself feel better. To play in Nocturne is to sign your death to the gods, and you know it."

I swallowed hard as he jumped up to pace the length of my family's living room. He'd been here plenty of times before, but I felt as if I were seeing him clearly for the first time. Our parents had pushed us together, and we were on track to get married after graduation. They'd arranged our union early on in my life, and I'd always known we would end up together. While my feelings for Theo were true, I couldn't help but wonder if there was something more that I was missing. Some vital experience that a carefully planned life wouldn't offer. My fingers twisted the simple ring with a small diamond that he'd given me two years ago when he'd asked for my hand. It felt tight around my skin.

"Theo, there's nothing that can be done. You know that. I don't wish to leave on bad terms, please."

His face looked crestfallen. "You're right. Why don't I take you to the gods' temple? We could pray for your safe return from the gods."

Internally, I felt annoyed by his suggestion. Theo knew that I adamantly avoided that place at all costs. The knowledge of how the gods played with our lives like we were nothing more than their playthings irked me. I'd never been one to give my loyalty to the gods, but my family and his were staunch believers. I knew it upset Theo that I didn't hold the same beliefs, and he was praying that one day I would. I didn't see that happening anytime soon.

He sat next to me then. He was so close that I could feel the body heat and anger wafting up from him. But it was the look on his earnest face swayed me to agree.

"Fine. We can go."

He grabbed me by my hand, his fingers fitting awkwardly against mine, as we set out down the road with the sun quickly setting behind us.

My legs were burning from climbing up all the stairs to the highest point in all of Paris. It was said that before the gods took over our world, us mere mortals created false gods to whom these buildings once belonged to. All evidence of them had been long wiped clean and the buildings were rebuilt with respect to the real gods that now ruled over us. The legend was that the gods had come down from the heavens after witnessing our strife amongst each other, in order to bring peace to our lands. They'd managed to set up a perimeter around our city, closing the gates off to any outsiders. To get into our borders, their approval must be given, and it wasn't given easily.

Personally, I didn't like the idea of being cut off from the rest of the world. But the gods had most people believing that it was for our own good. Many who lived in my city had become fearful of the outsiders because of their beliefs. We were constantly being told news of another war, another attack, another close call that the gods had saved us from. Our newspapers were littered with such headlines. Though, the more I paid attention to the gods actions, the more I wondered about the validity of their statements. Especially once I found a few books that told a completely different story.

I'd once discovered an atlas hidden in the school's library where it showed images of what the world used to look like. My city was practically untouched from the photos it showed, but seeing the places outside of here was like peeking into the forbidden. There was so much beauty and wonder that had existed in far off lands. I wondered if it was still true. If there really was such a thing as a Grand Canyon, or Cliffs of Moher, the Taj Mahal. I'd never told anyone what I had found and tucked the book back right where I'd found it. When I came back to look again a week later, it was gone. Then there were the journals of a monk that had jotted down what he called an invasion that had been printed and plastered all over our school's walls. I'd only read a few paragraphs before they were ripped down and Jenson Hellips was escorted off the premises, never to be seen or heard from again.

We knew that to question anything, would result in our same fate. So, I kept my reservations mostly to myself. Theo, however, had picked up on my lack of enthusiasm when it came to discussing the gods. He said he pitied my lack of faith, but was willing to commit to me anyways, certain that with time and prayer that I would change. We had an obligation to our parent's wishes after all.

The Sacré-Cœur, or the gods' temple, looked over all of Paris. It was a steadfast reminder of the gods' control, and the way that it leered over the city made us feel how insignificant we were in comparison. But I had to admit that climbing the steps to the temple granted us a breathtaking view of the city below.

Theo barely glanced over at me as we walked together, which was fine by me. His attitude over the summonings had pissed me off. It's not like I chose to be summoned. It was out of my control, and if I did have a choice, obviously, I wouldn't be going.

The temple was cold and nearly empty by the time we arrived— I assumed due to preparation of tomorrow's celebrations. It was an imposing structure with a large dome cutting into the quickly darkening sky above, and two smaller domes cast on each side. Inside was lined with lifelike carvings of all the gods, all made to be twice the height of a mortal. Dia, The Goddess of Spring, Axis, The God of War, Symph, The Goddess of Music, and so on were all placed in succession along the walls, looking down at their doting subjects. All exquisitely made with care and exceptional detail. The statues were depicted with a golden mask that represented their power. The same kind of masks we'd be forced to choose between come tomorrow. My stomach twisted anxiously as I contemplated which I would be saddled with as I passed them all. Would it be the power to grow flowers, or the power of strength? The power of invisibility, or even necromancy to move the millions of bones buried in the catacombs? I took a long breath in to calm my quickly spiraling thoughts.

As I walked by silently, I noticed there were some statues that had been left offerings at their base. Flowers, jewelry, meaningless trinkets to beg for their favor. The largest of all the statues was of course Reaper, The God of Death, who was said to be the most powerful of all the gods. His statue was featured prominently in the middle of a dais with a ray of light illuminating the stone. It looked as if he had been frozen in time for how lifelike the carving was. Like any moment he might blink and break free. The chiseled abs were on full display with nothing but a scrap of fabric covering his lower front.

There was one notable difference with his statue. Where the other deities were left tokens and offerings, some with so many that they were spilling onto the floor, his base where offerings should be, was bare.

I don't know what made me do it other than it felt wrong to see his left out in such a way, but I found myself kneeling at the bottom of his statue, head bowed and uttering the words of respect.

"Oh God of Death, the mighty, powerful, and revered, please grant me the desires of my heart." I slipped off the bracelet on my left hand that I'd always worn. It was made with small round beads of moonstone that were held together by a black string. The stones clinked loudly in the empty church as they dropped onto the statue's empty offering bowl.

"It's bad luck to invoke the God of Death, Dessa. Gods, you should know that," Theo chided me, gripping me hard by my elbow.

"For someone so concerned about the gods, you sure don't seem too concerned to be cursing in their temple," I spat back, my irritation at an all-time high. "I didn't even want to come here in the first place, and now you're mad at how I chose to show my devotion?"

"Let's just go," Theo said, glancing around worried about the scene I was causing. His fingers dug into my skin, and I glared up at him, yanking my arm out his grasp.

"There's no one here to impress right now, Theo." He looked as if I'd just slapped him, but I couldn't find it in me to care. Not when he was acting so awful, and I was over his temper tantrum. Too exhausted by the day's emotions to have to cater to him as well. "You're right let's just go. I promised Marley she could help me pack."

I turned on my heel and stormed off not caring if he followed me or not. His cries to stop, fell deaf on my ears. How could he be so selfish? Exiting the temple, I was greeted with the sight of the sun setting over the entire city. It felt as if the whole of Paris was holding its breath, waiting for tomorrow and what was to come. I came to a stop at the edge where a wire fence had been erected in a crisscross fashion, my anger rolling around tight in my chest. Lovers from all walks of life hung metal locks engraved with their initials on the fence, promising their love would be as eternal as the locket they'd fastened to the structure. There were so many that the fence curved from all the weight. My fingers clutched a random blue one and my thumb worked its way over the thin initials. E+M, it read. I wondered who they were and if their love withstood the test of time. Theo and I had never brought our own locket, and I'd never wanted to. Now, as I stood here with the tangible weight in my hand, the thought of wanting more bubbled violently to the surface. For the first time in my twenty-two years, I wanted something for myself.

I'd always slunk in the shadows of my family, being the diligent, quiet one. With Marley constantly getting into trouble and Jean being the athletic star, I was content to watch them shine. I did my duty of what was expected of me, going to school and being with a respectable partner. Never asking or wanting for anything that would cause waves. But now, I was singled out. Forced to examine the quiet life I'd become so accustomed to. Maybe Marley had a point, I just wish I didn't feel so utterly frightened by the prospect of participating in Nocturne. Only one could win the games, but could that be me? The odds were stacked against me, having never done anything remotely dangerous in my life. And now I would be venturing to one of the deadliest places someone could go— straight into the God of Death's dominion. The catacombs.

On the horizon, near the gates they'd erected far before I was born, movement caught my attention. A procession of black clad carriages being led into the city by what looks like a host of military members walked slowly past the large portcullis. I could tell they were military because of the distinct banners they carried with the gods' sigil— a stark white rib cage against a black background. I wondered at who was being escorted in with such protection. Someone important most likely. Maybe even the God of Death himself coming in from the battlefields to revel in the games he created. Knowing that all the gods would be invested in our progress set my already fragile nerves on fire.

"Dessa, please. I'm sorry," Theo said breaking my thought process and sounding out of breath. "I'm only thinking of you. You mean everything to me, you know that. Please forgive me. Let's forget I ever said anything."

I turned to take him in and caught his earnest expression. He grabbed my left hand running a finger over the engagement ring and brought my hand up to his lips. "I can't imagine a future without you in it."

My stomach clenched at his words. Picturing any future without him seemed unimaginable. We'd known each other forever. I'd always known that we'd end up together. It was what was expected. Only now my carefully planned out future was completely blown up by one singular paper. Perhaps it was the gods' way of reminding me that no matter how much I wanted my life to be my own, they were still in control.

"Fine. Let's get back before it's dark," I said as I reluctantly gave in to his pleas. Theo smiled, his cheeks dimpling with a level of charm that could melt away a glacier, and he led us down the steps. As we walked, I glanced back at the temple, watching the dimming light hit the tip of the spire feeling a chill in the air hit my skin and sent up one last hope that I would make it through Nocturne's deadly game. But even as I said my prayer, I couldn't shake the feeling that even if I were to make it through the games alive, nothing would ever be the same again.

MARLEY WAS WAITING for me in the doorway when I got back. I gave Theo a swift peck on the cheek, more so out of habit than anything. I was still so angry at him for the way he'd acted, but I was leaving tomorrow and didn't want to go on bad terms.

"Theo," Marley acknowledged with a chill to her voice.

"Marley." Theo replied with the same tone.

Those two had never really gotten along, and it made things awkward for me every time we were in the same vicinity.

"I'll see you in the morning. I'll be waiting for you by the entrance to the catacombs," he said before disappearing down the street. As soon as he was out of sight, I felt like I could finally breathe again.

"It's about time, come on. I've already gone through your whole closet and mine to pick out your Nocturne outfits. I was thinking we'd go with something simple for the parade, and then you can borrow my new black dress for the masquerade," she said, pulling me into the house.

Our home was a modest one, situated amongst a row of buildings that led up to the artist's district. It was rumored that long ago famous painters dwelled amongst these very buildings, but their works had been long lost to time. Their names scrubbed from the collective memory along with many other truths about our past. We were conditioned from a young age not to question what we were told, and those that didn't fall in line were punished for all to see. Their bodies strapped naked in front of the Notre Dame, their hands and legs tied wide as the sun burned every bit of them. Passersby would throw their garbage at them, or worse. Some would urinate on them or spit as they were made to endure the humiliation. The mayor held the public spectacles once a month to set an example of such prisoners. I always avoided the area during those times, not wanting to see the horror the prisoners were forced to endure.

Jean was helping Father in his workshop and Maman had long been asleep. I followed Marley, who was chattering a million miles a minute about the games. My head was too fuzzy to pay much attention, and I only caught every other word that she was saying.

Upstairs in my room looked like a bomb had gone off. Clothes were strewn about everywhere, and in the center of my bed was a suitcase propped open with several outfits hanging out like limp spaghetti noodles.

I pinched the bridge of my nose in frustration as Marley bounced on the balls of her feet with excitement. "Ta-da!"

"Wow... this is—"

"A mess, I know, but look!" Marley grabbed one of the dresses and draped it over my body, turning me to look in the full-length mirror. "Doesn't it just make your dark eyes pop? Put it on! I want to see how it fits."

Obliging, I turn to undress and step into the cumbersome looking thing. Once it was zipped in the back by Marley, I marveled at my reflection in surprise. Normally, I wore modest clothing. No frills or anything fancy. But this? This was a dress fit for a queen. Its sweetheart neckline plunged far lower than I ever dared to show. The waist was trim about the middle, accentuating the natural curves in my hips. The fabric flared out in a bell shape like I'd been plucked from the Notre Dame itself. The bottom was covered in a fine lace and the black material glittered against the dim light as I moved. My hands slid over the dress in awe. It looked as if the starry night sky had spilled onto my body in an array of twinkling starlight. I'd never felt so beautiful in all my life.

"Marley, this is stunning. Where did you even get it?"

She shrugged her shoulder. "I found it at the thrift store and was saving it for a special occasion."

"Thank you," I said, taking her hands in mine. "Really, this is going to be perfect for the masquerade. Help me get it off though? I want to try and get some sleep if I can before tomorrow, and I still need to finish packing. You didn't put any contraband in here, did you?"

Marley dramatically pressed her hand to her chest. "*Moi*?" It was typical of our city to speak in a mixture of English and French, sometimes melding the two in the same sentence. The elders, however, refused to adopt English, and spoke in French only.

"Yes, you. I don't want to get in trouble if you slipped a knife in there. You know how strict the rules are."

Marley rolled her eyes and patted me on the top of my head. "You're so dramatic. My little rule follower."

I glowered at her, and she put her hands up in surrender. "I swear. It's just the essentials. Clothes, hairbrush, a photo of the family. Honest. Now turn around so I can unzip you."

I did as she asked and tried hard not to worry that this might be my last night with my sister. Thinking like that would only get me more anxious than I already was, and possibly killed. No, I needed to focus on what I could which was putting these clothes away, finish my packing, and try to prepare myself for what awaited me tomorrow.

CHAPTER 3
ODESSA

All night, I spent looking at my ceiling, unable to sleep with dread boiling deep in my stomach. As much as I tried to push away the anxiety, it kept coming back tenfold. The city was eerily quiet, making me feel even more unsettled than I already was. Normally, I could hear the rumblings of people at all hours, but not tonight. Even in years prior before the games, the streets would be packed. I wondered if it had anything to do with that mysterious arrival at the gates. Since the war was ongoing and the gods were picky about who was allowed within our borders, we didn't get many visitors since our city was flanked by battles on all sides. Our high walls surrounding the city kept us safe, for now. But the Kings of Destar were relentless in their pursuit of our lands, wanting our people and resources for themselves. I feared that one day they would breech our defenses.

Jean would soon be joining the military ranks, and that knowledge filled me with dread. While he was strong, tall, and agile, he was still mortal. Most first years that get carted off to war barely make it past their training, and if they did, they were stationed at the front lines. Used as cannon fodder. They were nothing more than another body to place between us and the enemy.

Even with the war raging outside, the games were still scheduled to commence. For as long as I've been alive, the gods have hosted the games every year like clockwork. We're told it's a chance at a better life. One with magical powers and more riches than we could fathom. But I liked my life the way it was. Sure, there were things I wished I could change, like my mother's condition, but overall, I was content for the most part.

My mind whirled with possibilities of what was to come, remembering all the stories of the winners throughout the years. How they fought their way through the labyrinth of tunnels full of traps and ultimately clawed their way to victory. Many of the winners chose the strength mask, barging through the limestone rock and their fellow opponents until they reached the end. A few others chose invisibility which afforded them the ability to slink through undetected. If the healing mask wasn't available, the invisibility one might be my best bet at survival.

No matter how much I theorized though, I wouldn't be able to make a selection until I was down amongst the dirt and bones.

Light filtered through my sunroof alerting me to the new day. I dressed carefully in the outfit Marley, and I had chosen together the night before.

I'd chosen a simple black v-neck shirt with long sleeves, and hunter-green pants that were easy to move in and more my style than that of any colorful ensemble they might be expecting. My black boots were ones I'd worn in the winter months, that would be perfect inside the catacombs. They had a good grip, and held my ankle in place, which was extra helpful when walking on ice. I didn't know what kind of terrain to expect in Nocturne, but I figured these were my best bet.

The last things I put on were my necklaces that Marley insisted I take to give the outfit a little something more. Marley loved anything that sparkled.

My fingers worked with practiced movements as I tugged my long brown hair into a wispy braid. There. That should do it, I thought, taking one last look in the mirror as nerves skate down my spine, pirouetting along my limbs and finally settling into my core like a boulder. It's shape lumpy and cumbersome, and ugly.

Just as I was tucking my hair behind my ear, a loud bang came from downstairs, before muffled shouts could be heard. A stampede of feet clamored up the steps and before I could even inhale, three large guards burst through my closed door.

"It's your lucky day, sweetheart. Now grab your things and let's go," the tallest and meanest looking one with greasy black hair and pock marked white skin said, his black gun prominently displayed like the very real threat it was. He was across my room and in my face within two short strides, leaning down over me and flicking his soulless almost completely black eyes down the length of my body. I felt like I wasn't wearing any clothes from the hungry way he stared at me.

Certainly, I'd heard the stories of maidens who'd been caught in the crosshairs of the guards to either go missing or come back violated. People disappeared for even looking at a guard the wrong way. Their reputation was as cruel as the gods they served. It was best to steer clear of them altogether, but now, here were three of them in my room, with nowhere to run or hide. They smelled of body odor and gunpowder.

I swallowed hard, hoping they'd let me around them, but as I made to move, the tallest one grabbed me by the elbow and yanked me into his body. I could feel all my parts smash against his muscles, making me feel trapped, helpless, and panicked. His hot breath hit my neck and sent unwanted shivers down my spine.

"Such a shame that something so pretty should be forced to play the games. I bet you don't even last an hour." His hands roamed down my sides, and instinctively I took my elbow and jabbed it into his ribcage.

He doubled over, wheezing with surprise. "You fucking bitch! You're going to pay for that."

His large, calloused hand rose to slap me, but one of the other guards stepped forward halting him midair. "You know they don't like it when we're late."

"Watch your back you little bitch, I'd hate for you to end up dead before you even started the games," he sneered. Dread, cold hard dread settled into my stomach. I'd heard of accidents happening to contestants before. It wasn't uncommon for a few to end up dead before the games had even started, but his warning sounded like a promise he intended to fulfill himself.

"Davis, we gotta go."

The one called Davis flared his nostrils as he looked down at me one last time before righting himself. "You're right, this one's not worth it. She'll be dead soon enough anyway."

The guard's words followed me all the way down the stairs

and into the living room where my family waited for me with forlorn expressions, save for Marley, who looked like she would burst from the excitement. I clutched my suitcase in my hands so hard, that my knuckles were blanched stark white with the strain. My skin was still tingling from the guard's touch and my stomach was churning with nausea. I didn't even eat that morning for fear of throwing up.

"Remember to be ruthless, my darling," my maman whispered as I crouched down to kiss her cheek. I inhaled the familiar scent of lavender and hoped this wouldn't be the last time I saw her. Just in case, I memorized the faint lines around her eyes and mouth. The way her eyes misted over with tears, and her brown hair done in a similar braid as mine. It took every bit of strength I had to not break apart right then and there. Her thin hand cupped my cheek sending a sharp fissure in my resolve, but Davis was all out of patience. He hauled me away fingers tightly gripped around my arm, shuffling me out my front door to be shackled like a prisoner to the float. His cruel expression turned almost giddy as he pulled the metal tight around my wrists before locking them into place The restraints bit into my skin as he sneered down at my misfortune, happy to be apart of my demise.

"Don't trip," he taunted, taking up his position to escort the contestants to the catacombs, but not before knocking my side and making me falter in my step. I brushed away his words, not wanting the encounter to get under my skin. I had more important things to worry about, like how in the seven hells I was going to survive.

Maman stayed behind as the rest of my family boarded the parade float. I watched my mother's face disappear from sight with fear gripping my heart as I was yanked away by the chains as soon as the float began moving forward. It was a red and white beast filled with flowers and blue glittering ornaments. No matter how prettily they dressed it up though, it still was an open-air cage designed to drag me off to my uncertain destiny.

The parade to the game was long and grueling. We were required to pick up all the contestants along the way, and the temperature was quickly climbing. From my vantage point, I couldn't see them joining us but could hear the moment that they emerged based on the crowd's enthusiastic reaction. This parade was for the people, but the games? The games of Nocturne were for the gods.

The chains around my wrists were heavy and dug uncomfortably into my flesh, leaving angry red welts. That jackass made them too tight on purpose. I hoped he would someday accidentally shoot himself with that gun of his. Maybe in the groin. A girl could dream.

The longer we walked, the more my nerves rumbled around in my chest. The arrondissements were arranged in a circular pattern, twisting from one into the next. Several contestants had already been picked up, but there were still more to collect.

I could feel my exposed skin beginning to crisp from the unrelenting bright sun and it had me wishing I'd chosen another outfit. Maybe something with more breathability. I'd been preparing for the cool underground, forgetting the trek there would take hours through the streets of Paris.

The air smelt of sweat and freshly made bread as people packed the route to wave us off. Like lambs to the slaughter.The cheers from the crowd were nearly deafening. Everywhere I looked, there were glittering gold masks staring back at me as people waved enthusiastically from all over. Some were hanging off their balconies, some had climbed up light poles, but most were pressed along the barricades that lined the uneven streets, eager to see this year's contestants. Celebratory music pulsed throughout the city as we wove through the web of streets that led to our final destination.

We passed the Notre Dame crossing over the Seine where rows of boats were filled with spectators, dining, and drinking, and waving at us. There were several bodies on display, strung up for their crimes in the square, as a reminder of what becomes of those who cross the gods, but today? No one was paying their decaying corpses any attention.

Usually, I would spend this day tucked away inside, hiding from the commotion with my nose in a book. But today, I was the entertainment. Someone to take a bet on. I felt like a spectacle being picked apart as I walked by, escorted by the royal guards while the rest of the city celebrated the day off, grateful to have been spared or just elated to have an excuse to get drunk at nine in the morning. My brother, Jean, my sister Marley, and my father all accompanied me on the way, sitting in a place of honor on the float ahead of me. All the contestants' families had one while we were dragged from behind, tethered. Marley was in her element, playing to the crowd, while Jean and father looked on stoically.

As we moved, I could see more of who was being carted off to the floats. The time gave me an opportunity to examine my fellow contestants.

From where I was located, I could only make out about half of who would be playing, but from what I could visualize, I was in for some stiff competition. There were several heavily built men, whose muscles seemed cut from stone, and the girls had a cunning and quick look about them. One of the contestants in particular with dark unkempt hair and broad shoulders, kept looking over at me with a smirk on his lips like he might try and eat me for breakfast. It was unnerving and made my stomach roil.

Once we arrived at the gates, we were allowed to say our last goodbyes as spectators looked on cheering for us. A court jester was hanging above the crowd on a high wire, doing flips to the crowd's delight. There were dancers balancing on the tops of round hoops and jugglers spread throughout. A man blowing fire was stationed near the entrance and I made a mental note to sidestep him, for fear of singing off my eyebrows.

The entrance to the catacombs had been fashioned as a stone devil skull, with horns and its large mouth sat open wide, swallowing anyone who passed through whole. It sent a shiver of fear along my skin, knowing that once I entered those gates, I might not come back out again.

The guards unhooked our chains from the floats giving us agency to move about freely once more. My eyes swept over the crowd looking for Theo. He promised he would meet me here, but so far, I couldn't find him.

My father gripped me hard around the shoulders and pierced me with a serious look. "My darling girl, I know that you might want to go for the healer's mask for your mother, but I need you to listen to me. This place is a death trap. You know how the gods like to play. You must pick a mask that gives you a chance to survive. Your mother and I will understand. Just make it home to us, Pigeon." Unshed tears clung to his irises and gutted my already emotional heart.

I wanted to tell him what he wished to hear, but I also couldn't lie to him, so I just hugged him tightly, tucking my head against his chest wishing beyond all hope that this wasn't really happening, and I'd wake up in my bed. He smelled like the clay he worked with daily, though he was wearing his finest clothes as was expected, who he was at his heart shone through the spiffed-up veneer.

"I'm so glad we went with this outfit instead of the red dress, it would have gotten ruined in this heat," Marley said. I smirked, thankful for her lightness in that moment. I felt seconds away from crumbling or taking off, chancing the guards shooting me right in the back. Maybe if ran fast enough…

But I knew how that ended. The gods would have their due one way or another and there's no outrunning one of the gods once you've been summoned.

Jean clapped his large hand onto my shoulder. He'd be gone for training before I got out of here. If I got out.

His blond hair had already been buzzed giving his normally boyish appearance an edge. He looked so grown.

While we weren't as close as me and Marley, he was still my brother.

"Stay alive down there."

"You too," I replied, knowing that after training they'd most likely send him right to the border where the fighting was mostly concentrated. Every so often, the fighting would get closer to the city gates, but that hadn't happened in months. People still were acting as if everything was normal, just as long as the sound of the bombs were out of range, they could pretend we weren't in the middle of a war that was killing our loved ones daily. So many of the people I went to school with had already died because of it. At least twenty percent of my graduating high school class, but people still fervently believed the gods had our best interests at heart and were doing a great job protecting us. I didn't feel protected with numbers like that. What was most infuriating about the whole thing was when people genuinely looked confused when you brought up the war. They couldn't fathom why anyone would be concerned about it since they claimed we have the best army in the world. I couldn't relate to that type of thinking, and now here I was, saying goodbye to my brother worried for his safety. And for mine. Both of us being directly impacted by the whims of the gods. Him by being drafted against his will, and me being summoned against mine.

Taking a step back, I looked at my family trying to hold on to this moment for as long as they would let me. Memorizing each of their faces to tuck away for later.

"Contestants, please step through the gates!" A woman in a top hat and black fitted corset to match spoke through a long brass amplifier, her voice sounding shrill but commanding.

"Wait," I uttered, trying to find Theo in the sea of faces. His promise to meet me here before I was to be taken in rings hollow as I come up empty. He didn't show.

"Waiting for someone?" a deep timbered voice called from behind me, making my skin erupt in a sea of goosebumps.

I turned my head to see who it was coming from and caught the wild, dark-haired contestant smirking at me. His piercing blue eyes held a shimmer of danger, like he could watch someone bleed out and enjoy it.

Scoffing, I turned my attention back to the crowd,

wondering if Theo was just late, even though he was usually on time for everything.

"I don't think he's coming."

"What makes you think I'm looking for a man?" I asked, whipping around, my irritation getting the better of me. My nerves were frayed, and I was in no mood to deal with an arrogant prick. He had an accent that would suggest he came from across the strait. London perhaps. That was curious. For a brief moment, I wondered what his story was.

Instead of answering me, though, he just stared at me as if he could see every thought and feeling I've ever had. Those icy blue eyes stared straight into my soul. I wanted to ask him what his problem was, but my tongue couldn't seem to form the words.

"Step through the gates!" The woman with the amplifier called again, this time with more force. The guards took a step towards me, and I took the hint, turning my attention away from him.

"This is it. I love you," I said to my family trying to sound braver than I felt as they enveloped me in one final group hug. I shoved down my disappointment about Theo not showing up and reckoned it might be better this way— especially with how he acted yesterday. Unshed tears threatened to spill onto my cheeks, but I held them off by sheer will alone, not wanting my family to see me defeated.

"You got this!" Marley said, squeezing my arm.

A guard ripped me out of their embrace and shoved me forward. My feet tripped over themselves as I walked past the threshold. The guard kept shoving me in the back with the butt of his gun.

"I'm going!" I responded, hands up in surrender.

The contestants all began to file into the large, cavernous space as the cheers come to a deafening roar. This was it. There's no going back now. No running— just acceptance of the inevitable. Fuck, my stomach was alight with nerves. I felt like I might blow chunks at any moment.

The immediate temperature dip was a stark shock to my system as we passed into the tunnels. Out in the sun, I felt as if I were being baked alive, but in the open mouth of the cata-comb's entrance, the temperature plummeted quickly while a musty smell hung about the air. I couldn't hear the sounds of the crowd anymore as we were escorted deeper into the arched tunnels. Bones were stacked in intricate designs from floor to ceiling. A red neon glow began to emanate making the bones appear ominous and evil. There was an eerie swell of music that reverberated off the walls to a chilling crescendo. I stayed close to the middle of the tunnel, not wanting to accidentally bump into the wall of bones, knowing full well that they belonged to real corpses. A homage to those who walked these very same tunnels years before us.

One of the girls a few feet ahead of me had her head bowed in what looked like a prayer, her dirty blonde hair was a curtain around her face, but I could clearly hear her sniffling. At least I wasn't the only one scared as hell to be here. The dark-haired guy was a few feet in front of her, walking with a swagger that looked like he owned the place. Insufferable, I thought, rolling my eyes. Arrogance like that would only get you killed in a place like this.

The tunnel came to an end, spilling out into a large two-story rotunda. But right before we passed through, a plaque of black and gold was stationed right above our heads with the words, '*C'est ici l'empire de la mort!*' Etched into it.

Roughly translated the sign said, 'Stop! This is the empire of the dead.' A chilling reminder of whose domain we would be intruding upon.

But the contestants, myself included, continued to walk right past the sign and into the den of the gods.

CHAPTER 4
ODESSA

The rotunda was a spacious room with a large, vaulted ceiling and a glowing red rose chandelier hanging from the center illuminating the space in a sinister, crimson light. The red beaming light was a stark reminder of all the blood spilled in this place. The gods were stationed a level above us dressed up in their finery, milling about with drinks in their hands and laughter on their lips, their faces covered by golden masks. We were nothing more than this year's entertainment to them. A passing thrill. They loved to see mortals play with a drop of their power, fighting amongst each other for a chance to cling to it. Disgust churned deep in my chest at the unfairness of it all. I was more than just some disposable mortal, and I was determined to prove it.

The energy in the room was a mix between nerves and excitement. It was clear which contestants were chomping at the bit to compete, and which ones were wishing they'd never been summoned. Seeing their faces flickering in the red light filled me with dread. So many faces, all people with a life. Maybe loved ones back home just like me. How am I supposed to kill any of them? The concept seemed inconceivable, but if I wanted to make it home to my family, I might not have a choice. My knees quivered knowing that they're probably thinking the same about me.

A loud crackling boom of a microphone attempting to connect to the speakers ripped through the vaulted entombed area, making everyone cover their ears simultaneously. The music cut out suddenly and my spine straightened on instinct.

"Sorry, sorry," a short statured lion uttered into the mic from above. His scraggly mane was beaming in the red tinted light and his large snout twitched as he stood looking down at us. Talking magical animals were usually only found in the first arrondissement, coveted for their unique talents and hints of magick ability. Animals that were non-speaking were used to perform services , or as pets to those that could afford such a luxury. I'd never been in the presence of such a creature and felt a bit awestruck.

"Now, in just a few minutes, you will be escorted to your rooms one at a time, where you will inhabit until the start of the games. You will have the opportunity to train with your teams, or on your own. This will give you time to acclimate to your new powers. Remember, you can only accommodate a new mask, and subsequently its power, by killing the wearer." A few of us shifted uncomfortably at the reminder. "There is to be no foul play or fraternization with your fellow contestants while during the training period. Which means you keep your hands to yourselves. No sleeping together and no killing one another. Once the games begin, then all bets are off, and you are free to interact as you see fit. Anyone found guilty of breaking these rules will be subject to forfeit the games and sentenced to a life-time of servitude to the gods."

I swallowed hard, glancing around the room. Across from me stared the guy from earlier, his smirk firmly in place as he stared directly at me. I glanced away quickly, not wanting to already have been making an enemy. Why was he so fixated on me anyways?

"Please come forward when your name is called and choose your mask."

A procession of women clad in black fabric wrappings with harsh cut outs showing pieces of their skin with their faces obscured by the sheer fabric walked in. Each were holding a plush velvet pillow dipped in crimson with a golden mask affixed to it. The women circled the room once, then twice showing off the masks, tilting them to the contestants. You could almost feel the power pulsating off them as they passed by. My eyes snagged on the one representing the healer's magick – The Mender. I licked my lips nervously. So much was hanging on this one moment. My own survival depended on making the right choice. If I chose wrong, it could mean signing over my soul to the god of death himself.

The air tightened in my chest and my heartbeat pounded as the first contestant was called.

"Magnus Hartfield."

The name boomed loudly, and the gods stationed above erupted in polite applause. A blond-haired, well-built man wearing a tailored suit stepped forward with confidence and headed straight towards the mask named, The Enforcer. The power of strength.

As he placed it on his face and tied the ribbons behind his head, a blast of light enveloped his body shooting out of the tips of his fingers. It was nearly blinding, and I had to avert my eyes as the power settled into his veins. The glow dimmed and he took his place back in line.

A ripple of apprehension ran through me, wondering if I'd be the next name called. No such luck.

The next name out of the lion's mouth was the timid girl with dirty blonde hair that I had observed earlier. Her name was Lilly Perkins. She snatched The Ghost, granting herself the power of invisibility. The same effect happened once she placed the mask upon herself, and the gods applauded in response. They talked amongst themselves in a hushed whisper. I wondered if they were placing bets on us as they observed us.

Name by name was called and my stomach grew into a tighter knot, knowing that as each power was picked, my chances of survival became less and less. The Medusa, The Pyro, The Timepiece had all been claimed, but the healer was still up for grabs.

"Dex Bourreau."

The dark-haired man whose made it his mission to make me uncomfortable, stepped forward, hands shoved deep in his pockets as he considered his options. He took his time, weighing his options. He stopped over The Mender mask and every muscle in my body tensed. Almost as if he sensed my reaction, he looked up at me and held my gaze. Those icy blue eyes of his twinkling with mischief. Internally, I was begging for him not to choose that one. Any other one but that. His hand slowly reached over the pillow as my stomach plummeted past my knees and sunk deep into my toes. At the last moment, he diverted and snatched the one next to it— The Stag. A mask shaped like a skull with demon like horns coming out the top, giving him the power to reanimate bones. And in a place surrounded by over six million human bones, he'd have a lot at his disposal.

"Marcela Peroit."

A girl with wine-red hair and a prominent wobble to her step shuffled forward and made a beeline for The Mender mask and my hopes of being able to obtain the one thing that could save my mother from her illness, crumbled into a million pieces before my eyes.

I didn't have time to mourn the loss before I was called next.

"Odessa Deveraux."

The sound of my name jolted my entire body as I felt the eyes of everyone around me swivel towards my shaking form. Walking passed the glittering gold masks— I weighed my options.

The Bird, The Siren, and The Onyx were all solid choices. Controlling flight or water could come in handy. And the ability to control shadows might be able to make me as close to invisible as I could without that exact power. I pulled my bottom lip between my teeth as I passed Marcela, seeing the mask I had originally wanted firmly affixed to her face.

The only way to get that power now, would be to kill her in the games. Her violet-hued eyes caught mine and a moment of uncertainty passed between us before I focused my attention back on the remaining masks and their powers.

My hand hovered over The Onyx, noticing the prominent swirls etched along the face. The two holes for the eyes stare directly at me as if daring me to choose it. Before I even knew what I was doing, I felt my hand clasp around the mask. Choice made.

With a deep breath, I tied the ribbons around the back of my head, careful not to snag my hair in the knot. It tightened on its own securing itself in place. I braced myself for the blinding light, but it didn't come.

Murmurs from above began to reach my ears.

Did it not work? Was it broken or out of magick?

Just as I went to adjust it, wondering if I didn't tie it tight enough, the room plummeted into total darkness all around us.

My entire body felt like it was set on fire and a scream ripped free from my mouth. I didn't know for sure what was happening around me because the pain was so overwhelming, but I was distantly aware of bodies rushing about in the darkness running into each other in utter chaos. Shrieks are drowned out by my own scream. Power like I've never known rattled across my teeth and down into my every nerve ending. It was all consuming, dragging me down into its inky depths of untapped potential. Beckoning me to unleash it into the world. Whispers filled my ears urging me to give in.

Release, release, release!

Large hands gripped into my shoulders and as suddenly as the room darkened, it dissipated, returning to that eerie red glow from the chandelier above. The pain felt as if were sucked straight out of my body leaving me feeling dizzy and unsteady on my feet.

When my eyes finally focused, I saw the person holding onto me was none other than that cocky gorgeous bastard, Dex. His head was tilted to the side and the slits of his mask showed his icy blue eyes staring down at me with an intensity I felt all the way to my toes. His grip tightened a fraction of a second before he released me and returned to his spot in line like nothing just happened.

The lion cleared his throat, "Right. Well, if everyone can take their places."

The entire room seemed to follow me as I stalked back to the line and whispers filled the air as people righted themselves. Several had been knocked down in the fray. I stared down at the ground, ignoring them all, unable to shake the feeling that whatever I just experienced was not a normal reaction. Even trying to avoid the glances, I couldn't ignore the stillness emanating from the gods above. They'd gone from being jovial and excited to reserved and quiet. Their obvious attention on me, was the opposite of what I'd wanted. I'd hoped to slink in and be unnoticed. A blip, not worthy of their focus, but they were focused now, and it made my skin crawl. Having the gods' attention could be deadly. But something about the way my mask reacted seemed to have them on edge, and I didn't like the feeling one bit. I chanced another look to where they were stationed above in all their glittering splendor. They were still, but something was amiss. One, two, three... I counted the gods and there was one notable detail that had my blood chilling inside my veins— one was missing. Which god, I couldn't say, but there were only fifteen instead of the revered sixteen that usually attended. Had they been missing the whole time, or was it a recent development?

I pushed away the thoughts and averted my gaze once more, not wanting to be caught staring too long. People had been struck dead for less. All I wanted was to get through this competition and make it back home to my family, but I feared that I inadvertently had a target painted on my back from that little display of power. I searched my memory of anything happening like that in prior games but came up empty. I don't even know what it meant— if it meant anything at all. Maybe I was just overthinking things. It could have just been because the mask's power was rooted in producing shadows—nothing more.

After all the masks had been chosen, we were escorted to our rooms with instructions to meet in the banquet hall in the morning. There were three fully functioning bathrooms dispersed throughout the hallway, which made me cringe. I was well aware of how sharing a bathroom could go, having done it all my life with my siblings. Jean was the worst of us siblings, always hogging the room for hours at a time and leaving his hair all over the sink. It was disgusting.

The room the guard took me to that was to be mine for the next serval days, was down a long, arched corridor with flickering sconces placed at shoulder level to illuminate the path. There were black and white checkered tiles that looked as if they were several hundred years old lining the ground, and every few feet, a skull was imbedded into the stone walls.

The contestants were all quiet as we were escorted by armed guards one at a time. When I finally made it to my room, I found my suitcase I had packed waiting for me.

"If you need anything, just pull on this cord here," the guard gruffly instructed. At least it was a different one than had assaulted me earlier this morning. He left without another word, and I sighed, feeling relief sweep through me for the first time all day. I'd made it through the choosing ceremony. It had gone different than how I'd imagined, but now I could strategize and learn how to wield my newly gifted power.

The room was a modest one, but far nicer than the one I had at home. There was a full-sized bed filled with plenty of plush pillows, and a regal deep red comforter that had golden tassels hanging from the ends. A matching velvet canopy hung about the top of the bed that were tied back with golden braided ropes. A roaring fireplace heated the space, and several light fixtures lined the walls giving me enough warm light to see my surroundings. Despite the fire, there was still a chill that hung about the air, and a hint of damp that seemed to permeate through the floor. And of course, because we were underground, there were no windows to be found.

It had to at least be near supper time by now, and my stomach was still a mess of nerves. Though a low pang of hunger reminded me that I should probably eat something.

There was a small ice box filled with meat and cheese tucked away in the corner of the room. I rolled them up together and shoved them in my mouth suddenly ravenous. It's like I had been suppressing my hunger and finally realized I needed sustenance to survive. As I chewed, I went over to open my suitcase, wanting to settle in and rest my feet for the night.

But when I went to open it, a large dagger sat prominently on top with a note attached at the handle.

It read:

Just in case :)
- M"

. . .

FUCKING MARLEY.

Having this on me could get me killed or expelled from the games. Sentenced to a lifetime of servitude to one of the gods. My heart rate jackhammered into my chest as I whipped my head around trying to find a suitable place to stash it.

A knock on the door came and everything inside me panicked. The knife clutched in my hands would doom me before I even had a chance to fight.

The knob turned and my knees quivered in fear. I was a fucking goner.

CHAPTER 5
ODESSA

There was no time to hide the obvious weapon in my hand before a large imposing figure stepped through the door, making my jaw drop and anger rise.

Instead of the guard and chains I expected to see, a dangerous dark-haired menace walked into my room, taking all the oxygen out of my lungs with his sudden appearance. The door snicked closed behind him—the sound echoing off the vaulted ceiling.

"What the hell! Dex, I thought you were a guard."

He tilted his head to the side examining me like I was a specimen under a microscope, and he was a scientist desperate to discover my secrets. His golden horned mask gleamed in the flickering light, making him appear ten times more devious and dangerous than he had earlier. The ghost of his touch on my skin still lingered, remembering how he had steadied me when the shadows swirled all around me. I still didn't know if I had caused that to happen or if it was something else.

"You asshole, what are you even doing here?" I seethed, trying to calm my erratic heart rate.

The icy blue hue of his eyes locked on the dagger I held in my hand. Immediately, my brain caught up to my body and I hid it behind me.

Too little, too late. It was clear by that insufferable smirk that he'd seen it.

"What, are you planning to do with that? Stab me with your contraband? Might I suggest aiming for my heart if you do. It's the only way to get the job done."

"I—I'm not planning on stabbing *anyone*. My sister packed it without my knowledge, and now I don't know what I'm going to do. If they find it, I'll be kicked out and jailed. Or worse. Hung up in the stocks and made an example of."

I plopped down onto the bed and stared at the weapon in disbelief, not sure why I just unloaded all that on him, other than I was still clearly in shock. How could Marley put me in this position? I swore, if I got out of here alive, I was going to personally wring her little neck.

"That would be a shame, not being able to face you in the games due to a stupid rule. Have you thought of, I don't know, maybe hiding it?"

I glared up at him.

"What are you doing here anyways?"

"I came to see if you wanted an escort to dinner."

A loud snort came out of my nose, and I quickly covered my mouth. "You did not."

"Fine. But it's a good line." I narrowed my eyes at him, waiting for him to tell me the truth. "What about stashing the dagger in the light fixture right there?"

He pointed to the light above my head, and I turned to look at it. It could work. Standing on the bed, I carefully placed the blade into the back part of the fixture, watching as it was swallowed whole, only showing the smallest part of the handle. If you only glanced at it, it seemed like it was a part of the design. I was keenly aware of Dex's presence, watching me carefully with his muscular arms crossed over his wide chest.

"You're not going to squeal on me, are you?" I asked, coming down from the bed and using the poster to help keep me steady. When my feet were firmly planted on the ground, I couldn't help but notice how tall Dex was. He towered over me in a way that made me feel small and vulnerable.

"Not if you don't tell on me, too. No fraternizing, remember?"

I huffed out a breath of annoyance. "We are not fraternizing. I was minding my own business—

"By breaking the rules."

"—and you burst into my room. I could have been changing."

"That would have been horrible," his eyes run down the length of my body, and I felt my cheeks heat.

"You're a scoundrel."

He let out a deep throated laugh, his eyes twinkling with amusement, "I've been called many things, but being called a scoundrel might be my new favorite."

I huffed out an annoyed sound. "We could be arrested for you just being in here."

"Does that scare you? The danger?" He took a step closer to me and I backed up, only to have my thighs hit the bed frame.

"I think it does. Just look at that beautiful flush crawling up your neck."

I raised my hand to slap him, but he caught it easily in his large hand. "Careful, vixen. I might like it too much if you hit me."

His focus caught on my ring as he held onto my hand, and his gaze seemed to flash with an indescribable emotion.

"Well, would you look at that—" His skin was an inferno against mine as he turned my hand to get a better look at the simple diamond that Theo had given to me. My heart beat wildly against my chest as Dex tightened his grip. "You'd think your betrothed could have sprung for a better ring instead of whatever this is."

I yanked back my hand and rubbed it on my pants to erase the feeling. "Get the hell out of my room." My voice sounded firm but inside my stomach was doing flips. My skin tingling from his touch.

The moment stretched between us, his subtle but intoxicating musk invading my senses and making my head spin with the proximity. We were locked in a challenge of wills and mine was slipping. But I'd be damned if I let this agitator ruffle my feathers. Who did he think he was just waltzing into my room like he belonged in here? And judging the ring from Theo when it cost him a month's worth of work to save for. I bet he couldn't fathom the sacrifice.

Dex looked down at my lips and I felt my breathing stall in my chest, my body leaning towards his like an invisible tether was pulling me towards this insufferable, arrogant man. The energy coming off him was palpable and confusing. I couldn't understand this pull he had over me that was making me forget myself.

"It seems whoever gave that ring to you really holds the key to your heart."

The moment between us popped with those words and my anger came rushing back.

"Make sure the door hits you on the way out."

He dipped his head in a mocking bow and exited the way he came. I ran to the door and locked it behind him, grateful for the barrier between us. I didn't need some cocky asshole messing with my head and my emotions, derailing me from focusing on how to survive these games.

No good could come of entertaining a rake like Dex. No matter how tempting it might be.

What the hell was I thinking anyways? I had a fiancé back at home. And even if he didn't show to say goodbye, I'm sure it was for a good reason.

It had to be.

THE DINNER BELL rang throughout the halls like a death knell. It was an ominous sound and the vibration of it rolled throughout my entire body. I double checked my braid and nervously pulled at the black laced dress I'd put on for the evening. The sleeves wove a delicate floral-like pattern all the way down to my wrists, giving the illusion that inky black spiderwebs were coating my skin. The dress was floor length, covering my ballet slippered feet with the long fabric. Giving myself one last look in the oval shaped mirror, I deemed myself presentable enough. This would be the first time I'd be able to assess the competition since I was too stuck in my head earlier to pay much attention. I feared I'd already made an impression on them all at the mask choosing ceremony, and I needed to ascertain just who I needed to watch out for.

Guards lined the hallway, ready to escort us out to dinner. Dex emerged from his room at the same time, and I felt like my dress became two sizes smaller as he gave me that knowing look like we shared a secret. I hated that he knew about the dagger. He could turn me in at any time and lead the guards right to it, but for some reason I didn't think he would. I felt like a toy he was playing with.

His eyes traveled the length of my body, taking in my outfit change with a smirk pulling at his lips. He was dressed in the same clothes as earlier, only his hair looked mussed as if he'd just rolled straight out of bed. Oh, to be that unaffected by being here. He exuded a level of confidence I wish I could tap into for myself. I would just have to fake it, I decided.

The dining area was the most elaborately decorated room I'd ever stepped into. It was hard not to gape at the pure opulence that surrounded us. Glittering gold appliqués of the *fleur-de-lis* lined the dark walls. Candles flickered in the corners and along the long table. Statues of the gods were lain out just like they had been at the temple, reminding us of who's domain we were in— as if we could forget. High backed elegantly designed chairs were placed on either side of the table, complete with a plush *fleur-de-lis* patterned cushions that matched the walls. There were sixteen seats total. Just enough for all the contestants.

Thankfully, Dex was seated on the other end of the table, and I was able to get a reprieve from his overwhelming presence. Though, across from me sat the one person who picked the strength mask, Magnus. I could feel the power wafting off him from my spot. Though the gods only gave one drop of blood to our masks, some of their powers were more potent than others. It was clear why the strength mask usually won the competition. If I could feel it from here, there's no telling what that kind of power could do in action. Magnus glared directly at me with his pasty white hands gripping the edge of the table.

I swallowed hard, imagining the worst.

Thankfully, the food was brought out swiftly, stealing his focus. Whatever it was, smelled absolutely divine and had my mouth watering instantly. My meager rations in my room weren't enough to quell the raging appetite I'd worked up in my nervous state.

I was seated between The Siren mask wearer, who was a petite girl with ebony skin and jet-black hair that swung in intricately woven braids below her waist, and The Spider mask wearer, who was a boy with a tan that suggested he worked the fields. He seemed the same age as my brother with a similarly cut hairstyle as Jean, and deep green eyes, that had me feeling all kinds of homesick.

The servants were the same women who'd brought out our masks earlier. They balanced trays expertly on their arms, plating our food in front of us with blank expressions and eyes that looked as if they were unfocused. It was unsettling. What could have happened to them that caused such disassociation?

A simple roasted chicken with rosemary seasonings and a side of mashed potatoes, covered in a rustic white cream sauce was placed in front of each of us. A few of the contestants were chatting amongst each other, but all seemed to hold a level of nervousness that was palpable. It was hard to forget that the majority of these people around me would most likely be dead in a few days. It was rare for more than a handful of contestants to emerge from the catacombs with their lives intact.

I cut into the meat delicately removing a bite sized piece feeling my nerves rear their ugly head. These contestants that surrounded me could be the reason I didn't make it back home. I had to pay attention. I'd already clocked the biggest threat as Magnus, and he seemed to still be unnervingly fixated on me, watching me through the small slits in his mask as he devoured the chicken off the bone with his bare hands. The juices from it running down his chin. Gross. I had to stop myself from throwing a napkin at him. That was sure to guarantee me becoming even more of a target. His intense gaze made me want to slink down into a puddle just to avoid his notice.

"What I want to know is which one of do you think is going to die first?" he asked, not wavering in his penetrating gaze. Chicken rolled around in his mouth as he threw the bone onto his plate with a clatter.

Ice sluiced along my veins feeling the implications of his words. The threat lay there between us clear as day. He meant for it to be me. I hoped to all the gods he wasn't on my team. When I looked up, his eyes stared directly into mine. I quickly looked away and focused on my plate. Picking up another piece of chicken.

The two contestants on either side of me visibly tensed at

Magnus's callous words. The Siren had a crust of bread paused halfway to their mouth before they set it down onto their plate with disgust.

"Probably someone who can't keep their mouth shut," a reply came from down the table.

I didn't have to look over to see where it came from, though. I knew that voice and felt my heart flutter on its own volition.

Sure enough, Dex got to his feet and circled around until he planted his hands on Magnus's muscular shoulders with his long fingers digging into his flesh. The golden horns of his mask gleamed against the soft candlelight making him look far more threatening than the man he stood over. Dex had the look as if he could snap Magnus's neck and go right back to eating without breaking a sweat.

"Do you know what kinds of things can happen down here to people who don't make allies, Magnus? They end up dead. Now I know you're feeling all kinds of big and strong because of that mask you have on there, but I promise that magick can only help you so much. All of us here now possess ways in which to kill each other." Dex slapped him hard on the back and Magnus flinched at the contact. "It would serve you well to remember that."

Dex smirked and revealed a concealed dinner knife in his sleeve. He leaned down to Magnus's ear and whispered just loud enough that I could make out his words.

"One wrong move in here, and you're dead." The knife slammed down mere millimeters from Magnus's meaty hand. The whole table shook with the force, and a guard emerged from the shadows, gun poised and ready to eliminate the threat.

Dex put his hands up and walked calmly back to his seat, but not before catching my gaze and winking at me.

I didn't know why a part of me found that so damn attractive, but I squashed the feeling deep inside as soon as I recognized it for what it was and remembered the ring around my finger. A promise that I belonged to Theo. I had no business finding anyone else attractive. Plus, Dex of all people, was just asking for trouble. No, it was nothing but a small slip in judgement. A primal instinct and nothing more.

"What team did you get?" The Siren asked after the shock of what just transpired before us wore off.

"Hearts, you?" I asked back, making polite conversation.

"Spades. My name's Céline."

"Odessa."

"I'm on Diamonds," The Spider answered. "Name's Uric."

"Nice to meet you," I responded just as an eight-legged creature emerged from the tips of Uric's fingers stringing a web behind it.

"Shit," he cursed, smashing it with the palm of his hand. "Gotta get the hang of that." He had a boyish charm to him. The tips of his ears pinked up with embarrassment.

"Good thing we have a few days to practice," The Siren, Céline, said.

For that I was grateful. Practicing how to work with our new powers would make the difference between life and death.

"Do you think the gods will be watching us? As we train, I mean?" Another girl with two golden braids plaited down both sides of her head asked. She had The Ghost mask on— the power to disappear.

"Fuck, I hope not."

Being watched and judged as I fumbled my way through trying to control this new power I'd been saddled with, wasn't something I was looking forward to. It felt awkward enough during the choosing ceremony, which I'd been working hard to forget.

Everyone started out the games with their teammates, before being lowered into the labyrinth. Many champions chose to eliminate their teammates and face the games on their own. Doing so was a risk, because teaming up with others could mean they would be able to assist if you found yourself in trouble.

I pegged Magnus as the type to eliminate his whole team and could only hope that I was placed as far from him as possible. Magnus seemed to boil with anger ever since that little display Dex made earlier. The knife was still lodged in the table, a reminder of just how unhinged he was.

"Who do you think is going to win?" Céline asked, taking a sip of red wine.

I shrugged, "It's anyone's game." And it was. Luck could be as big of a factor when it came to survival.

"Contestants, you will be escorted back to your rooms where you are expected to stay for the remainder of the evening until we come to get you for training in the morning," an announcement crackled over the speaker system. I looked down at my barely eaten food and shoveled a few more forkfuls into my mouth even though my hunger had abandoned me. I knew I would need my strength for what was to come. We all would.

CHAPTER 6
ODESSA

The shadows refused to come out of my fingers no matter how much I willed it. Frustration laced my chest as I tried again, and again. The tether I'd felt as tangibly as my own skin, was now decidedly absent. It felt as if it went into hiding and every attempt to access that magick, failed miserably. While the rest of the contestants practiced honing their skills with precision, I sat, facing the reality that I might be in real trouble here. If I couldn't utilize my power, I would be nothing more than a sitting duck. Ripe for the slaughter.

At least the gods weren't here to watch my failure.

Come on Des, I told myself, it's just like when you're studying for school. You keep at it until you get it. Only instead of worrying about a final exam, I was worried about my fellow contestants. Failure was deadly.

Right about now, I would have been taking those exams that I'd studied so hard for, instead now, I'm far below the city in a musty room full of sweaty bodies training to kill.

I wondered how my family was doing, but most of all, I worried about my mother. The failure of not being able to secure the one power that might save her ate at my conscious. Though, technically, I still had time to secure it for myself if I was willing to murder the wearer for it. My eyes slid to where Marcela sat cross legged, cutting her shin with a knife and using The Mender's mask to heal the injured skin. Just one moment with that power, could save my mother from her terrible fate.

All around me, contestants were practicing their power. The air was rank with sweat and desperation. Each of us wanted to win, even if we hadn't wanted to be summoned in the first place— winning meant a lifetime of safety. Guaranteed riches beyond our wildest imaginations. And while I had been content with my life, I couldn't help but want the chance to save my mother. If I made it home, power and riches intact, maybe, just maybe I could save her.

My team of hearts consisted of two guys and one girl. Reed, Killian, and Natalia, who preferred to go by Nat. Reed had the power of flight and was currently floating effortlessly over a pile of foam mats ready to catch him if he were to give into gravity and tumble. Reed made it look so easy as he flashed his bright white smile down at us. His blond hair fluttered as he swooped low and landed on his feet like a cat.

Killian had the power to duplicate and had a pile of rocks spread out in front of him. His two-faced mask sat snuggly against his brown skin while his black hair was shaved close to his head. The rocks doubled as his power surged.

Nat had chosen, The Medusa, and was currently turning items into stone with just one look. She was the one that scared me the most out of our teammates. She had an edge to her that let me know she would do whatever it took to win this competition. There was an air of ruthlessness about her that she carried in the way she walked. As if she would gladly turn my entire body to stone if I were to even sneeze near her. Nat had a sharp bob cut right at her chin that got shorter in the back. Her hair was dyed a neon cerulean blue, and her pale skin was adorned with a smattering of freckles. Her narrow waist moved easily through the obstacle course, dodging each impediment skillfully. She dropped down into the splits just as a boulder came swinging past intent on crushing her to pieces. As she reached the end, her eyes found mine and she winked right at me. I made a note to keep a wide breadth when around her.

While we were technically a team, we all knew that only one person could win this whole thing. Any of us could turn on the other in a moment, making our fragile connection tentative at best, deadly at worst. I could be in the room with my future murderer right this second. And there would be no judge and jury to condemn them because it was legal. We would do whatever was necessary to win. Even if that meant committing the unthinkable. At least it was unthinkable to me. I'd never even so much as harmed a spider, choosing instead to scoop it up into a cup and set the creature free outside where it belonged.

While we weren't allowed to cause other contestants harm during this training period, mysterious accidents weren't outside the realm of possibility. Which was another reason why having access to my magick was vital. How was I expected to protect myself if I couldn't even produce a whisp of power?

Reaching inside my core once again, I searched for an ember of that power I had felt before and worried that maybe I'd spent it all during the mask ceremony. Perhaps we were gifted a finite amount and I'd stupidly used it up But that couldn't be true since the other contestants were using a fair amount training and no one else seemed to be struggling as much as I was.

"Need some help, Deveraux?" Dex's voice asked, making the hairs on my arms raise. I hated the way my body seemed to respond to him.

"Not from you," I grumbled, trying again to make my power work.

"You wound me," he gripped at his chest as if I'd physically maimed him. I rolled my eyes at his antics and went back to ignoring him. Only, he wasn't ignoring me. He came up behind me and whispered in my ear.

"Just let go, love. You're too in your head." His breath skated across my neck and goosebumps detonated along my skin and my stomach clenched in response. I cleared my throat loudly and took a step away from him which only made Dex chuckle. It was deep almost like a growl vibrating in his chest.

"I'm not your 'love'. I'm not your anything." I crossed my arms over my chest feeling my anger rise.

"Yet," his tone was biting yet playful.

"We'll see about that." Though my words were harsh and said with force, they seemed to have no effect on the object of my annoyance. Instead, he watched me even more intensely as I tried and failed to work even a spark of magick to my fingertips.

All night, I had tossed and turned worrying about the dagger I'd hidden, but a thorough check of the space afforded me with the answer that the light fixture was the only possible hiding place. Meaning Dex still knew its location and could use that information against me if he so chose. Being in a foreign bed was also difficult. I'd only ever slept over at friends' houses and my sister's bedroom. Here, I was underground. Alone, and facing the biggest challenge of my entire life. At least the mask was able to come off at night in order for me to sleep. I couldn't imagine trying to get any rest with that thing affixed to my face, digging into my nose and pressing against my forehead. It was bad enough that it had to stay on all day. Being made of gold meant it was heavy enough to be a burden. At least my design was less elaborate than others. Dex's must have been giving him a headache with those horns jutting out at the top.

Those long dark eyelashes of his brushed against his mask with each blink and distracted me from the task at hand. No one had any business being that — hot. Fine. I could admit that Dex had a certain allure that most girls would find appealing. Objectively.

"You need to feel it from here." Dex's fingers splayed along my stomach as he pulled me flush against him. Shock reverberated throughout my body at how well we fit together. The warmth of his hand striking a chord deep inside my core while my breathing hitched, my diaphragm tightened with a mixture of desire and fear. As his fingers lingered on me, a tiny flicker of smoke danced along my fingertips. I shouldn't be letting him touch me at all. He had no right to, but fuck, it felt amazing. And the power I felt strumming inside me was just as intoxicating. Shadows built until I could hold it like a ball in my hand.

"You see how it grows from your emotions? Feed it. Build on that feeling," he instructed.

My head swam as Dex's hand held onto me. I feared that if he were to let go that I would crumple to the floor. All my emotions flew to the center of my soul where that thin tangible string glowed from within, the power building with each passing moment. I fed it my fear, my desire, my very essence as the shadows began to leak onto the floor. Everything in me vibrated with a need for more. My head tilted back and found the hard planes of Dex's large chest. He inhaled sharply and dropped his hand as if he'd been burned.

As quickly as he pulled me to him, he let go, backing up a step and putting his arms behind his back straightening his spine. The shadows disappeared instantly from my hands at the lack of contact.

What the hell was I doing? I must have been more sleep deprived than I realized.

"Seems you got the hang of it, now. You're welcome."

I raised my chin defiantly, annoyed that he was able to manipulate me so easily. "Why don't you just leave me the hell alone for once?"

Stumbling over my own feet, I fled in the opposite direction wishing those shadows were back so I could hide inside of them from how embarrassed I felt. Making a fool of myself was not a part of the plan. I needed to focus on winning, or at least staying alive. Being down here, away from the life I always knew, was messing with my head.

Once I felt I was far enough away, I chanced seeing if I could access my power on my own. Sure enough, the shadows appeared easily, as if they'd always been a part of me.

I didn't know what vexed me more. Knowing that I was able to access them because of how Dex showed me. Or that I enjoyed every second of his instruction.

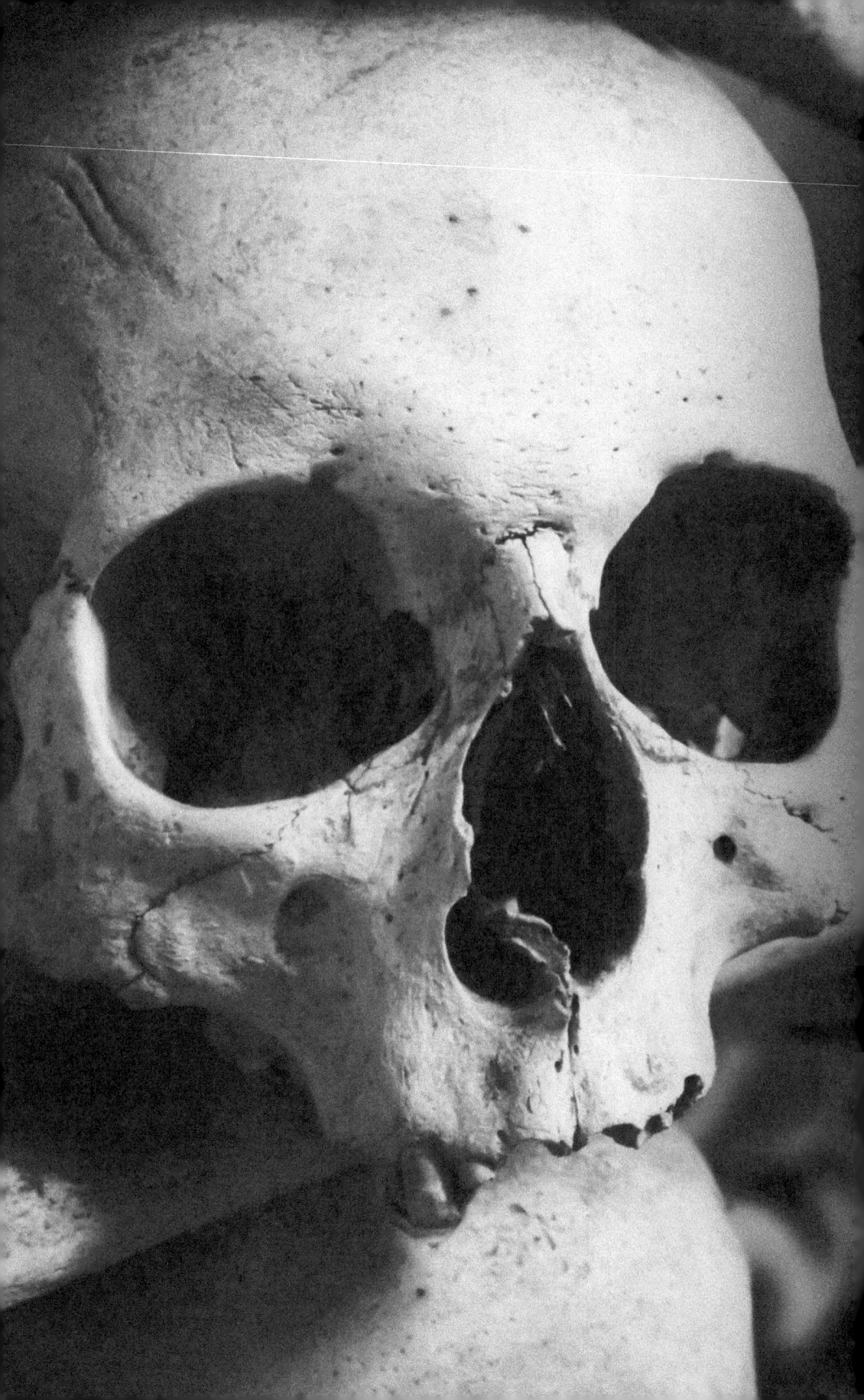

CHAPTER 7
DEX

I was her enemy in every sense of the word. Not only was I here to make sure I walked out with all the powers the masks had to offer, but I knew that doing so meant I would be killing each and every contestant. No one had achieved such a feat before. The most a contestant had acquired in past games was a grand total of seven. To behold all sixteen, you had to be downright insane to even attempt it. Good thing I'd never been accused of having my shit together. It was going to be an absolute bloodbath.

But holding onto Odessa and feeling how affected she was by me, had me questioning my grand plan. I supposed, there was no reason I couldn't enjoy her while I eliminated the rest of the competition. Once the games started, all rules were thrown out. Anything you could imagine was allowed. Even fucking her against the catacomb walls. I bet she could make the most delicious noises from that slim breakable neck of hers. Her sweet jasmine scent still lingered even long after I'd let go of her.

Watching her from where I was after she stomped off clearly as affected by me as I was her, I could admire her uninhibited. Her tenacity was adorable. I admired how hard she was trying to get that magick of hers to work. From the Mask Ceremony, I knew she was more than capable of accessing that dark and twisted part that resided within us all. She just had to not be so afraid to embrace it.

Not everyone can accept it as easily— the darkness. It's like a second skin for me. Melding perfectly with my already questionable soul. The power sat right at home within my chest, running up and down the length of my nerve endings and surged to life at my command. Odessa would pick it up soon enough. It was addictive—these feelings of control and power. My soul longed for more, and I knew just where to start.

That Magnus made himself my first target with that arrogant mouth of his. Men like that think that having strength makes them invincible. It'll be his fatal flaw and it works well in my favor. He thought no one would dare to cross him because of his chosen power. Well, he thought wrong. I'd have him buried so far beneath the bones that make up this place that they'll never find even a trace of his body.

He looked at me then, as if he could see inside of my thoughts. My mouth tugged up into a smirk knowing his days were numbered. His gold gleaming mask was a farce upon his face. For his strength training he'd chosen to lift boulders above his head and have them come crashing down with a loud yell, making everyone around him uncomfortable and jumpy. Even his own teammates had decided to leave him alone, working amongst themselves on the opposite end of the room. Him being by himself would make it easier to catch him by surprise.

Shadows began to curl around Odessa, snagging my attention and my mouth turned into a full-blown smile. They built slowly, gathering around her feet like snakes, then crawled up her luscious curves, enveloping her body in a fine mist of onyx. I knew she would get there. Giving her that little push was more for my own enjoyment than anything. She felt so damn pliable beneath my hands and a part of me ached to feel it again. Her pleasure at succeeding was palpable from here. I bet I could wring that out of her with just a few well-placed strokes of my fingers. Her shadows enveloped her completely, obscuring her from view, looking as if she had never been there in the first place. Then she reappeared with a smug as fuck smile on those plush lips. Her brown eyes danced with glee, realizing that she had finally done it on her own. She spun around and found me lurking, that smile faltering for a moment before it dropped from her face completely.

Internally, I grumbled, knowing she had every reason not to trust me, but wanting that shred of happiness to be shared with me all the same.

We still had a few days of training before the masquerade ball that the gods and goddesses would be attending as well. They liked mixing amongst the lowly peasants, picking their favorites to bestow their favor upon, if they so chose. Not many were ever found worthy of such an honor. Not that it did much good. If someone was destined to join the dead, there was no escaping such a fate.

"You want to go over strategy?" Regis asked. He was on my team of spades and had chosen The Manipulator, giving him the power to influence the emotions of others around him with just one thought. I could feel the cool film of it falling over me

75

now, making a part of me believe that it would be in my best interest to talk with them. I bit down on my tongue to keep it from revealing my secrets as I strode over to where they three of them had gathered. They were seated around a small round table clearly discussing their plans for succeeding together. I knew better than to trust anyone in here, but I could humor them.

Regis was seated with his leather gloved hands pushed together under his weak chin. He was a small man, no more than twenty given his lack of facial hair and somewhat acned complexion that dotted along his alabaster complexion.

Also on my team were two girls named, Céline, and Genevieve. Céline had chosen The Siren as her mask and was swirling a droplet of water around in the palm of her hand as Regis droned on with possible scenarios.

One thing I knew for sure was that no matter how much someone planned, the unpredictability of the game always won out. You could train as hard as you wanted— fate would always have the final say.

Genevieve, bless her, interrupted Regis's droll musings by turning to me, and asking what I thought about all of this. Her flame like crown intertwined with her mask almost matching the hue of her long hair. She'd be one to keep around. Light was always a useful tool. Especially in the dark catacombs.

"I think we're doing far too much talking, and not enough practicing," I answered, wanting to see these teammates of mine in action. The more I could study their strengths and weaknesses, the easier it would be to take them out.

"Agreed," Céline says, not waiting for a response. Instead,

she pushed away from the table and sauntered off to where an obstacle course sat unused.

It was made with an uneven terrain that led to a cracked and jagged wall that only went up about halfway to the large ceiling. The entire thing had random bits of bone sticking through it. Some skulls, some that looked like ribs. One thin rope dangled from the top, but it looked as if it would snap with the smallest amount of weight. No, the only safe way up would be to climb using the crevices in the natural stone. From there, water sat on the other side, waiting to catch anyone that fell. The water continued down a narrow passage with a cage like structure sitting on top and was lined with barbed wire, sure to cut anyone that grasped it. A narrow exit was placed at the end of the water that was thick with mud and small rocks. Anyone that wanted to fit through there would have to crawl on their belly.

"We were here first," I heard Regis's nasally sounding voice complain.

He had his arms crossed over his chest, looking up at one of Odessa's teammates. Clearly, they'd had the same idea to train here as well.

"You're not using it," Nat, I think her name was spat back. She was a fiery little thing. Too bad it wouldn't save her from me.

Odessa hung off to the side, watching the interaction with her shoulders bound tight like a rattle snake about to lunge for an attack.

"No use fighting over it, why don't we both use it. We'll send one person from each team in at the same time," I said making both parties whip their heads in my direction. I shoved my hands into my pants pockets, glad I chose something less tailored since it looked as if I was about to get neck deep in mud.

"Fine," Nat gritted out. "We'll pair off one teammate at a time. I'm going first."

Regis took up the spot next to her and dipped down into a crouching position, ready to run.

"First one to make it to the end wins," he said, determination coating his every fiber.

"Count us off, Killian," Nat instructed to the guy wearing The Duplicator.

"Oh, uh, yeah okay." He shrugged as if he couldn't care less about what we were doing. "3,2,1.... go!"

Both Nat and Regis took off at a sprint while the rest of us looked on. A few others seemed drawn to the commotion and peered over, their curiosity getting the better of them.

Nat was nimble on her feet, stepping over the uneven ground easily. Regis, was not so lucky, stumbling several times. It slowed him down, having Nat reach the wall first.

It was a straight climb up and she lunged for the rope.

Big mistake.

The rope gave way, and her body came crashing down into a heap at the bottom. Her leg jutted out beneath her at an odd angle as she cried out in pain. Regis paid her no mind and stepped over her body, gripping onto a piece of bone to hoist himself up.

"Can we get a mender over here?" Odessa called out.

No one moved though. They just watched as she writhed in pain.

Regis found purchase on the wall and began his assent.

"You. The one with The Mender mask, why don't you

come over here and help?" Odessa asked, striding across the room with purpose. The girl she was speaking to, glanced up, annoyed to be interrupted.

"She'll be fine," the girl responded.

"You don't deserve to have the healing power if you won't use it to help others," Odessa spat out loudly. Her anger practically sizzling off her.

She turned on her heel and made it over to her teammate and leaned down.

"Grab my hand," she told Nat.

The set of Nat's jaw was tight, clearly experiencing pain as she took Odessa's extended hand.

Nat's arms had several cuts along them, superficial ones, but it must have stung. She leaned on Odessa as she hobbled towards the starting line.

Regis, didn't even look down as he scaled the wall, making it about halfway before he seemed stuck. The next plausible grip seemed right out of reach for him.

"Here, have some water," I said to Nat as she made it over and collapsed onto the ground. We each had been given some at the beginning of our training session.

Odessa glared at me, but Nat took the small container without question and slugged back the contents.

"Couldn't be bothered to help before?" Odessa asked, fury sparking in her eyes.

"You seemed to have it handled. Besides, didn't you tell me to leave you alone?"

She huffed and her dainty nostrils flared. "That doesn't mean you should stop being a decent person!"

Just as I was going to retort that I was nowhere near decent as I took a step closer to her, Regis fell with a loud crunch. His small mouth screaming out in pain at the top of his lungs.

The other contestants around us barely even batted an eye.

It couldn't have been more clear that everyone here, was out for themselves.

There could only be one winner.

All I had to do was kill every single person in here, taking their powers for myself, and that winner would be me.

CHAPTER 8
ODESSA

I'd been watching the other pairs run through the obstacle course intently— learning from their mistakes. Going for the rope was a death trap. Only one other person from Dex's team fell. The rest found their way over, the most impressive being, Céline, using her power to control water to lift her over the top. It carried her safely almost the entire way, sputtering out just as she hit the middle of the other side. She dropped hard into the belly of the water waiting below. Thankfully, it seemed deep enough to sustain a higher fall since there didn't appear to have any other way to get down from the top other than to jump off. Reed and Killian managed to scale it without issue, though, Reed hesitated at the top of the wall. When he fell, he hit the water stomach down with a sharp slap. It sounded painful.

I made a note not to do that and swallowed hard, knowing that my fear of heights was more than intact. There's nothing to do about it though, so I'd have to handle it— somehow.

Suddenly, it was our turn. Of course, Dex positioned himself in line to be paired up with me. I couldn't figure out what his angle was, and why he liked picking on me so much. It irritated the shit out of me. I couldn't think of anyone that could rile such a response out of me. Normally, my temperament favored a calm and collected one. But since being here and meeting Dex, a match had been taken to it, burning any notion of me having myself together. Marley would be thrilled to see her big sister coming apart at the seams. She always did think I was too buttoned up for my own good.

When it was our turn, I took up the spot on the faded white line, one foot in front of the other, ready to make a dash for it.

Dex, however, lazily unbuttoned his shirt as if we had all the time in the world, and I couldn't help but notice his well-defined chest. That was the body of a man who'd spent time working on his physical appearance, and clearly, it was paying off. He even had those two divots that pointed in a v shape at his hips. I quickly averted my gaze to not appear as if I were gawking over his chiseled physique, but it was too late. He had a self-satisfied grin upon his mouth as his blue eyes twinkled with mischief.

Arrogant prick.

"See you on the other side, Deveraux," Dex's sinfully deep voice said, sending a shiver down my spine unbidden.

Fuck this guy, I would make him regret deciding to mess with me.

As soon as Killian said, "Go!" I was off, feet flying effortlessly over every dip in the ground. I met the wall and hoisted myself up using the uneven parts, anchoring my foot against the lowest section.

Sweat pooled between my breasts and my heart hammered hard against my chest, knowing that one wrong move could land me in a heap of broken limbs, just like Nat.

The guards had finally sent a mender to assist, but they took their sweet time doing it.

Right above my head sat a piece of bone that looked as if someone had lodged a femur into the stone. Next to me, Dex effortlessly climbed, his sculpted muscles on display for everyone to see. He was way ahead of me, and with little to no upper body strength, I didn't stand a chance.

My hands gripped around the bone, shaking with the effort to pull myself up. It took everything I had to move even an inch.

Fuck. Why wasn't I the type of person that worked out?

There was no way I was getting over this thing on strength alone.

Suddenly, the bone in my hands began to violently shake.

My grip started to slip, and my foot slid out from its position on the wall. The ground beneath was far enough away that if I were to fall, I'd probably die.

Above me, Dex looked down from the top of the wall with his hands on his hips.

Was he using his motherfucking power on me right now?

As if a switch had been turned on inside me, shadows materialized around my body, gripping me about my waist like a harness. They hoisted me to safety and set my shaking form on top of the wall.

I always thought of shadows being mere wisps, not something tangible.

There was no time to dwell on my newfound knowledge though. Time was ticking and I wanted to win.

Dex, starred at me with his mouth quirked up in that annoying way that dimpled his cheeks.

"Try to kill me again and I'll cut your dick off."

"Is that a threat, love?"

"That's a promise, jackass. And stop calling me love."

We're so high up— higher than I anticipated and my stomach roils with nausea as I looked down into the inky black water below. It didn't feel like I could access the shadows with how jumbled up I felt, so I would have no choice but to jump.

"After you, your viciousness" Dex gestured in a mock gentlemanly bow.

I had half a mind to shove him off here, but I didn't think the guards would take too kindly to me intentionally maiming a fellow player. Dex might not have cared about getting caught, but I certainly did. The risk of being arrested wasn't worth the reward. Besides, we only had a few more days of training before the games officially started, and then I could maim him all I wanted. I could make him bleed and beg for mercy.

Right now, I had bigger things to worry about. Like how the hell I was going to make it off here.

With a wink, Dex stepped off the ledge and plummeted below without even breaking a sweat.

Dammit.

I was behind again. The water below seemed to zoom in and out in the field of my vision making my head swim. My toes crept up to the edge, kicking small pieces of the wall off. If I slipped right now, I'd probably crack my head open and die. Goodbye world.

No, I needed to jump far enough away that I cleared the jagged wall, but not too far that would land me right on top of the barbed wire cage. There was only one way down from here, and it was to jump off this wall.

Decision made. I leapt into the air, eyes closed and stomach careening up into my ribs. Wind whipped around my body as I hoped with everything inside me that I would make it.

What seemed like an eon later, my feet touched water and I was enveloped fully into a freezing vat of muddied water. The cold was a shock to my system, and I fought against the instinct to open my mouth under the water. Instead, I kicked with a ferocity to break me free of its clutches. I still had to swim to the other side without getting caught up in the barbed wire, and Dex was already halfway there.

Staying low, I pushed off the wall, took a deep breath, and ducked beneath the surface to avoid the long reach of the wires that dipped into the water like hands ready to grip onto me with one wrong move, just like Killian. He'd gotten wrapped up in one of the tendrils and now had slices all down his neck and back.

The water was far too cloudy for me to make out anything clearly. My lungs screamed out for oxygen, but I had to keep going. I was almost there, I had to be. Black spots dotted my already limited vision as my body demanded air. *Just... a little farther*, I told myself putting everything into kicking.

Just as I was about to make it free and clear, a barbed wire that I didn't see, grasped me by my braid, yanking me back.

My mouth opened, letting in a torrent of dirty water as I screamed soundlessly out in pain. Bubbles escaped as water filled my throat. It burned so fucking bad and panic, hot, raw panic pounded against my chest as I fought to get free.

A small wisp of a shadow emerged then, wrapping around my body and unhooked my caught locks from the wires.

I was able to claw my way out, getting cut down the length of my back as my hands were ripped into ribbons trying to free myself. It felt like burning knives digging into my soft flesh, but I had to keep moving despite the pain. If I didn't, I would die here. Blood streamed from my wounds as I swam. Tears pricked at the back of my eyes, but I wouldn't give into the agony. For myself, for my family, I fought to reach the end.

Finally, my knees hit ground and I crawled out of the mud, covered in my own blood, dripping wet, and half frozen.

Sputtering a breath of oxygen, I wheezed and collapsed onto the finish line as I involuntarily coughed. My lungs and throat felt like they wrecked on fire.

Dex looked down at me, hands shoved in his pockets. His horned mask appearing more devilish than ever in the dark lighting.

"I thought you'd never make it."

Anger like a hot poker stabbing my chest bubbled up inside me, but I didn't have the energy for a smart retort. Instead, I glared up at him and wished I was back home, snuggled up in my bed, not stuck down here in this hellscape.

Everyone seemed to be picking up their things and heading to the tunnel, but not Dex. He just stared down at me with the same intense expression that had me wishing I could read his mind. The man was an enigma but figuring him out might be the death of me.

"Here, let me help you up," Dex said offering his hand.

I smacked it away with what little strength I had left.

"Fuck off."

He chuckled darkly.

The effort it took to get myself to standing was monumental, but the sweat gathering down my back and dotted across my forehead was worth it to not accept help from a man who would have gladly watch me drown.

I was in desperate need of shower and a good night's rest, but we still had one more challenge. With the way I was feeling I didn't even know how I would have enough energy to even make it back to my room without collapsing. Each breath was labored, sounding wet with the muddied earth that rattled around in my lungs.

I may have lost to Dex today, but I was still standing. My mom was right, there was a strength inside me that I just needed to cling onto. It might be the only thing that helped me make it through to the end.

THE MENDERS PATCHED me up as best they could before they led me down the tunnel where the rest of the contestants waited in an arena. The room was rounded at the top and had one long ray of light that illuminated what looked like a fighting ring. There were several slabs of concrete that could be used to hide behind as well as nine sharp iron poles jutting out from the ground that encompassed the outside of the ring.

"Ah, now that we're all here, we can begin," a voice called from the lower level. A woman with large elaborate braids wrapped around her head stood with her hands on her hips. Her ebony-colored skin glistened in the minimal light. She was muscular and had a formidable presence. She was wearing the same standard issue uniform as the guards, marking her as one of them. The only difference was where most uniforms held a white rib cage, hers was embroidered with a golden hue. I'd never seen a distinction like that before, but it's not as if I try to associate with the god's army. They were known for their maliciousness.

"I am Captain Thiel. You will address me as such. Now, you'll be facing off as teams, demonstrating your new powers. The last one standing, will have won their team a five-minute head start. You may be wondering why we train our contestants at all. Well, there was a time before any of us were born, that contestants were sent into the catacombs with no training at all. However, the gods found that the lack of proper training ended with almost all the contestants dying rapidly. To ensure that you have a proper chance at winning, we allow three solid days of getting used to your magick. And then of course you have the masquerade, where you'll be mingling amongst the gods and goddesses themselves. It will be a chance for you to win their favor, and that can make all the difference when you're neck deep in a pile of shit."

"Yeah, we'd hate to die too quickly for the god's entertainment purposes," Nat quipped, only to earn herself a deadly stare from the captain. Nat was mouthy and bold in a way I could only dream of. It was an admirable quality, but in this case, possibly deadly. The gods' army members weren't exactly full of compassion and empathy. They were cruel. Obedient. Soldiers that thrived on keeping us in line.

Making my way down to where the rest of the contestants were, I almost tripped over my own feet from how exhausted I was. If my team were to be allowed five whole minutes of access to the catacombs ahead of everyone else, it could make a huge difference. It might not seem like much, but every second counted when it was a race to the end. The first one to touch the wall with the engraved word '*Fin*', marking the end, would be declared the winner. The only trouble was getting there. The catacombs were a maze of tunnels and rooms, filled with booby traps and pit falls. If your fellow contestants didn't finish you off first, the catacombs just might.

I found an empty spot next to my teammates where Nat was visibly struggling to stand. How we were supposed to fight against the other teams right now, I had no idea. With Nat still recovering, and myself still reeling from the obstacle course, I was wishing we'd never gone up against Dex's team.

"Team of Diamonds, please step forward."

Four contestants stood looking just as beat up as I felt. Clearly, today had been rough on us all.

"Team of Spades, where are you?"

My eyes found Dex easily as he stepped forward with the rest of his team. His gaze caught mine as he walked into the cage and my stomach involuntarily flipped. Nat gave me a wary look, but I schooled my features to feign indifference. What did I care about Dex? Nothing, that's what.

"You have ten minutes to defeat your opponents. Remember no killing is permitted until the games officially begin. Failure to abide by the rules will result in your immediate removal from the games."

A shot rang out and the potent taste of magick filled the air all around us. Dread coiled within me. I had an ominous feeling that someone wasn't going to make it past today. Selfishly, I hoped it was anyone but me.

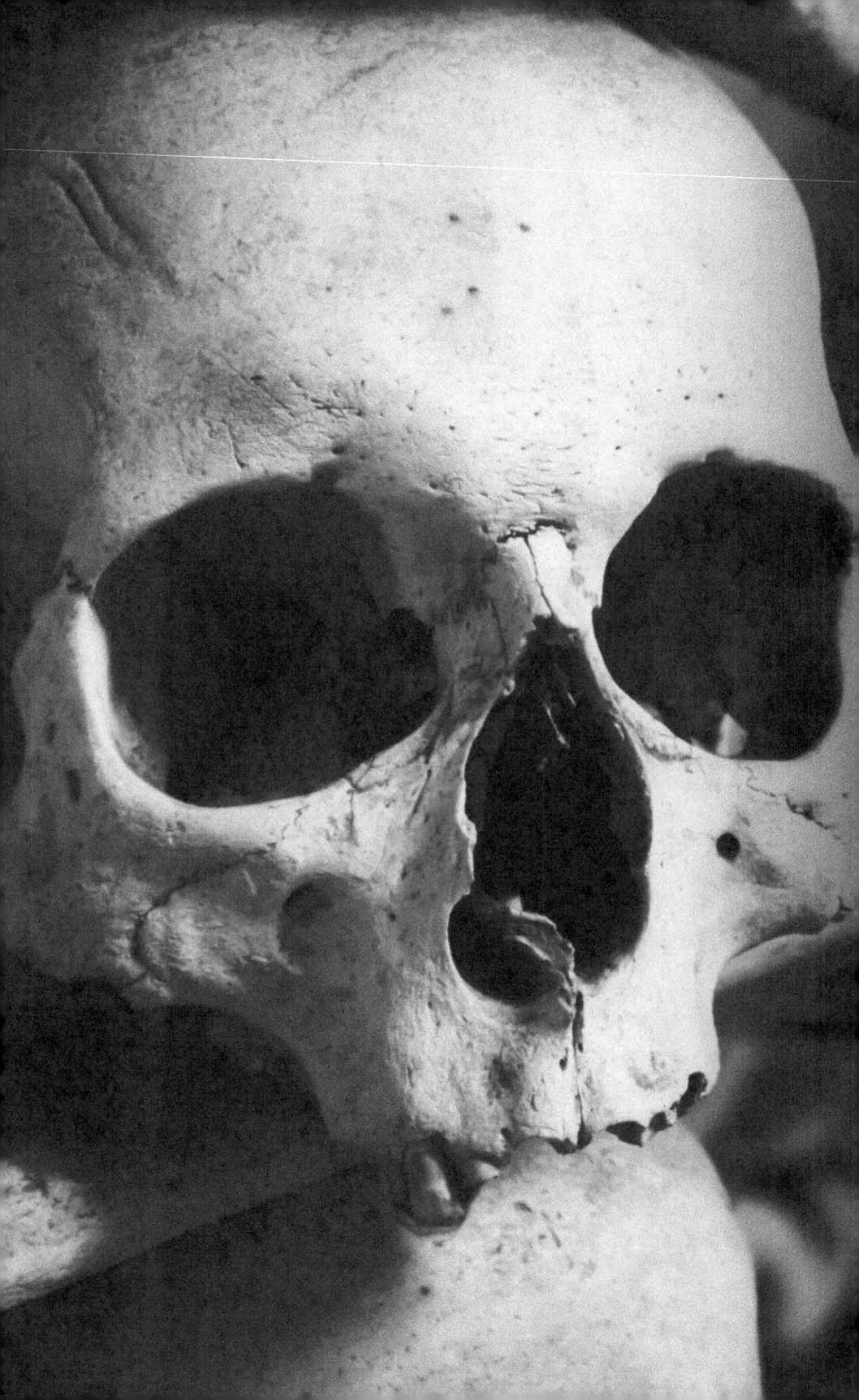

CHAPTER 9
DEX

I could feel her watching my every move. Her eyes tracking me felt like a caress against my skin. Was she worried about me or hoping that someone hit me with a fatal blow?

Probably the latter.

The moment the shot went off, magick came flying at us from all directions. Immediately, I took cover behind one of the concrete slabs and tried to formulate a plan. Céline, Genevieve, and Regis had paired off against the opposite teams, leaving the one asshole I ached to take down free for me— Magnus. He had looked at me like he wanted to snap me in half, but I wasn't about to let that happen.

My magick was limited to being able to manipulate bones, and without being allowed to kill someone else for their power, I felt constrained in what I could do. I had to think outside of the box. Good thing I was an expert at solving problems.

The rules never stated that I only had to use what was in the ring, and we were in the catacombs. There were skeletons buried all around us. Reaching out with my power, I locked onto the closest bone I could find. It was above us, small in size and embedded in the rounded ceiling, but it was something.

A loud crack echoed in the cavernous space as the ceiling cracked and a partial piece of what looked like a mandible with some teeth still attached careened towards my outstretched hand. Bits of ceiling came down with it, and I dodged them before they crushed me.

A blinding beam of light hit me square in the eyes and caused my vision to instantly become obscured as Genevieve's magick burst forth. I dropped to my knees, eyes shut tight as my palms pressed to the outside of my mask, hoping that the damage wasn't permanent. Staying low, I attempted to open my eyes only to be met with spots and a large fist crashing into my ribcage by none other than Magnus. My body went flying with the impact and I felt my ribs become dislodged as his strength pummeled into me. The taste of blood flooded my mouth as I scrambled to stand.

The area around us had been reduced to rubble. My head swam and my lungs wheezed.

Magnus loomed closer, a sneer coating his cruel mouth, golden mask alight with the singular sunbeam's fading light. I swallowed hard trying to figure out my next move.

The jawbone that I had summoned with my power lay a few feet away. If I could just get there in time, I could use it as a weapon.

Magnus moved, his size was a burden though, giving me enough time to clumsily scramble for the shard of bone. The magick beckoned me forward, directing my steps while my eyes were still struggling to adjust. I scooped it up just as Magnus clasped the back of my shirt, yanking me back hard enough that my feet were no longer touching ground.

The neckline of my shirt buckled against my throat, choking me.

My arm swung on him, the jawbone slipping in my weakening grip. But I managed to land a solid punch to his face. Bone hitting bone, his own jaw crunching beneath the mandible causing him to drop me. My ankles twisted on impact, and I went down onto the concrete ground hard.

"You're fucking dead!" Magnus screamed as blood dripped down the side of his face.

I became vaguely aware of the chaos that surrounded me. Magick shot out from all around us. Contestant versus contestant were in a bloody brawl, all for the chance of five extra minutes. I couldn't imagine what it would be like when the real games finally started if this is how we were acting for a measly five-minute head start.

Magnus reached down and grabbed me by the front of my shirt this time, arm raised and ready to strike. With his power of strength, it wouldn't take much for him to punch a hole in my head and I'd be dead upon impact. My head turned to the side and my eyes caught Odessa's horrified expression. Her hands covering her mouth and her dark brown eyes blown wide with worry.

Worry for me, I realized.

With a renewed energy, I used every bit of magick I could access and shoved it out. In that moment I realized that the bones I could control weren't limited to dead and buried ones, but the very much alive ones.

Magnus's beady little eyes rimmed with malice, widened the moment I locked onto his skeletal form. He became a puppet in my hands. I made him set me down with ease and I felt my lips quirk up into a smirk at my newfound power. His strength was no match for me.

Cracking my knuckles, he began to move at my command. A lunge here, a pirouette there.

He looked utterly ridiculous and the snickers behind me from the other contestants watching had his cheeks reddening with embarrassment. I fucking loved it.

After a minute or two of exerting my power over him, I finally made him crouch down before me—kneeling before his master. He looked up at me reluctantly and that malice was replaced with the most delicious shade of fear. I had him by the balls and he knew it.

"Do you have anything you want to say to me, Magnus?" My arms were locked behind my back as I stood tall over him. The fighting around us had stalled out. Everyone was watching this moment, wondering what I would do.

I knew I couldn't kill him— not yet anyway.

"Fuck you," Magnus muttered.

"What was that? I couldn't quite hear you?" I leaned down and wrapped my hand around my ear. I knew what he said but wanted him to feel just how helpless he was.

"I said, fuck you," he spat, and I let him go. His body fell into a useless heap, and the crowd around us cheered. I lifted my arms out wide and took a bow.

My eyes locked onto Odessa's, and I saw on her face a moment too late that I had let my guard down. Turning my back to a rabid dog like Magnus was a mistake.

"Watch out!" She cried, and I turned around to see a sharp piece of rock lifted in the air and aimed right at me.

Genevieve jumped in front of me, arms raised and light shining, but Magnus couldn't stop and my magick that I had been wielding was slow to respond. I had no choice but to watch the tip puncture through her chest and come out the other end.

The arena fell into a stunned hush as blood bubbled out of her gaping wound and down the corners of her mouth. It had gone right through her heart. Magnus ripped the makeshift blade from her body, and she crumpled at his feet.

"You!" The captain cried out, pointing her finger at Magnus. "Guards, seize him. The rules were clear. No killing fellow contestants until after the games have begun."

"It, it was an accident!" Magnus grappled as the guards grabbed him about the arms and cut the ribbons from his mask off. It fell onto the ground with a clang echoing off the ceiling.

We watched on in horror as Genevieve's still body was carried from the arena, her hands dragging on the dusty ground below. The guards removed the crown of light from her.

She had saved me.

Jumped right in front of the danger. Part of me wondered if it was of her own volition, or if I'd inadvertently been the one to move her there. Maybe with this mask, I was more powerful than I realized. While I'd planned to kill everyone in here eventually, the actuality of death was far different than the hypothetical.

"The punishment, I fear, will be your life," the captain said, removing the blade strapped to her back. With one strong arc of the blade, it sliced across his neck removing flesh and bone. His head ripped free from his body with a sickening wet sound, cutting his scream short. Blood sputtered free soaking the floor and spraying those closest to him, making a few of them retch. We watched as Magnus's head rolled across the stage landing at my feet. His dead eyes were staring up at me while his mouth was stuck open in a voiceless scream.

The entire room went deadly silent.

I couldn't tear my eyes away from the bloody head that laid at my feet.

The captain strode over to where Magnus's decapitated head was and gripped it by his dark hair as if she were plucking a flower from the Earth.

"This is what happens when you don't follow the rules of Nocturne. You're playing a game of the gods. Never forget that you are but mortals in their realm. You're all dismissed for the day."

"What happens to their powers?" Regis asked with more audacity than I could pretend to have.

The captain turned with a feral smirk splayed upon her lips. "Those powers are forfeit. Now get out of my arena."

She didn't need to tell me twice. I dipped my head and scrambled to get the hell out of there. Maybe I was in shock, but all I could think about was what a shame it would have been to die before having the pleasure of tasting Odessa's lips against my own. As if she knew my thoughts, her gaze found my own. We kept doing that. Finding each other in a crowd as if we were the only two that really mattered. I didn't hate it.

CHAPTER 10
ODESSA

D inner was quiet. The only sounds to be heard were
the scrapes of forks against plates and a few groans
of pain. It seemed that everyone was run down
from training, but also grappling with losing two contestants.
The empty spot across from me where Magnus once sat felt like
a dark reminder of just how deadly and volatile this contest was.

I didn't realize that the learning curve to utilizing my
magick would be so grueling. I'd just assumed that the moment
I put on the mask it would be easy and that I could wield the
shadows without a problem. How wrong I'd been. It took skill
and patience and a surprising amount of energy to harness the
wild sparks of power that now resided within me. But once that
mask came off my face, the power seemed to fizzle out into
nothing. Only winning the competition would allow that
magick to remain with or without the mask, or so I'd been told.

I forced myself to eat every bit of meat and potatoes that lined
my plate, even though I felt queasy from ingesting the dirty water

during training. My strength would be needed to not only get me through the training sessions, but the competition itself. The beef burned on its way down my esophagus. The inside of my throat was still raw from how hard I'd coughed to expel the water from my lungs. I chased the food with a swig of wine, hoping to dislodge it from where it felt stuck. It went down hard and had me longing for the roast my mother used to make before her illness. How we would all clean our plates of every crumb when she would make her famous roast. Usually for a birthday or celebration Thoughts of my mother soured my already irritable stomach and I pushed my plate away, trying not to focus on my family and what they might be doing. Or if my mother was still with us. I tried and failed not to think about it and the life I'd left behind.

To think right above our heads laid an entire city. Bustling and alive with people and carriages. While we were down here in the flickering candlelight, surrounded by the long dead and buried. Living and training in the domain of the gods.

The upcoming masquerade was only a few days away and the gods would be in attendance. While I was certain the dress I'd packed for the occasion would be perfect, the knowledge of having to interact with our city's rulers and reason for this competition gnawed at my anxiety. How could I look them in the eye and know they only saw me as a chess piece? A mere moment of fleeting entertainment in a lifetime of endless charades meant to make their immortal lives less boring.

Dex's gaze locked onto me then, wine glass paused on my bottom lip as I remembered I was in a room full of my potential murderers.

I glanced around at the contestants nervously as I shakily

put down the glass harder than I intended to, causing a small splash of liquid to career over the side and drop onto the wooden table beneath.

Dex watched me curiously, and while I actively tried to avoid his attention, I couldn't deny the warm feeling that accumulated in my chest and down my spine every time he looked at me as if I were the only person that existed in this crowded room.

Since the start of the competition, he'd singled me out for whatever reason. The weight of his gaze simmered under my skin as if my body liked the way he looked at me. Like he was undressing me in that handsome head of his.

The thought was insane. I couldn't possibly like someone like Dex. Not when I had Theo at home waiting for me. Sweet, devoted, Theo who I'd known all my life. It was just the stress of this place getting to me. Maybe the lost oxygen had gotten to my head and had me entertaining wild ideas.

I could practically hear what my sister, Marley, would say about the situation. She'd tell me to forget Theo and have some fun for once with the devilishly handsome stranger. She'd always found Theo dull and didn't understand our relationship. But I did. With his family's station, Papa wouldn't have to work as hard. I'd be able to provide and have a security that we lacked. Sure, my father's designs were well sought after now, but I remember a time when our stomachs groaned with hunger because he wasn't selling anything and the bills from the physicians kept piling up. How my father would go out at night and beg when he thought we were all asleep.

Being with Theo would alleviate the worry that lingered in

the back of my mind. ~~Gods knew Papa wasn't~~ getting any younger.

A loud gong rang throughout the room announcing the end of dinner. No one made a noise as we shuffled back to our rooms, eyes downcast and shoulders slumped. Whatever illusions of how easy this competition would be were snuffed out today. Even Dex looked slightly defeated and that had me worried. If the most arrogant among us was feeling that way, I didn't know what to expect once the games started. I could only hope that I would master my power before the shots that signaled the start of the games rang out. No matter what happened, any illusion of being able to walk out of this unscathed were dashed to pieces. There would be blood on my hands by the end of this, I just hoped it wouldn't be my own.

"AGAIN!" Nat called, sparring towards me with a blast of power. I'd narrowly dodged her attack and rolled onto my back avoiding being turned into stone.

"Nice to see you're all healed up," I wheezed, struggling to get my feet underneath me.

"Yeah, well, the healers did what they could."

Nat bounced energetically on her feet waiting for me to get back in position. Her chin length hair swished with the motion as I put my hands up and readied myself for another attack. She was fast and strong, making me work hard to keep up with her.

Yesterday was a grim wakeup call that I was woefully unprepared for this competition. Theo's words haunted me on a loop inside my head, reminding me that even he didn't believe in me enough to make it out of here. That's probably why he didn't show up to say goodbye. He knew I was dead meat.

But there was another voice, a stronger, gentler one of my mother's reminding me that I had a strength inside. It was the only thing pushing me forward.

"Looking good, Deveraux," Dex's voice crawled over my skin as he walked past.

"Drop dead, Bourreau," I snapped, losing control and feeling the embers of my magick coat my hands. Shadows danced along the tips of my fingers ready to strike.

I was in no mood for his shit today. Muscles I didn't even know I possessed ached. Every inch of me it seemed was worked to the bone in yesterday's training. The healers merely took the edge off, but it wasn't enough. I could still feel the dregs of my near-death experience clinging to the periphery of my mind, taunting me.

"Aw, don't be like that. I know you secretly like me." I rolled my eyes and almost missed the moment Nat decided to strike. The magick hit my shield and it became instantly ten times heavier as it slowly morphed into stone. I dropped it with a resounding clang and called for a time out.

"Almost got you," she said with a smirk.

"Yeah, well good thing you didn't, or you'd end up like Magnus." I shuddered, and she did too.

While we were on the same team, and working together for now, I couldn't let myself forget that the moment the games started she could turn on me. It didn't look like I'd be making any real friends here soon with that kind of environment.

Dex crossed his arms over his chest as he watched me drink from my canteen of water.

He looked at me as if I were the most interesting thing he'd ever seen, and it did funny things to my insides.

"What?" I snapped, feeling a dribble of water drip down my chin.

He caught it with his thumb, wiping it away with a swipe, only he didn't let go. His hand cupped my chin and angled my head to look up at him. My heart stuttered and I swallowed thickly.

His nostrils flared as he stared down at me, almost like he was angry at me for something, but I didn't know what.

"Try to be more careful. Wouldn't want you dying already when I haven't even had the chance to play with you yet."

"You disgust me."

"Oh, yeah?"

My chest heaved. "Yeah." I shoved him backwards, needing space from how fuzzy he made my head.

"That's too bad."

"Why?"

He shrugged his toned muscular shoulder with a bored expression glinting behind that mask of his. "If I disgusted you so much, you wouldn't want to find out."

I harrumphed angrily.

"If the two of you are done with your foreplay, we have training to get back to," Nat said with her hands splayed on her narrow hips.

I gaped at her, but Dex just chuckled like she'd said the funniest thing in the world. Even with his dimpled smiles and intense way he paid attention to me, I couldn't shake the feeling that I was in the presence of something dangerous every time I was around him. It was like being locked in the same room as a sleeping bear. Sure, they were cute and asleep, but at any moment they might wake and maul the ever-loving life out of you.

Perhaps I was being overly paranoid, and the nature of Nocturne was starting to get to me.

I was painfully aware that we only had one more day before this thing kicked off into full gear, and we'd be in the middle of an all-out war against each other.

Just as we were about to spar again, the captain entered the room with her entourage of personal guards. The training area fell silent, and we all stood up straight.

While Dex's danger felt buried, the captain wore hers like a second amor. It was palpable in every calculated move. Even the slightest glance from her felt like it might be your last.

"Follow me," she instructed.

We did as we were told, getting corralled by the guards as if we were a herd of cattle being led to slaughter. The tunnel had a short ceiling and confined walls, not allowing us much space to maneuver as we walked not knowing what exactly we were in for.

A large wrought iron door sat at the end and opened with a wave of the captain's wrist. She must possess some type of magick, I thought. Maybe the ability to manipulate metal.

We filtered inside the small dark room that was surrounded by human remains. Skulls and bones were embedded into every crevice. Only the faint flicker of a candle illuminated the tight space. At the end of the room lay an open casket that was occupied by a skeleton.

Was this a tomb?

The very air around us smelt of decay and damp mold. It made my skin crawl. I wanted nothing more than to get the hell out of this small space, feeling panic take root in my stomach as the captain's eerie smile was illuminated from the bottom as she held a single candle below her chin.

"While we are now two contestants down, it will only get worse from here." The people around me tensed at her words. "Practicing your magick is only one aspect that you'll need to survive the games. Wit and physicality are also valuable assets that will see you through to the finish line."

Uneasiness rolls through my gut in anticipation for what she's about to say next and how that would apply to where she's brought us.

"Your next training session will leave you locked in this room with your teams, with clues hidden in which you will need to decipher in order to break free. Since you failed your last test, the winners from this round will have the opportunity for the same prize. A five-minute head start." Her smile was cruel as she walked out into the tunnels and turned back around. "Oh, and try not to kill anyone this time."

The lights flickered out and the door shut with a clang leaving the remaining fourteen contestants in a tomb surrounded by skeletons.

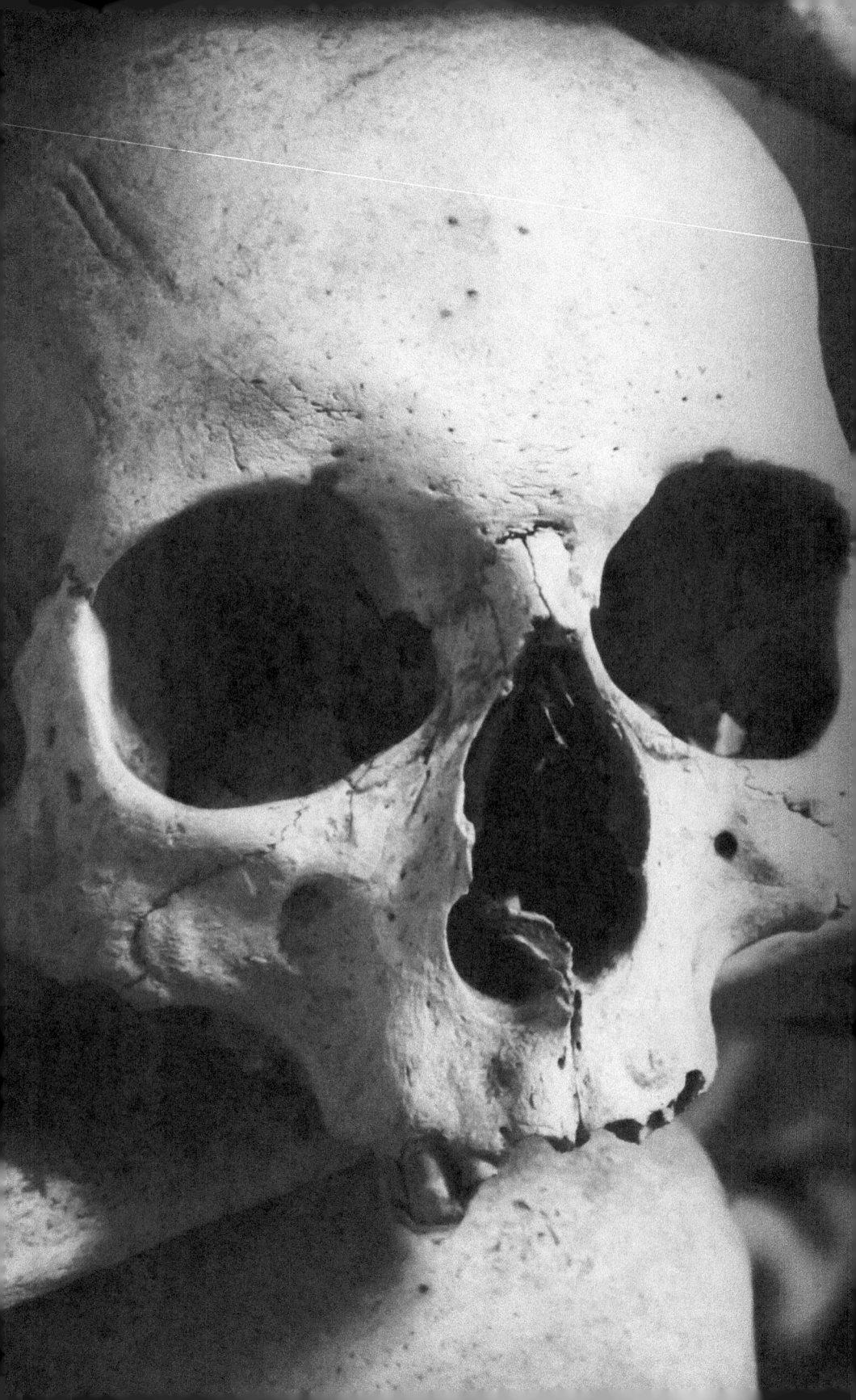

CHAPTER 11
DEX

There wasn't much that could rattle me, but claustrophobia just happened to be one of my weaknesses. The room we'd been brought to was small for normal standards, but cram fourteen desperate contestants inside, and well, I was sweating my ass off.

"Who the fuck has the power of light?" An irritated manly voice asked.

"She fucking died yesterday," I snapped, the panic of being trapped building inside of me. *Died saving me because of that fuckwad,* Magnus, I thought bitterly.

"Oh, right."

"I have fire," The Pyro muttered, coaxing a flame into their hands. It illuminated his stark white face and dusty blond hair.

It wasn't much, but it was enough to make out the expressions of the people around me. Most looked freaked as hell, not that I can blame them. The golden glow of their masks in the faint firelight gave them a sinister appearance, reminding me that no one could be trusted down here.

The door was firmly locked and no amount of hitting it with my shoulder was going to knock it down. We had to find another way, and it was taking everything in me to appear stoic, like I wasn't seconds away from combusting.

I knew coming down here that this would be a possibility. Tight spaces were a given when you're dealing with over two-hundred miles of underground tunnels. There were bound to be small spaces. But I still fucking hated it. It reminded me too much of what I'd been through to get here, but I couldn't think about it now. I needed to focus on how to get out of this fucking room. There were fourteen of us shoved in here. It was too much. I was knocking elbows with some sweaty short guy who possessed the power of time and reeked of body odor.

"Let's find those clues so we can get out of here," Regis said, acting as leader again. I didn't mind. I'd let him think he was in charge, before I snapped his neck with my bare hands and took his power. Not that I could act on it now.

Odessa was off to the side, standing with her arms wrapped around her middle and her bottom lip pulled between her teeth. Guess she didn't like small spaces either. She seemed preoccupied by the casket, not taking her eyes off it for a moment.

"Bring that light over here, I think I found something," Regis said.

Right. We were supposed to be looking for clues. There wasn't a lot of room to move but the more my eyes adjusted to the dim light, the more I could make out.

I focused in on the wall. From up close it looked like a

nonsensical arrangement of skulls and bones, but from over here, I could faintly make out a word being spelled out by the shape. It looked like it spelled out the French word for death— *la mort*. But with one notable difference. The 't' was upside-down.

The fire went out abruptly and more than one person grumbled in frustration.

"Sorry," The Pyro apologized. "I put my hand down for a second."

Was the air feeling tighter in here than it was before?

Sweat began to gather at my temples as I slowly started to lose my cool. As soon as the fire flickered back into existence, my heart rate steadied out. My eyes instantly went to where Odessa had been standing, but instead of being where she was before the light went out, she was standing over by the casket staring down into its contents.

Her hand hovered precariously over the actively rotting corpse as if debating if she wanted to touch it or not.

"What are you doing?" I asked her, making my way over to where she stood by squeezing past several bodies. No one seemed to know what they were doing and were instead poking around and hoping for the best. Like a clue would jump right out at them any second.

"Why would this be here? It doesn't make any sense. Most bodies are kept as decoration. Placed into the walls. But this one? It's displayed prominently. There has to be a reason."

I swallowed hard watching as she dipped her hand into the open casket, searching for a clue that would get us the hell out of this room.

It was more ~~tomb than room~~ to be honest, and that one singular thought had my panic rearing up again.

You're not back there, I told myself.

While we were supposed to work as teams, mine were too busy checking the cracked checkered floor.

I stared down into the occupied casket. Who was this person to be granted such an honor as a casket in this place of the gods? The skeleton was freshly rotted, with most of its face decayed, with the exception of a thin wisp of skin that stretched over the right side of its cheekbones. It wore a long musty smelling dress that at one time might have been a vibrant blue, but now was a dusty faded gray. Then I noticed that the skeleton's gnarled boney hands were clutching onto a small box placed directly over their chest.

"We should look in there," I declared.

"Well, you're the necromancer, so move the bones," Odessa said still searching the fabric laced sides.

I cracked my knuckles and reached for my magick making the bones in its hands release the box. It did as I willed, giving up the box as if it were handing it straight to me. Upon further inspection, it had the known insignia of the gods etched into the top of the lid and some words carved onto the side. *Même le dieu de la mort ne peut pas nous séparer.* Not even the god of death can separate us. Interesting to find something that directly insulted the god of death while we were in his domain.

The box was light in my hands, and I shook it, listening for anything inside.

"Don't shake that, what if there's something breakable in there that we need," Odessa hit my stomach with the back of her hand forcibly.

I chuckled. "What, do you think they hid a glass key in here or something?"

She rolled her eyes. "Well, are you going to open it or not?"

The lid took more force than I anticipated to pry open, but finally after sticking the small bit of my nail into the slit, it was free. Inside laid a small worn paper.

"Hey, Pyro, bring that light over here, would you? I can't make out what this says."

They obliged, getting close enough that we could see the word 'la mort' written in ink. The 't' matching the one on the wall. Upside-down.

"Can we hurry up? I don't know how much longer I can keep this fire going," the Pyro warned.

"What do you think it means?" Odessa asked.

"Not sure." My brain whirled, wondering what the significance was. If we didn't solve this soon, the small quarters were sure to send me into an all-out panic, and I couldn't slip up with the persona I'd been so careful to convey. If my fellow contestants saw me as weak, I'd be made into their target instead of the other way around. With two powers now permanently out of the games, I couldn't afford for any more mistakes. It was vital I secured as many as possible.

"Hey, what did you guys find? *La Mort*?" Regis asked grabbing the paper from my hands.

As soon as the words left his mouth, the wall shook sending dirt and bones collapsing into a heap. The casket disappeared through a trap door and the ceiling began to lower. The only way out was through a small door that had appeared with the toppling of the bones.

"Quick! Through here!" Odessa exclaimed, grabbing my arm on instinct.

She pulled me through the panicking throng of contestants. Each of us trying all at once to get to the same exit. With every second that passed the ceiling grew closer and the room grew smaller.

One of the contestants shoved us hard, and suddenly a deluge of spiders began crawling all over us. Screams erupted as something bit my leg, causing instant numbness.

"I-I can't. I can't move." Every muscle in my body seized up on me, as I was shoved hard onto the ground. Odessa's grip on me was lost and she was swept through the door, her brown eyes catching mine as she disappeared. More spiders crawled over my skin, as the numbness spread up my body.

I glanced above me and watched in horror as the ceiling dropped closer. The very real possibility of being crushed to death was staring me in the face. No matter how much I willed my muscles to move, they refused.

Suddenly, hands were on my shirt, and I was being dragged through.

My vision swam and I could barely make out who was helping me. Though the soft scent of jasmine clued me in.

Odessa had come back for me, even when I hadn't done the same for her. Even when I'd been actively plotting her demise along with everyone else here. She came back to save me.

I couldn't form words, but if I could I'd be expressing my gratitude.

"Holy fucking gods, you're so much heavier than I thought you'd be," she groaned, finally getting me safely through the door.

She fell back and it was then that I'd realized we were back in the tunnels.

"Congratulations, Team Spade. You've earned yourself a five-minute head start. As for the rest of you, you'll be starting at the normal time. Now, you have one more day of training, so rest up and refuel. You'll need all the strength you can get."

Our team had won, but I could barely find it in me to care. Not when the effects of the spider's bite were churning through my veins at an alarming rate. I think I could feel my heart rate slowing.

"Let's get you a healer," Odessa said.

Her face was the last thing I saw before I blacked out.

CHAPTER 12
ODESSA

I was in desperate need of a shower, but with only three available I had to wait my turn. Just like back home, I thought with a pang. Every muscle in my body ached and my head swam from the harrowing experience in the tomb. I needed the feel of dirt and bones scrubbed from my skin.

There was a moment when I didn't think I would make it out of there, and for the second day in a row, I walked away with my life— grateful to still be here. Most unexpectedly, though, was the way Dex handled the challenge. I didn't know why it ate at me so. Maybe it was the humanizing aspect. I'd grown so accustomed to hating him, that seeing a vulnerable, mortal side to him did funny things to my insides. Shameful things. Things I shouldn't even be thinking about or feeling. Try as I might to stuff that down, it kept popping back up again.

They'd whisked him away to be seen by a healer, and that's

the last I heard. We went straight to dinner and then back to our rooms. But he hadn't shown.

In truth, I'd never met anyone like him before, and my feelings surrounding him confused me. Maybe I'd been more sheltered than I realized growing up, because while there was a dangerous energy about him, I kept finding myself intrigued, and almost drawn to it. Though, I wondered if saving him would end up biting me in the ass.

I'd forgotten that we were all out for ourselves here.

There could only be one winner after all.

I don't know what possessed me to go back for him. Maybe I was too soft like Theo claimed, but I didn't think I could live with myself if I just left him there to be crushed.

They'd expelled The Spider for causing Dex harm, and a part of me felt relieved that the competition was already getting slimmer. The less people I had to go up against, the better.

Guilt gnawed at my conscious as I thought of Theo. I realized that I hadn't even been missing him. While thoughts of my family were frequent, Theo hadn't really crossed my mind. I wonder what that said about me. Surely, it was just because of the stress of being down here. If I wasn't training, I was either eating, drinking water, or stuck in a state of anxiety over what was to come. That had to be it.

After some time had passed of me stressing out in my room, I decided it was safe to chance a shower, entering the first one I crossed. The door was unlocked, and as I stepped inside, I breathed a sigh of relief. That is until I realized that it was in fact occupied already, with a very naked, very wet, Dex.

He seemed back to normal. The healers must have done a thorough job, because he moved as if nothing had happened.

His body was a specimen to behold. The muscles this man possessed were hypnotic and sinful.

I couldn't seem to look away, though I knew I should.

I shouldn't be seeing this, but I couldn't make my feet move.

My mouth hung open as I watched his powerful, large hands wrap around his impressive length. It was bigger than I thought possible, but I only had limited experience with Theo, who always pushed me away saying we should wait for marriage.

Now that I was here, I didn't know if that day would ever come.

Oh gods, I could die a virgin. Now, that would be tragic. Damn Theo and his stupid principals.

Dex placed one of his hands against the tiled wall as the water from the shower cascaded down his muscular back. His forearm flexed with the effort of jerking his long cock over and over again, and I couldn't help but wonder what it would feel like to have it inside me. Filling me. Making me come.

Wetness gathered in between my legs. He still hadn't noticed me, and I wasn't sure if I wanted to be seen or not.

Animalistic groans echoed off the tiled walls as he thrusted into his own hand.

"Odessa."

The word was quiet, but loud enough to flip my stomach at hearing my own name on his lips in such a way. It sounded like a prayer or a plea, with so much passion attached to every syllable.

It was erotic and wrong to be intruding like this during such a private moment— but he had said my name. And it did things to me. I should have been ashamed, or maybe angry that he was thinking of me like that. But I wasn't. I was flattered and turned on by it.

He wanted me.

I was afraid to admit that maybe, just maybe, a part of me wanted him too.

"Are you just going to stand there, or are you going to join me?"

His head hadn't turned around, but he knew I was there all the same. For how long, I couldn't say, but hearing his question popped whatever trance I'd been under, and I found myself scrambling for the door. Desperate to get out of there.

Heart hammering and breaths coming in short panicked waves, I ran back to my room and shut the door behind me. Try as I might, I couldn't scrub the image of how he looked and how he had sounded from my mind.

Dex had somehow wormed his way into my brain, taking up space that shouldn't belong to him.

My face felt like it was on fire from the embarrassment. How could I look him in the eye after this?

I yanked the mask off my face and paced my room. The shower would have to wait. There's no way I was going back out there now.

The only option I had was to stay in here for the rest of the night and sneak out in the morning to clean up.

I'D LAID DOWN, needing a moment to rest and closed my eyes. My breathing steadied, and all the worries that have been plaguing me drifted away from me. After what seemed like minutes, the door to my room opened, though I could have sworn I'd locked it.

I knew who it was without having to look. His presence was palpable. He carried a distinct energy with him wherever he went. That dark and dangerous air was practically electric.

"What are you doing in here?" I asked Dex.

"You know what I'm doing here, Odessa," he growled my name like he had earlier in the shower. With possession and passion.

Lust for him overwhelmed me.

I knew I shouldn't want him, but those icy blue eyes locked onto me, taking in my body like I was the most beautiful thing he'd ever seen. My nerve endings lit up with sparks like I'd never felt before as he perused my curves. The desire evident on his face.

He wasn't wearing his mask, and his hair was still damp from the shower. He smelled of soap with a masculine undertone. Sandalwood perhaps.

"I can't stay away from you, Odessa. I won't pretend that I don't feel something for you. And I think you feel it too. No, I know you do. You saved me when you didn't have to. You grabbed me by my arm earlier and pulled me to follow you out of danger. Don't tell me that you don't feel this pull between us. From the moment I saw you, I felt drawn to you in a way that's distracted me from why we're really here." He sat at the edge of my bed and took my hand in his. My hand with a very noticeable, very meaningful ring. His thumb grazed the ring and my breath caught in my chest. "I know you feel it, even though you've promised yourself to someone else, your body betrays you."

His free hand rested on top of my ribs, right between my breasts. I was certain he could feel how hard my heart was beating. The staccato pace of each beat at wanting more. Every single nerve felt hypersensitive. I was acutely tuned into him, waiting to see what he would do next. I licked my lips in anticipation.

"It's only fair, you know, that you let me see you like how you saw me." His words stole my breath. "What do you say, Deveraux? Why don't you let me see what a gorgeous body you're hiding behind these clothes of yours."

I don't know what made me do it. Curiosity? Desire? But before I could think twice, my head nodded my consent.

His nostrils flared as his hand drifted to the side with my permission, mapping the prominent curve of my breast as he pulled my shirt down, exposing my naked flesh to him.

Dex inhaled and ran his thumb over my pert nipple. "Fucking gorgeous just like I knew it would be."

I could feel his touch radiating all the way down to my toes. I should be pushing him away and telling him to stop, but my mouth couldn't form the words.

"Tell me to stop. Tell me you don't want this," he pleaded, not stopping for a moment. He seemed to be possessed with the need to touch me, his eyes aflame with want.

My mouth seemed to not work still, but I bit my lip, eyes wide, pleading for him to keep going, urging him on.

His hand dipped lower, caressing my stomach, my sides, lifting my hips to help guide my pants off.

I let him.

Gods forgive me, I let him touch me like I was his, while still belonging to another. In all my time with Theo, not once did he make me feel desired. I felt like an obligation. The means to an end. But Dex? I felt like a choice. There was a pull between us like no other that I had fought to deny.

Once my pants were a pile of fabric on the floor, Dex stared down at me while I opened for him. The wet desire evident between my legs. He crawled over to me.

"I've never seen anything more beautiful," he said taking me all in. "Gods, you're going to be my undoing."

My shirt was hardly covering me, and I was naked from the waist down. I'd never been so vulnerable and so free with anyone. I'd always been pushed away and made to feel shameful for wanting intimacy. But now? I felt desired. I felt wanted. And Dex wanted me. Fiercely.

His large hands grazed the skin on my inner thighs as he came down on his elbows, his mouth so incredibly close to me. I could feel his breath skating over my clit. There was no denying that Dex had a wickedly magnetic presence that had captivated me.

If I allowed this, then the good girl that I'd been when I arrived was as dead as the bones that lined these catacombs. She'd be replaced with a newer, more daring one that tip toed on the edge of danger, stroking the flames just to see what would happen. Was that something that I really wanted?

One look at Dex, and I had my answer.

Yes.

"I've wanted to taste you. Wondered what it would be like."

"I haven't showered yet," I realized, suddenly feeling embarrassed. Remembering that I'd been running around all day training.

"I don't fucking care. I want to taste you. All of you."

Just as his mouth came down on my bundle of nerves, I jolted awake.

The room around me was still. The only sound I could hear was my own breath, panting.

My hand clutched at my chest, and I sat up. It was just a dream, but it felt so real.

More real than any moment I'd experienced in my life this far, and I feared how much I liked that.

CHAPTER 13
ODESSA

The dress I had picked for tonight sat snuggly along my frame. While Marley had originally bought it for herself, I couldn't deny that it fit as if it were made especially for me. The sweetheart neckline accentuated the curve of my breasts and the black fabric glittered with each small movement, dancing like liquid starlight had been draped over my body. It was, in a word, dreamy. Shame I had to wear it to such a foul event. Oh, everyone was supposed to act excited, and I'm sure some were. But I couldn't find the feeling of excitement. All I felt was dread.

After this evening was over, we'd be forced to begin the games and I knew not all of us would make it out.

I lined my eyes in a black eyeliner and painted my lashes with a few coats of mascara. The golden mask glowed in the warm candlelight. I'd almost gotten used to its weight, liking the way the magick flowed into my veins. It was addicting. For the first time in my life, I felt powerful. Maybe that was why I'd fantasized about Dex like I had. The mask could have been influencing me with a darker, more dangerous part of my psyche than I realized. Most of the magick wielders were known to be callous and sometimes even cruel. I chalked it up to needing a ruthless nature to win the games, but maybe the magick had something to do with it too. There was no denying the way I felt once I had gotten the hang of it. Accessing that thread of magick within had become easier and easier the more I practiced. Each time I used it, I could feel the power blossoming within me— growing and becoming more settled into my very fiber. We were enmeshed together, this power and me. And I liked it. Maybe too much. It made me realize just how someone would be willing to kill another in order to keep it. What should scare me, sent a thrill through my body.

The dread I'd been feeling was discarded and a wholly new feeling had replaced it. There was a gleam in my eyes that shone back at me in the mirror. I hardly recognized myself from the girl I'd been when I first received the summons. I'd been frightened. Skittish. Worried.

But lying dormant beneath my chest cavity was a gold thread of power that thrummed with my mother's reminder to be ruthless. I could feel it within me, alive and thriving — ready to strike. All I needed was a target.

I lifted the mask away from my face with a frown, looking at it with concern at how dark my thoughts had become.

I'd been able to snag a quick shower after training today, spending the majority of it avoiding Dex and his annoying smoldering. The man made glowering hot. The knowledge that I had not only seen but then... well, never mind. It wasn't important. I just needed to focus on getting through the night in one piece. The gods were to be in attendance, and that knowledge had my nerves aflutter.

To make things worse, rumors of random room searches had been making the rounds at dinner, and I debated taking the dagger with me. I could strap it to my thigh and hope it stayed put. It was either I take it with me or risk getting it found while I was at the masquerade.

Fuck it. It wasn't worth getting caught.

The belt to one of the dresses Marley had packed might just do the trick. Without second guessing myself, the decision was made. The cool metal of the blade sat against my thigh as I wrapped the black fabric belt around it, binding it to my body as tightly as I could.

I took a few practice steps and jumped up and down to see if it would hold. So far, so good. Now it just had to stay there for the entirety of the evening. Placing the mask back on, I took one last look in the mirror as its power surged in my veins filling me with a confidence that shone back at me in my reflection.

THE ROTUNDA WAS PACKED with servers and opulently dressed contestants. Neon lights illuminated the space, similar to the very first day we'd arrived but now with hues of blue mixed in with the red. When they merged together, they created the most gorgeous shade of purple. Music played distantly from above, and I could scarcely make out the band from here. All the contestants I could see, had chosen their very best outfits, but when I scanned the room, my eyes caught in horror at the three very prominently displayed heads that were hung above the entrance to one of the tunnels.

Magnus, Genevieve, and Uric.

Their names had been etched into stone beneath them, while their faces still were adorned with the masks they had chosen. If you looked closely, you could see the bones of their neck still attached and protruding from the freshly severed wounds.

Was that to be our fate should be fail and die down here?

Our bones to be made a part of the catacombs forever. A reminder of how insignificant we really were in the grand scheme of things. I didn't think that when Uric was escorted away earlier, he would end up like this. It was vile and cruel.

Dex was nowhere to be seen, but I was too preoccupied with the visual of our fellow contestant's remains to focus on anything else. A deep voice that carried a menacing tone, skittered to life in my head.

Less people we have to kill, isn't that exciting?

My mouth dropped open at the intrusive thought, and I pushed through the crowd feeling slightly panicked as I grabbed onto a long flute of champagne one of the servers had on their trays. I tilted the glass back and drank the contents in one gulp.

I didn't have time to ruminate on the grotesque scene I'd seen and that chilling voice, because the neon flickering lights dimmed, and a reverent hush washed over the crowd.

The gods had arrived.

They were even more breathtakingly resplendent than the last time we had seen them. But like before, the God of Death was notably missing.

Not much was known on how exactly they entertained themselves with the games, but most assumed they were able to watch somehow. Using a magical recording device to relay live images of the games. Some had claimed that they used rats to follow us through the tunnels. Some others had sworn that they knew because they were gods, and therefore, all knowing of what was happening with the contestants.

I'd rather have the rats to be honest. The thought of them seeing me at my most intimate moments sent a shiver down my spine, but I supposed that's part of how they maintained their power. Through vague stories of their lore, meant to invoke fear and obedience in their subjects.

To top things off, they'd erased all our history of our time as a people before their arrival. They'd scrubbed our monuments and replaced them with their own likeness with a demand to be worshipped. And many did without complaint. Now any mention of the time before was banned. People were executed for committing such an offense. Looking at those three heads above was just another reminder of how volatile the gods could be, and I was right in the thick of it.

The gods moved like the ethereal beings that they were, almost like they were gliding over the black and white tiled floor. Each of them was dripping in opulence and proudly displaying a mask to match their power. I realized our masks were replicas of theirs. It seemed they were pairing themselves off to their matching power. My spine straightened as the God of Shadows, otherwise known as Kage, came to stand right in front of me, offering me his gloved hand. His mask matched mine in every way, The Onyx.

I took his offered hand with a curtsey, dipping my head into a bow to show the reverence required. Sweat gathered on my lower back, aware of the secret weapon I'd concealed beneath my dress. My power met his as soon as our hands collided, making me take a steadying breath.

Standing, I could see he was wearing an opulent black jacket that swept down to his knees. It was embroidered with intricate swirls that mimicked the very shadows he was known to wield. His shirt was well fitted, and his black pants were pleated and tight. He was devilishly good looking in an otherworldly way but simmering beneath the surface was a feeling that if I made one wrong move, I'd be nothing but a pile of ash at his feet. His dark wavy hair was styled neatly to frame the mask he wore, and his tanned skin seemed to glisten in the light, adding to his allure.

"Shall we?" He asked looking amused while he gestured to where the other gods and contestants were lining up.

I nodded my head and took his elbow letting him lead me. My eyes darted around the room, but still, I couldn't locate Dex. Not that I cared. It was just interesting that I hadn't seen him yet.

"How does it feel to have my power running through your veins?" Kage, The God of Shadows asked, and I nearly tripped over myself at his words.

"Um—"

He chuckled, throwing his head back as if he was so amusing. "Don't lie, I know you must love it. The rush. The surge of power. And it's only a drop of what I'm capable of."

His arrogance was almost tangible. My mouth nearly turned into a grimace, but then I remembered just where I was and who I was talking to.

"I am very grateful. Thank you."

"I bet you are." His smile was wolfish and dazzling at the same time. It was easy to forget that while charming he may be, he was also deadly. It took effort to reign in my contempt that I felt for these ethereal beings that fucked with our lives for fun. Without them and their stupid games, I'd be at home right now.

He let go of my arm and took up his station on the opposite end where the divine all had lined up. A low rumble of a bow being dragged across the strings of a cello reverberated in the rotunda, building as more string instruments joined in.

A waltz, I realized. We were expected to dance together. Nerves tumbled freely about my body, vibrating just beneath my skin at having to keep myself poised in the gods and goddess's presence.

He bowed slightly and I curtsied in response. Our bodies came together in a swirl and his large hands encompassed the expanse of my back. His skin felt oddly cold, leeching through the thin fabric of my dress as if I were in the arms of a corpse. A shiver ran down my spine as we turned around the dance floor. Thankfully, our school dances had prepared me for such a moment, the muscle memory kicking in on where to move and when. I rose my arm as gracefully as I could muster following along to the steady beat of the music, loathing every second of it.

Every movement had my mind singularly focused on the weapon strapped to my leg. Hoping beyond all hope that the knot I tied was sufficient enough to keep it in place. The distraction made me slower, having to scramble to keep up with the dizzying dance. Kage seemed completely unaware of my struggle, too busy acting important and impressive.

That might work in my favor, I thought, trying to keep it together as we spun. Only two more movements around the room, and I would be free of him.

"You are quite the dancer, Ms. Deveraux," Kage said, dipping me.

"Thank you," I responded, averting my gaze as was customary to show respect. Truthfully, I just didn't want to look at him, afraid that if I did, he would see right through me.

As he brought me back to standing, the music thankfully came to a halt, and I clapped along with the rest of the room, showing our appreciation to the talented musicians.

"Enjoy my power, I know I will enjoy watching you attempt to wield it," The God of Shadows said with a bite to his words. He turned on his heel and left me in a daze.

Taking a steadying breath, I swiped a mushroom cap from a nearby server, popping the tasty morsel into my mouth. I tended to eat when I felt stressed, and right now, my stress was at an all time high. The games were tomorrow. But no amount of mushroom caps could make me feel better about being tossed into the middle of a massacre. The mushroom cap was larger than I expected and I was pretty sure my cheeks were resembling those of a chipmunk right about now.

Of course, that's exactly when Dex decided to show his annoyingly handsome face, coming over with a smirk, his hands shoved deep into his pockets making his muscles pop prominently in his tightly fitted button-down shirt. It should have been illegal for him to look that good.

I chewed quickly, pocketing the food in my cheeks feeling

them stain with heat as he came near. All day I'd been able to avoid him, but now I was being cornered with nowhere to run off to.

My eyes darted around the room looking for an escape. Nat looked cozy with her goddess, Mediah, The Medusa and the rest of my team, Killian and Reed were showing off their powers to a few of the female contestants. I rolled my eyes at their sad attempts of flirting.

"Fancy seeing you here," Dex said.

I swallowed my food down and avoided his gaze, trying with all I had not to think of how I'd found him in the shower, saying my name. Yep, I was failing hard because that was all I could think about. Another server came by with a tall glass of champagne that I grabbed gladly, chugging the contents back.

"Aw, still feeling embarrassed over last night? Did you not like hearing how hard I came picturing you beneath me?"

I choked on the liquid I'd been drinking, feeling a burning in my chest and a dribble of the alcohol down my chin.

"What am I going to do with you?" He asked, wiping my mouth with his thumb. Everything in me stilled at that small touch. It brought me right back to that stupidly hot dream I'd had of him. One that he could never find out about.

I smacked his hand away, which only made him chuckle and those icy blue eyes of his dance with glee like I was a challenge to him.

"Excuse me," I said gathering my dress trying to get past him. He grabbed my wrist, gently, but with enough force that I stopped, turning to look at him. My breath felt caught in my chest. I knew I should run in the other direction. He was trouble waiting to happen, but his touch felt so damn good against my skin.

"You don't have to run from me, you know," he seemed sincere, but this was Nocturne. No matter how sincere his words may be, I knew I couldn't trust anyone. Least of all a devilishly handsome rake that if I were to entertain would only cause me heartache.

"Yes, I do." I'd been reckless with my feelings, allowing him to somehow slip behind my defenses. Imagining the things I had and liking it. The visual of us together on my bed still so fresh and seared into my brain.

I was glad then that he didn't possess a power to read my mind. The shame that I felt over fantasizing about him in the night was all consuming. The guilt was as palpable as my own heartbeat. I shouldn't be thinking of him like that at all. But here I was, wrist being held by him as if that was exactly where I belonged. Next to him.

It wasn't possible. I was taken, and we were on opposite teams. He could as easily kill me for my power, as I could for his. But for some reason, I wanted that all to not be true. I wanted the chance to know what it would feel like to give into these forbidden feelings that had taken root in my chest. And that was the most shameful thing of all. A betrayal of the highest kind to Theo, the man I was promised to. And I couldn't forget that.

"I can't," I said eventually, pulling my arm away from him, feeling the ghost of his warmth still wrapped around my wrist. He shoved his hands back into his pants, his jaw clenched tightly as if he wanted to say something further but was refraining. I turned, walking blindly away from him, with no destination in mind other than away. Discarding the glass in my hand as I walked, my face felt red from the thoughts whirling in my head.

Just as I turned my head to look behind me, my body collided with The God of Shadows.

"Kage," my mouth said before I had time to think about how disrespectful that was. To call a god by their first name as if we were friends could be a fatal mistake. I realized my blunder immediately, bowing my head. "My apologies, my divine ruler."

My heart was going a million miles a minute, waiting for him to decide my fate. One look up, and I saw what looked like amusement dancing upon his smile.

"I never hear my name anymore, it's refreshing really. I almost forgot that's what it is. Everything is always divine this and god that. Don't fret, child. I won't punish you for your mistake."

An unspoken, 'this time', hung in the air and I bowed again showing my gratitude.

"Would you like to dance?" He asked, though it sounded more like a command.

"I would be honored to," I responded. When I took The God of Shadow's hand for a second time that evening, Dex's stare was boring into me with a simmering anger that followed us as the dance began. Oh, Dessa, what a mess you've gone and gotten yourself into now.

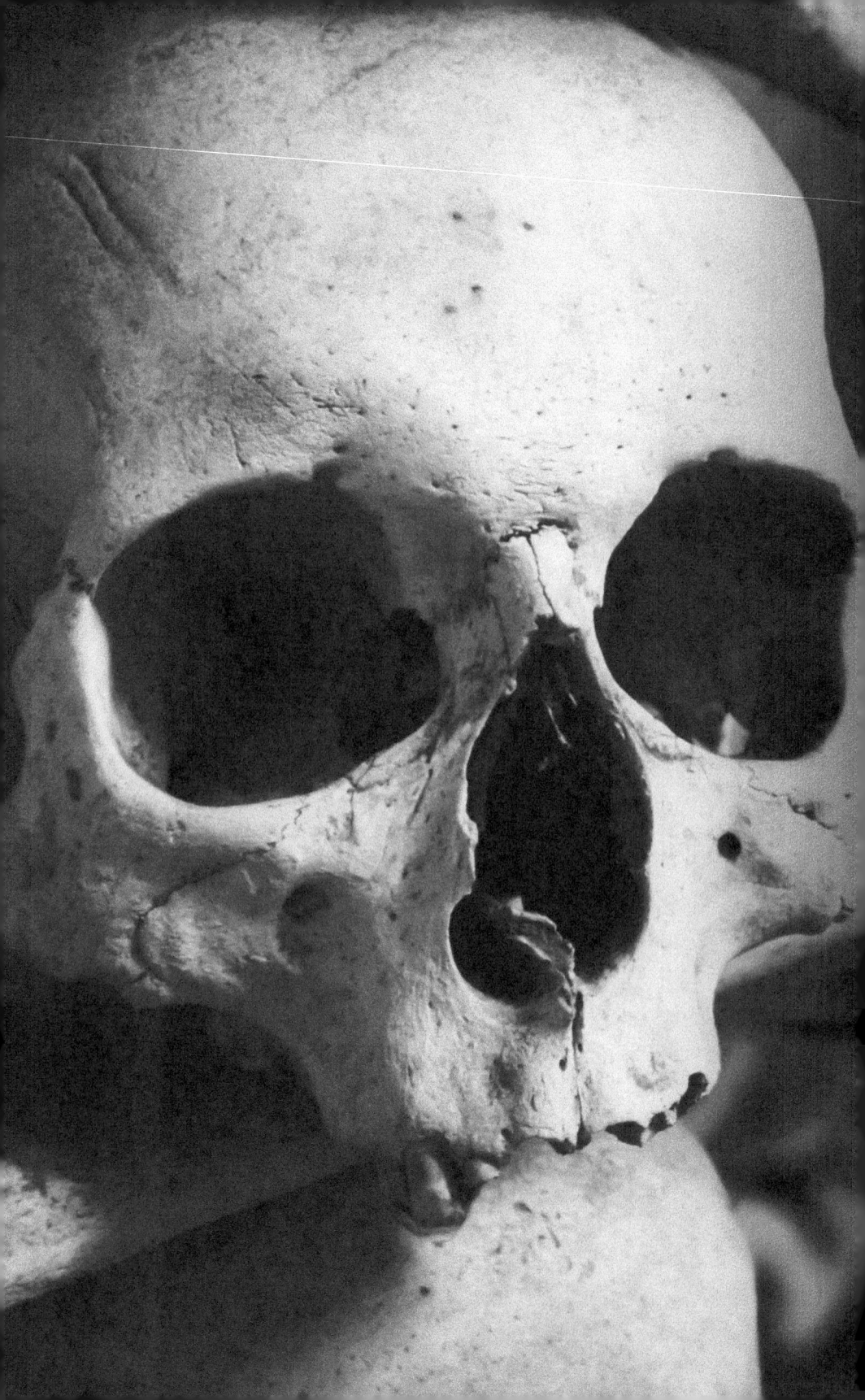

CHAPTER 14
DEX

She was a vision. Like a demon and angel had made a baby and the result was her. She was all parts beauty with equal parts danger. I don't even think she knew all that she was capable of yet, but it was palpable. Just one look at her, and I could tell that she was formidable, even if she didn't quite believe it herself yet.

The games would change that.

I'd scared her, though, I knew she felt this pull between us, just as much as I did. Maybe it wasn't me that she was scared of, but what it meant about her. A truth in herself she wasn't ready to face yet. That she liked this dark and dangerous part of her. I could tell she'd spent her life being good for everyone else, but down here, nothing else mattered. She had to stand on her own two feet with no one to cater to but herself. Maybe for the first time in her life too.

I could only hope that there could be a way that we both made it out of here, no matter how unlikely that might be.

Nocturne was unpredictable and unforgiving. She hadn't seen me yet, having snuck in later than I should have.

"What are they going to do with those masks?" I heard Regis asking.

"None of your business," the Goddess of Spring replied in a chilling tone.

Eyeing the masks on top of the decapitated heads also had me wondering the same question, but the Goddess's clipped response was telling. Clearly, we weren't meant to know, which made it all the more interesting.

A part of me wondered if I'd be able to sneak back in here after everyone had gone to sleep. They'd told us the only way to obtain the power of another mask was to kill the wearer, but they'd told us many blatant lies that they covered up with finery and an active destruction of information. I'd learned that the Divine were more interested in serving their own interests than helping their own citizens. Transparency wasn't something I could expect from them, and the Goddess of Spring's curt response had me intrigued enough to find out for myself.

A loose plan formed in my mind to take those masks for myself. The three powers alone would be worth it.

It was genius really. If there was a way to obtain those mask's powers, displaying them in plain sight like they were a sure way to make us feel like they were forever out of reach. A reminder of our insignificance.

Well, I had a feeling that I would call them on their bluff.

Odessa's deep brown eyes finally locked onto me, and I went towards her as if pulled by an invisible string. I couldn't help myself when it came to her. Every time she was around, I seemed to forget everything but her.

She'd been avoiding me all day and it thrilled me to know I'd gotten under her skin. What she walked in on, I hadn't meant for her to see, but the fact that she had, that she knew the truth of how I felt about her, was in a way freeing. If only she wasn't so frightened of her own feelings.

After a brief as hell interaction, she ran from me, right into that god's arms. They spun around the room, dancing as if they were the only two in here.

It ate at me, watching them when I knew she belonged with me. Even if she didn't want to admit it to herself yet, she knew it. Deep down. She had to.

Anger and possession coursed through my body like I've never known, until he whispered something in her ear that made her smile, and fuck. I couldn't take it anymore. Before I knew what I was doing, I found myself tapping on his shoulder as if he were just a mortal man.

"Can I cut in?" I asked boldly.

His emerald, green eyes flashed in surprise, and Odessa stared at me open mouthed.

"Why not," The God of Shadows replied, offering me Odessa's hand stiffly.

It was clear he wasn't happy being interrupted.

Odessa fit snuggly against me, her jaw set tightly as if she knew we were being watched and couldn't say what she really wanted to.

As soon as we started dancing and were far enough away from anyone that would eavesdropping, she snarled up at me. "Are you out of your mind? Provoking a god like that?"

"Provoking? I thought I asked nicely."

"You can't just go and ask a god to cut in!" She talked

through clenched teeth, keeping a fake smile in place, playing the part like nothing was amiss.

"I think I just did."

She shook her head, and I spun her out, bringing her back in. Her backside became flush with my front and there was a very noticeable item poking at me from her thigh.

I chuckled. "Speaking of things you shouldn't be doing—"

"Not a word."

"Wouldn't dream of it." She spun again, this time coming to face me. She was a good few inches below me and had to strain her neck to glare up at me. Then I watched as her eyes went wide and she awkwardly clenched her legs together.

The knife was slipping.

If she were to be found out, her head would be up on that wall along with the other contestants, and I couldn't let that happen.

I brought her body close to mine, covering the fact that she was clearly struggling to keep from dropping the damned thing.

We moved together in tandem, her eyes darting around the room in a panic. I gripped onto her thigh, feeling the outline of the dagger.

"Just go with it," I pleaded with her.

"Fine, but if you fuck it up, I'm taking you down with me."

She had no choice but to trust me. With my hand pressed against her thigh, I dragged my hand up to her hips, the knife moving with me. Thankfully, she had something protecting her skin from being sliced otherwise, I'm pretty sure she would have gotten nicked by the sharp blade. Finally, with my other hand coming to clutch the knife, I yanked it through the tight fabric that cinched in at her waist.

It wouldn't hold for long, but it was something.

The song came to an end, and she bowed politely then took off, headed in the direction of the bathrooms. I let her go, watching as she left. In fact, most everyone had stopped what they were doing to watch us. I hadn't noticed, too focused on the temptress in my arms. I wasn't ashamed for wanting her. She was gorgeous and had a spark that made me want to fan until it was a raging inferno.

Tomorrow, the games would begin, and we'd be plunged into the depths of this volatile place. I wondered if that was the last, I'd see of her until we were officially opponents, playing against each other for the chance to win.

CHAPTER 15
ODESSA

I ran straight from the ballroom making a beeline for my room, hoping that no one would notice me slipping away. No such luck. The bastard guard, Davis, that had brought me to this wretched place blocked my path down one of the dark hallways, with his arms crossed over his chest and a smile that was devoid of any kindness. I was toast.

"Good evening," I tried for a sweet tone and a dip of my head.

"Where are you running off to in such a hurry?" he asked taking a step closer.

We were alone, the two of us, and with no audience to see what he would do, I took a step back as well trying to keep a healthy distance away from him. His cruel eyes gleamed knowing he frightened me with that one step back.

"I've been meaning to check on you since I brought you here. You're not trying to hide something from the guards, are you?"

My heart was hammering a million miles a minute as he came closer. This time, I stood my ground.

The dagger sat between the fold of the dress's fabric and my skin, feeling like it might loosen at any moment.

"No, sir," I responded trying to figure out how to get away from this creep.

"Mmm, I like the way you say, sir. You know your place and how utterly insignificant you are."

He grabbed me then, twirling me hard against the stone wall with his hand in my hair and his hot unwanted breath at my ear.

"Tragic that a sweet, sexy thing like you won't stand a chance. We can have some fun before that, though."

Before I could say, stop, his hands were hiking up my dress and a very noticeable bulge prodded at my backside. Vomit threatened to spill up my esophagus as my body shook.

"Please, sir, I was just trying to get some sleep before the games tomorrow. If you'll just let me—"

"Shut the fuck up. Now! You'll do as I say, you hear me?"

I nodded, knowing that to attack one of the guards was to sign my own death.

My brain whirled trying to figure out what to do and how to get out of this situation.

"Now, where was I?" he asked, squeezing my ass in his hands. If he were to look to the right, he'd see the wrapped dagger, but he was too preoccupied with violating me.

A telltale sound of a zipper being undone filled my ears and a whoosh of my magick erupted from my chest, knocking him back so hard that his head hit the other side of the hall, smacking into the stone wall. I whirled on his slumped figure, and reared my arm back, punching him right in the face.

This place might have me killed for it, but no one was to touch me without my permission.

"Fucking bastard," I said with a snarl.

He seemed to be passed out from the impact, and I ran, leaving him there as I shook with the adrenaline coursing through my veins.

I closed and locked the door behind me, hands shaking. My back was flush against the door as my heart rate came back down to a normal rhythm. Clearly, while I'd been out my room had been ransacked, and I knew then that taking the dagger with me was the right call.

"Fuck," I said aloud in disbelief at what had just happened. I could only hope that the bastard guard felt too embarrassed at getting taken down by a girl that he didn't report me.

It took a good amount of time to clean up the space around me, but once I did, I fell back onto the bed, still dressed in my masquerade outfit. I was far too tired to remove it, and I couldn't help but replay the events of the evening over in my mind.

Spinning around the dance floor with Dex and Kage was something I hadn't expected, but it was the surge of protective power and attack from the guard that gnawed at me the most. Would they know it was me that did that to him? Would he tell? Would they believe me if I told them what actually happened?

And to think in the morning, I was expected to fight in these games for a chance at riches and power. The power thrummed in my chest like it knew I was thinking of it. Was it enough to kill another person over? I didn't want to dwell on it. Though, that dark part of me answered a resounding yes for me.

I didn't want to think about anything.

What I wanted was to wake up in my own bed and to have had this all been a bad dream.

But I wasn't that lucky.

If I died in the games tomorrow, I hoped my family would know how much I tried to get back to them. Seeing the truth of how easily people perished down here, had me wondering if what we knew about Nocturne was the truth at all.

I'd never expected to see my fellow contestants' heads mounted to a wall like that. The image wouldn't leave my mind. And I'm sure that's exactly the effect they wanted. Why else display such savagery?

And that voice in my head?

A part of me hoped it was a figment of my imagination. Just stress from the games starting. But I knew that was bullshit. Something, or someone, had been speaking inside of my head, and it scared me most of all.

I fell asleep still dressed, and tormented by my own thoughts, wrapped in anxiety and dread. The games were starting tomorrow, and there was no getting out of it.

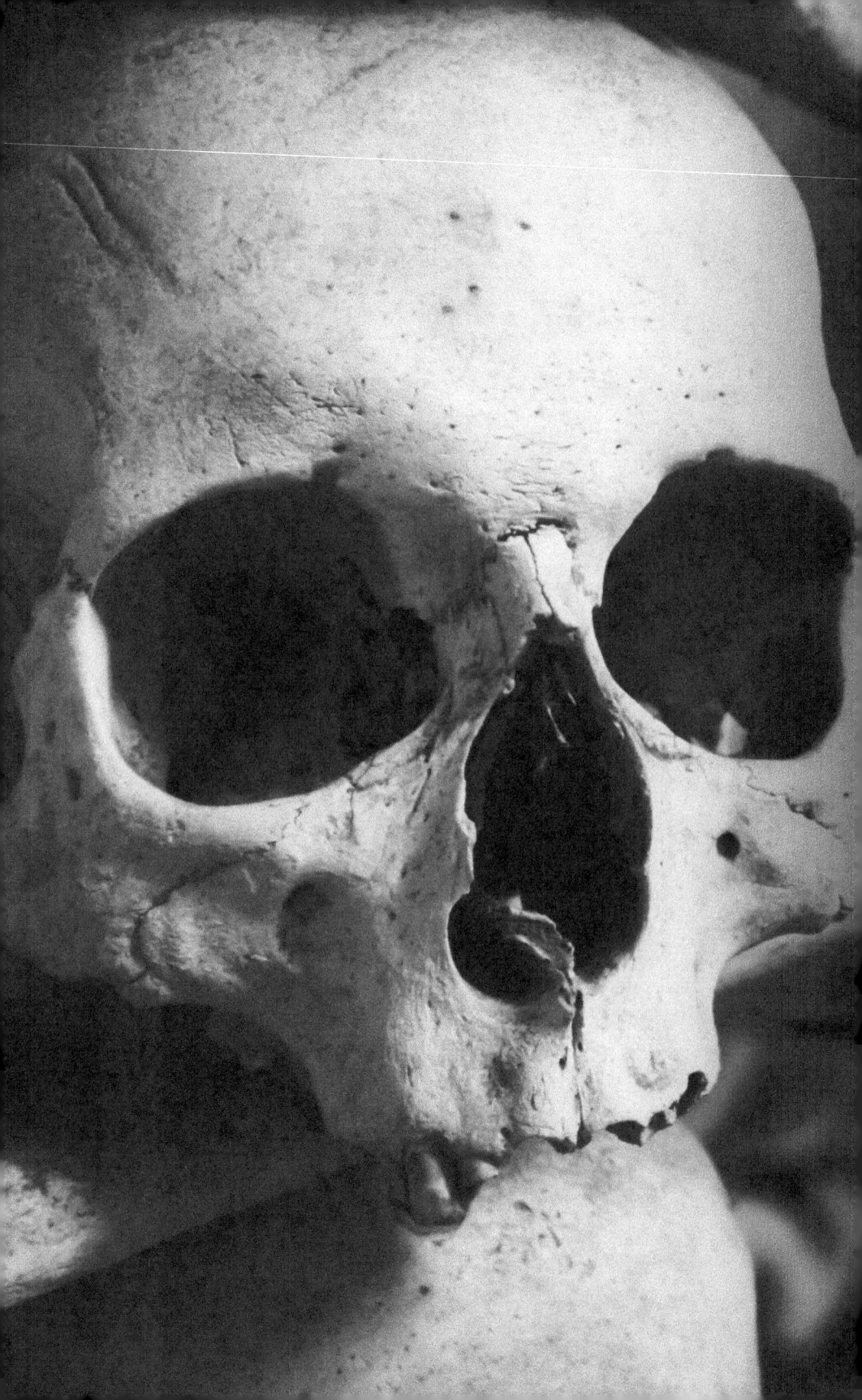

CHAPTER 16
DEX

The rotunda was empty save for a few discarded servant trays and random bits of uneaten food that littered the floor. But right where they'd been left, were the three heads— masks still affixed to their faces. I'd managed to sneak out without anyone noticing and now, I was so close to obtaining the powers I sought. At least, I hoped my theory was right. I was taking a huge risk to find out, but it would be worth it.

Carefully and quietly, I pulled on my power, using the bones in the walls to create a makeshift ladder for me to climb. The bones held my weight as I made my way up to where Magnus's head sat as a decoration and warning. The mask came off easily, revealing the deformed and already eroding state of what remained of him. My stomach roiled, threatening to empty the contents of the rich party food I'd consumed earlier, but I couldn't afford to waste time. Who knew how often the guards patrolled the tunnels. I didn't want to find out.

I was lucky no one had caught me yet as it was.

Odessa hadn't come back from the bathroom, and I assumed she'd gone to bed early. Smart move really. I should probably have done the same, but I couldn't pass up the chance at obtaining the powers while I could. Not when they were so close.

Genevieve's was next. Her mask was tangled in her golden hair. The crown wrapping around her soft curls. I gripped the mask by its ties and held it together in the hand that held onto Magnus's.

Uric was last. His was the furthest and required me to strain from where I stood in order to reach it.

Soft voices began to fill the corridor, and I froze. My fingers were barely brushing against the golden edges. I could run back right now and not get caught, but I was so close to having all three masks.

As quickly as I could, I undid his mask, and stashed it with the others, climbing down the makeshift ladder, using my magick to push the bones back to where they'd been.

"Poor bastards probably won't even make it two minutes with the new additions they installed. That acid water? Instant killer," a voice murmured getting closer.

Acid water? My ears strained to hear what the guards were saying as I pressed my body tightly against the wall. I crept quietly into the hallway, hoping the shadows would keep me covered. All I needed was enough time to try one. Then I would know if it worked.

Two guards seemed to linger just out of sight. Quickly, I took off my mask and put on The Enforcer, tying the string behind my head. Just like with mine, it tightened, and I felt a surge of power running through my veins.

Those lying bastards, I fucking knew it.

Most contestants were too tired to find out that our powers worked even if we took the masks off. The magick was dimmed, but still entwined. Working at our behest, we only had to know how to call on it.

Quickly, I slipped off the mask and put on The Crown, then The Spider.

"Hey, weren't they wearing masks before?"

Shit.

"They probably took them into storage."

"Right."

My heart was hammering a million miles a minute as I slipped back in my room. The masks hung from my hand as their power thrummed in my veins.

"What happened to your eye, by the way man?"

"Some bitch contestant wouldn't let me fuck her."

I stilled.

"Which one?"

"That brown haired one with the braid."

"Oh man, yeah. She's hot."

All the powers I'd just absorbed shot to the surface in a blinding rage. They were talking about Odessa. And one of those assholes had tried to hurt her. It seemed she'd been able to land a punch, which filled me with pride. But a punch wasn't nearly enough punishment. I stepped out from where I was hiding with a deadly smile on my face.

"Can we help you?" The tall one with the shiner on his eye asked.

Yeah, this guy was going down.

"I was on my way to the bathroom, think I got turned around," I said, putting a fake drunken swagger on as I walked forward.

The guards looked at each other like they were annoyed.

"Yeah, buddy. The bathrooms are back that way. You shouldn't be out here. It's off-limits," the tall one said, putting his meaty hand on my shoulder.

Immediately, I pounced on him.

"And you shouldn't be assaulting women," I said twisting his arm behind his back and kicking him straight in the elbow. The bone gave a satisfying pop before he crumpled before me in a heap of agony.

"You're fucking dead!" the other one cried, going to put a whistle to his thin little lips.

My power had him frozen before he had the chance to move. It settled deep into his bones as his eyes went wide in shock. The thing about some of these guards is that their position has made them think they're untouchable. I was more than happy to shatter that illusion.

"What's worse than a guy who assaults women?" I asked, moving around him, yanking his knife from his belt. It was cool to the touch as I raised it to his throat. "Anyone who excuses and supports that kind of behavior," I said, slicing clean across his jugular.

He went down clawing at his neck to no avail as he bled out at our feet within seconds.

I turned on the assaulter who was cowering.

"Listen, man. I'm s-sorry. I didn't hurt her. Swear."

"I really don't care what your opinion of the encounter was.

I heard you. She wouldn't fuck you. But you've got me instead. And while I won't fuck you, I will make you wish you'd never been born."

"Fuck—"

I slammed my powers into him, using all the force I had to break him apart bit by bit until his bones were emulsified and his skin looked as if he had been melted.

To get rid of the evidence, I turned that light power on so high that their bodies dissolved into piles of ash.

All that was left of the guards could be swept away by the maids.

Now I just needed to prepare myself for the start of the games in the morning. From the sounds of those guards' conversation, it was even worse than I was imagining.

With the guards' now dead, I was able to sneak the masks back where they belonged, hiding their powers deep inside me to use when the time was right.

Four powers down, twelve to go.

CHAPTER 17
ODESSA

I've braided and unbraided my hair seven times already before deciding on a low-slung French braid that I could pull off to the side. No one had come to take me away in the night, so I assumed, for now, I was safe from that wretched guard.

My fingers shook trying to pull my hair into place, which is why it had taken me so many tries. My nerves were on edge, and I knew that every second was bringing me closer to when we'd be taken down into those tunnels.

I found a way to keep the dagger on me by shoving it into the side of my boot, hiding the outline with a thick sock. It wasn't much, but it would have to do for now. Leaving the dagger wasn't an option. And if I had to use it, I'd pretend I'd found the thing in the catacombs. All items within were fair game after all.

Thoughts of my family. Of Marley and Jean, Papa and

Mama flittered around in my mind like a caged butterfly. And Theo... Fuck.

I knew that they were waiting on me. That I'd promised to make it back to them, and I always kept my promises. But being here had made me realize that the life I'd been living— the one I planned for and loved, wasn't as great as I thought it was. I'd been living my life according to their rules. Fitting into a box they provided for me. Making myself small to appease everyone around me. If I did make it back, I didn't think I could just go back to that. I was different now. Stronger. Would they accept me for who I was becoming? Would Marley still wrap her arms around me if I wasn't the sister she remembered? Would Papa? Jean? Would Theo and I survive as a couple now that I'd been finding myself pulled to another?

So many questions that had no answers.

All I knew was that all of it had to wait. The most important thing was getting through the games.

My body felt exhausted. Over the last several days, the training and anticipation had taken a toll on me. The masquerade would have been enjoyable under any other circumstances. But with the heads of the fallen contestants watching over us, it was a constant reminder of what we had to face today. And every breath I took, reminded me of my own mortality.

I spun my engagement ring around my finger nervously, the light from the fireplace catching against the simple diamond. When Theo had given me this ring, I'd accepted whole-heartedly. Knowing that in doing so, I would be making my family proud. He'd planned a small meal for both our families at our favorite restaurant, which was a huge splurge for my family, but par the course for his. My Papa had told me not worry about the cost because it was a special night. I remembered the way the waiters all gathered around our table waiting expectantly as I pretended to be surprised by the ring floating in my champagne glass. Marley had spilled the beans and told me that Theo was proposing that night.

Her exact words were, "Please don't make that butt wipe my brother-in-law."

But what I remembered most of all was the feeling like I didn't have a choice and a nagging question inside of me that wondered what it would feel like if I just said no.

Both our families were watching us with unwavering attention as he asked me to be his wife, knowing that their plans of putting us together had worked. My face had pulled into a smile I had practiced many times over that it was second nature when I did it again to say yes to the man kneeling before me.

If I made it through Nocturne, I'd be expected to pick up right where we left off. With wedding plans and a future that felt like it no longer fit.

Could I really go back like nothing had happened?

There was a rapt knock on the door and my stomach sank.

The games were about to begin.

WE WERE MADE to change into a uniform, so all that preparation this morning was for nothing. The outfits were long sleeved, black jumpsuits that cinched at the waist. The material was thin enough that it was easy to move around in, but heavy enough that it would keep us warm in the chilled catacombs.

I left my suitcase behind as instructed. They told us that if anything happened to us, they would send our personal effects home to our families. It was clear that's all they would be sent back, because our bodies belonged to the gods now, and if we died down here, here we would remain.

Reaching the end of the maze alive was the only way out.

I carefully hid my dagger as I changed, swapping the sock I was wearing for a different standard issued one. It fit snuggly in my new black boot, hidden with the help of the jumpsuit.

We were then given a matching knapsack, filled with gear that we might need. There were food rations wrapped in silver packaging, one small canteen like the ones we used in training, flint to start a fire, and a blanket. The pack had a belt that clipped around the front of our middles, keeping the weight evenly distributed.

Killian popped open one of the food rations and sniffed it before taking a bite. "Ugh, tastes like cardboard."

"Nutritional cardboard," The captain's voice rang out, making us all stand taller. "That stuff is your lifeline between starvation and living, so treat it accordingly," she warned.

Killian sheepishly wrapped the food back up and placed it back in his pack.

"As you may recall, Team Spades, will be getting a five-minute head-start." My gaze instinctively found Dex where he stood with his thick arms crossed over his broad chest.

He'd saved my ass last night, helping me cover for the dagger that almost slipped right out of its bindings. He could have made sure I was eliminated right then and there, letting it clatter to the ground, but he didn't, and I wasn't sure why.

Maybe he felt ending me like that was an unfair advantage, but there was a secret underlying part of me that hoped it was for other reasons. Despite the fact that I knew nothing could happen between us, I still found there was a deep part of me that wondered what if. Which was incredibly stupid of me. We were rivals. Enemies. Both of us competing for the same outcome— to win these deadly games. But only one of us here could win.

"Follow me," the captain ordered.

And we did. Down into the tunnels, with nerves settling like a rock deep in my stomach. Guards flanked us on all sides. There was nowhere for us to run and hide. We had no choice but to walk forward into what could be our own demise. This was it. Everything we had been training for the past few days.

Gods, had it only been a few days since I'd been brought here?

Time felt so elastic and untethered here. The constant darkness that surrounded us made it feel like one long perpetual night.

We stopped right outside what was known as 'The Alchemist's Gateway'. It was an arched section of the tunnel that had been changed over time to resemble the open mouth of the gods. With teeth bared and sharp as if we were being swallowed whole. There we were shoved against the wall into our four teams. Each team had its own alcove where we were placed on top of a platform. Stepping onto it, I could feel the springs beneath my feet, shudder with our collective weight. I swallowed hard.

Dex was right across from me, waving.

I rolled my eyes that he would find this so amusing to wave at me right now when all I wanted to do was vomit.

Then, two guards strode over to where a large wheel sat right outside of Dex's team's wall. I recognized one from when they had ripped me from my room. He'd urged that scum Davis to not torment me, but now when he looked over at me, there was nothing but contempt behind those eyes. Those bastards seemed to be enjoying seeing us off like this— all nervous and off kilter. Not knowing what to expect next.

The guards gripped onto each end of the wheel and began to turn. As they turned, Dex and his team were lowered into the ground.

The only tell that he might be anxious was the quick rise and fall of his large chest as their team inched further out of sight.

Now we had to wait.

Each second that ticked by felt like torture. Nat, Killian, and Reed all looked as nauseous as I felt. I adjusted the pack on my back, trying to get comfortable with the new weight digging into my shoulders. No one said a word as we waited for our turn. We all seemed locked inside our own heads, playing out imaginary scenarios and trying to prepare ourselves for what lay a few feet beneath us. Just when I thought I couldn't stand the silence anymore, the captain motioned to the guards.

"Show time mortals. Enjoy the games. Try not to die," she said with a menacing smile as we were lowered into the cata-combs and swallowed up into the inky black darkness.

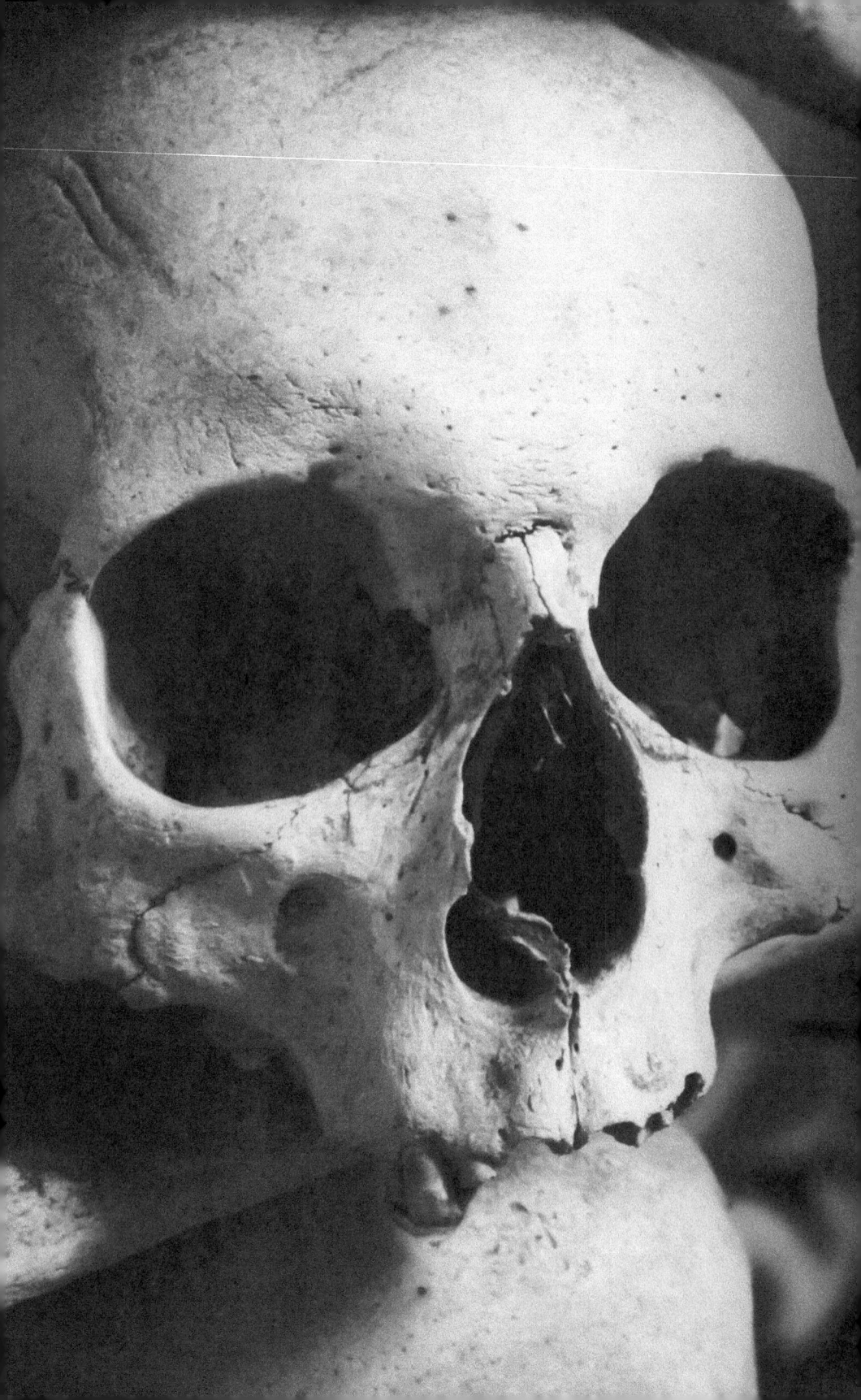

CHAPTER 18
DEX

P lans of what I needed to do swarmed deep in my mind. The darkness enveloped us as the platform lowered. The smell of damp and mold permeated the air. And something else that I couldn't place, almost acidic in nature like a chemical.

There were three of us left on our team. Regis, Céline, and I. Genevieve had been eliminated early on, and now I carried her power of light in my veins. Our masks were firmly tied about our heads and our packs weighed heavy upon each of our shoulders.

Odessa had looked downright terrified up there, and it twisted my gut seeing her like that. But she had every right to be terrified. A part of me felt it too. That anxiety coursing inside me, only I would use it as fuel to help me win. No amount of winking or my smiles could help her now, though. We were in it, and we'd be lucky as hell if we both made it out of here. It'd been done before, but rarely. Even if we both made it out, there could only be one winner.

The platform rumbled to a halt and a faint, dim red light illuminated a long tunnel ahead. There were two narrow concrete paths on either side of some water that ran the length as far as I could see. The top of the ceiling was rounded, and the walls were made of pure bone. I could feel my power awakening down here, strumming to life with electric energy.

A sudden burst of red light from above sliced through the air with a loud booming shot, and a male sounding voice echoed off the tunnel walls.

"The Games have begun. You have a five-minute head-start. Use it wisely. If you shall perish, may your soul be granted the God of Death's favor."

Here we fucking go.

The lights went out for a moment, and we all stood there struck dumb or too scared to move. But then the dim light returned with a flicker and Regis, always the first to take charge, leapt into action, plunging into the water from off the platform, only to scream out in agony.

Smoke rose from the part of his legs that were touching the water as he thrashed around, scrambling to get out. "Help me!" He cried, falling to his knees with a rotted hand outstretched. His skin was sloughing off his body and his bones were beginning to poke through as he became engulfed by the steaming water in seconds. It splashed onto Céline and hit her square in the thigh. That one round splotch ate through the cloth on her pants, burning her skin with a sickening sizzle.

And right before our eyes, Regis was eaten away bit by bit by the water.

Acid water, I thought, remembering the guard's conversation from the night before. There wasn't time to grab him out. He'd just perished, the water bubbling like a stomach digesting a large meal.

The rest of the teams would most likely make the same choice— to trudge straight through, not knowing that the water was a death trap.

Odessa was all I could think. Someone had to warn her.

"Are you coming?" Céline asked, making her way on the right side of the tunnel. It was a narrow fit, but she could place her feet side by side comfortably enough. The slope of the ceiling might be a problem for me with how tall I was, but I couldn't make my feet move.

Odessa would be down here at any moment, and I couldn't let her end like that.

"No," I responded, my hand reaching out and engulfing her small neck. "I'm sorry." Her eyes were wide with terror as I yanked her mask off and pushed her into the vat of acid with a scream upon her lips and a sinking in my gut. I knew the cost of being down here, and it was kill or be killed. And there was only one way Céline could be parted from her magick.

I rolled my shoulders as her body disintegrated with a sickening hiss. I didn't want to look as she died, but I couldn't look away. That fear and betrayal that flashed in her eyes before the light went out of them. The power to control liquid was now mine.

If the gods weren't entertained yet, they would be soon.

The tainted water was practically roiling now while it ate through the two bodies of people I'd called my teammates. I wondered how many more would be its victim. From the sixteen we'd started with we were now down by five. There were just eleven of us left and the odds of winning were getting better and better with each passing moment. If only I could make it to the end, wherever that lay hidden.

Now I just had to sit here and wait for Odessa's team to get here, and hopefully I could intercede before she wound up walking straight into a trap.

I knew I didn't owe her anything. And my goal hadn't changed. In fact, now that the games had officially started and I'd already bagged another power, that desire to have it all was only growing. But there was no reason I couldn't bring her along with me while the others floundered amongst themselves.

A mechanical clicking sound alerted me to the three other platforms being lowered.

Fuck, which one was she in?

My eyes strained as I watched intently, wanting to spot her before any chaos erupted. And it would too. With three teams converging on a small tunnel that was filled with acid, there were sure to be casualties.

I could see the tips of feet appearing. Her team had four people so that immediately eliminated the platform in the middle. There were only two other possibilities, and each were on opposite ends.

Legs appeared next, and to the right I spotted her with a small, almost unnoticeable bump on her leg. That fucking dagger.

I dashed over to where her platform was lowering just as they hit the bottom.

"Games are now commencing," that same voice said, drowning out all the other voices. The red light pulsated, and

Odessa's eyes found mine before we were plunged into total darkness.

Screams started filling the air from all around. Small hands gripped onto my forearms and pulled me down. Fire ripped through the area, making us duck and roll in the small landing space as the scent of burnt flesh stung my nostrils.

I cradled the small figure against my body and knew immediately who it belonged to. My hands wrapped around her braided head of hair, protecting her.

"Stay out of the water. It's full of acid," I warned, loud enough for her to hear. Her whole body was fucking shaking under me. "Follow me, now, Odessa." I pulled her to standing and shielded her as best I could from the magick that was being thrown about without a thought of who or what it might hit.

Tell-tale sounds of people being gutted and thrown into the acid rang out between screams and the moans of the injured. I pulled Odessa by the wrist onto the lip of the tunnel.

The lights flickered then in that ominous red hue that made everything around us look sinister.

My feet moved quickly as I dragged us out of the fray. Her team members were right on our heels, but that was fine. As long as they didn't attack us, because I wouldn't hesitate to end them.

"How do you know about the water?" Odessa asked when we were far enough away from the fighting. A rogue bit of magick went whizzing past, barely missing us.

Sweat gathered beneath my jumpsuit where the pack pressed down onto me.

"My team. They both went in. They didn't come out."

"Are you kidding me? What a crock of shit," Killian responded from the other side of the tunnel.

"Feel free to test it out yourself, but don't come crying to me when the acid eats your flesh and bones."

Killian swallowed, but kept moving, his eyes darting from the the small path in front of him to the water below.

The further we went, the more distant the voices and screams from the other teams became.

I wondered how many were lost. There was no way to salvage their powers, and I'd made peace with that. There were plenty of powers still up for grabs. Two more and I would tie for the record number that had been acquired.

Odessa still clung to my forearm. I didn't even know if she realized she was doing it, but I didn't mind. It warmed some cold dead part inside me to know that I brought her comfort. During our time here, she'd burrowed beneath my defenses and brought out a protective side that I didn't even know I possessed. Maybe it was the way she looked at me, or her fight against herself to hate me that did it. All I knew was that we were here now, and I wasn't going to let her go anytime soon.

She was the only one in Nocturne that could claim they were safe from me. No matter how many times I went over it in my mind, I couldn't bring myself to envision her any harm. Doing so sent me into a panic worse than what I experienced in the tombs. Leaving without her wasn't an option and I'd kill anyone that dared to cross us.

I'd even foiled my chance of getting more powers just to make sure she didn't plunge into that river of acid. No one had ever come between me and my goals before. It shocked me that I was able to compartmentalize those feelings of loss, moving quickly to assure myself there would be more opportunities. And there would be.

There were at least three powers in my vicinity now that I could take for myself, but we had to keep moving to get out of danger first.

Gods only knew what other traps might lay ahead, but for some reason a part of me felt that getting through the beginning was the easy part.

CHAPTER 19
ODESSA

It felt as I had been walking for miles. With how long and winding these tunnels were, that probably was the case. No one had spoken in hours, each of us trudging cautiously along the sides of the tunnel. Careful not to disturb the water below. Occasionally, small bits of rock would slide off from one of our shoes and ripple the top of the still murky black water, echoing off the short, rounded ceiling.

"We should stop to get some rest soon," Nat said.

"Oh, yeah? How are we supposed to do that? We touch that water and we're dead," Killian retorted.

I shuddered, imagining the worst. It might have been foolish of me to trust Dex, but I didn't think he was lying. Plus, he'd helped me more than once when he didn't have to. Staying behind to warn me just so I wouldn't be engulfed by the acid. There's no knowing what would have happened to me if he didn't take the time to do that, maybe even to his own detriment. He could have gone off and had a head start if he wanted to. But he didn't. He stayed, and I knew he stayed for me.

I could feel my emotions shimmering just beneath the surface threatening to spill over and take the wheel, but I couldn't afford to break. Not down here.

"There's got to be a break in the tunnel sometime. It doesn't just go on forever, nitwit," Nat snapped, bringing me out of my thoughts.

Though it did feel like the tunnel was endless. There hadn't been a turn or anything that we could see yet. And knowing that the other teams were right behind us, didn't make me feel like we could stop. At least not safely.

While our alliance between each other was fragile at best, it was a whole lot better than facing the other teams alone. There was no telling how many of them were even left after the kind of bloodbath that was unfolding before we peeled out.

"I think I see something!" Reed said.

And sure, enough just ahead there was a fork in the tunnel, breaking off into three separate directions and no way to know which one was the right choice.

The water became shallow and eventually nonexistent. The floor turned into an uneven cobblestone, making it difficult to walk without twisting an ankle. At least the boots they gave us had good traction.

As we got closer, shapes carved into the limestone arches appeared. One of an anatomical heart, another that had the gods' symbol of ribs, and the last one that resembled leg bones made into an 'x'.

"Which one do you think is the right way?" Killian said,

holding the straps of his pack and tilting his head back to study the symbols.

"Obviously, it's the gods' symbol," Reed said.

"Wouldn't that be a little too obvious?" Nat replied.

"I think it's the 'x', for 'x' marks the spot," Killian interjected.

"What do you think?" Dex asked. His tone was low enough that I knew his question was just for me.

My brow furrowed as I studied the markings. The gods symbol would make the most sense, but it also seemed the riskiest. They were known for playing tricks, and that's what made this such a difficult choice. They'd be just as likely to point out the right way with their own symbol as they would to use it as a trap. It was impossible to tell.

"I think we should follow the heart," Nat said. I still hadn't given my opinion feeling a wave of overwhelm at it all. The sounds of people dying still echoed in my ears. No amount of anticipating the worst could have prepared me for the reality of it. I'd seen dead bodies before, but they were in funeral homes. Those were staged. Calm. Their corpses looked peaceful. Not like the gruesome annihilation that I'd witnessed in the start of these stupid games. And I knew it was far from over. How many of us would even make it out of here?

Nervous glances were exchanged between several of us as the discussion heated up. I found myself chewing on my bottom lip as I swiveled my head, looking at all three tunnels. Weighing the options.

Knowing that the other team could be right behind us had me feeling the pressure of choosing quickly. We had to keep moving, but I had to admit my legs were tired and I didn't remember eating breakfast. With how dark it was down here, there was no way to really keep track of time. And my stomach was stabbing me with how hungry I felt.

"I think we should rest first before we move on. There's no telling what kind of traps are in any of those tunnels," I said finally.

"Yeah, let's do that. But we can't linger long," Nat agreed with a sigh, dropping her pack and sitting cross-legged on the ground. She rolled her shoulders and dug into the food that had been provided.

I joined her, taking a much-needed drink from my cool canteen. The icy water slid down my throat and into my empty stomach. There wasn't much it could hold, and I knew that I needed to ration it.

"Fine," Killian said joining us on the hard ground.

Dex stood with his muscular arms crossing his large chest, looking down at us before patrolling the perimeter. The way I'd jumped into his arms should have felt embarrassing, but there was something about him that made me feel oddly safe. The way he blocked me by using his body made my insides all warm and squishy.

Above the tunnel we had just come out from, I noticed there was an etching of a hand. I wondered what each of those etchings could stand for, because one of them had to led to the end of this maze.

"How many people do you think are left back there?" I asked, digging around for the food rations. Finally, my fingers brushed up against the silver foil and I pulled it towards me.

"Seven of them went after each other back there. There's no

way they all made it. Especially if what you said is true about the water," Reed said.

Dex eyed him and nodded his head. "It's true. I had no reason to lie about it."

"What do you think they're doing up there right now?" Killian asked, taking a seat beside Reed and gesturing to the ceiling above. The two of them reminded me so much of my brother. He'd be in training about now. Preparing for the war that raged just outside our borders.

"I think they're sitting down for lunch. Or running off to grab some cheese with a side of some crusty bread," Reed answered sounding wistful.

"I'd kill for some bread right about now. My mother always said that there wasn't much that couldn't be fixed by a good piece of bread," Nat said, biting into her ration with a grimace.

I swallowed my stale piece of granola, the texture grating across my tongue like sandpaper as I thought of my own mother. Was she even still alive?

In my heart I felt like I would have known if she passed. Or at least I hoped so. The two of us were so close that if I were to lose her, I don't know how I would cope with it. While a part of me knew I couldn't keep her forever, there was another part that hoped I could have more time. A selfish part of me wondered if I would get the chance to take the healing mask. I'd been too frightened to do anything but run for my life earlier.

If I came past the healing mask again, I don't know if I would hold back, or if I would try and take that power. I was afraid to find out what I would do, because would the power be worth it if the cost was another's life?

"We shouldn't linger long," Dex warned, watching the tunnel we had come from.

I knew he was right, but the adrenaline that had been coursing through my veins seemed to have dried up. My body felt exhausted and all I wanted to do was sleep.

"You think they purposefully made the worst tasting rations on the planet?" Killian asked struggling to chew the hard bits of granola.

Suddenly a burst of flames came careening down the tunnel, narrowly missing Dex. He had just enough time to tuck and roll before it turned into a wall of flames that were quickly encompassing the entire room. Reed wasn't as fast, and his arm was overtaken by the flames. Charred flesh and smoke filled the small, rounded room making my lungs burn.

His screams pierced my ear drums filling my heart with ice-cold dread.

My instincts finally kicked in and I sprung to my feet, shoving the rations back into my pack. I hoisted the heavy bag onto my shoulders in one swift move.

"We have to move!" I cried out, stating the obvious but my teammates were all trying to help Reed put out the fire on his arm that had crawled up his face and singed his hair.

The wall of flames covered the entrance to two of the tunnels and was quickly edging into the third. We had no other choice but to take off down the tunnel marked with the god's symbol and hope to high heaven it was the right one.

CHAPTER 20
ODESSA

Dex was right beside me, pushing me into the smoke-filled tunnel. I didn't look behind me to check if anyone else was following. My feet pounded on the hard ground trying to escape as the large wall of flames grew closer, licking the top of the tunnel.

The Pyro planned to burn us all alive, I realized, and nearly had taken out Reed in the process. The heat from the flames penetrated through my clothes as sweat began to gather on my skin. Running as fast as my tired legs would carry me, I pushed deeper into the dark tunnel. If I stopped, I would die.

Smoke and flames chased us through the narrow space. I couldn't stop coughing and my eyes were tearing up, making it difficult to see.

The sound of someone tripping and hitting the floor filled my ears. Fuck.

I turned, finding Reed crumpled on the ground next to

Killian trying to lift him up. Nat kept running ahead and Dex pulled at me to follow.

My eyes bounced between the growing flames and my fallen teammates.

"No," I said, rushing to their side and pulling Reed to his feet.

This might be a cutthroat place, but I couldn't leave them behind like this.

Reed leaned on both Killian's and my shoulders as the flames continued to grow at an alarming rate behind us. We had to keep moving.

"Ow, fuck. You should just leave me here. Go on ahead," Reed insisted.

"I'm not leaving you," I said, struggling to hold up his weight. My legs were shaking with the effort to keep going.

"Give me him," Dex said, pushing me ahead, and taking over for me.

There was a silent moment that passed between us then, and I mouthed my thanks.

I didn't hesitate to run once Dex had ahold of Reed. Just ahead, a wide expanse opened, and Nat stood near the edge of a cliff.

There was nowhere to go.

We were standing at the edge of the abyss. A partially collapsed drawbridge could be seen swinging several meters away. Far enough that there was no way to reach it without magick.

Magick. Right.

I'd almost forgotten that I even had that power inside me. The mask on my face felt almost like a second skin at this point.

"How do we get across?" Nat asked, her eyes blown wide as she looked down into the inky expanse. It seemed to stretch on forever as if night itself had settled beneath our feet and taken up residence in this cave.

The flames were still growing and would be upon us in moments.

"Do you think you have enough power to fly across?" Nat asked Reed, whose power was The Bird- the power of flight.

He looked to be in rough shape, but maybe, just maybe he could find a way across.

Reed stepped forward, shrugging out of Dex and Killian's hold.

His burned arm shook as he struggled to keep his balance.

"I can try," he said taking a deep breath that resulted in a coughing fit.

"I don't know about this," Killian said, the worry evident in his tone. I felt it too, but what choice did we have?

Reed took a few steps back, steadying himself.

"Here goes nothing. If I fall, tell my family I love them."

"You're not going to fall," I reassured him, but I didn't know if I was lying to him or not. I hoped I was telling the truth.

Reed took off, power flowing through his veins as his feet lifted off the ground. He was doing it. He was going to make it. He was halfway across and almost there.

But then, he coughed hard and started tumbling down into the dark abyss below. I let out a gasp as we all watched his form become eaten up by the darkness. Horror gripped my heart as I watched him, helplessly frozen to the edge of the cliff.

"Reed!" A cacophony of voices called after him, mine included.

Fire from behind us threatened to send us tumbling after him.

Then, a crumpled looking Reed shot out from below barely making it to where the drawbridge lay hanging.

"Oh, my gods, Reed! Are you okay?" I called out. My voice echoed across the expanse.

I could hear a faint coughing and then, "Yeah. All good."

"Is there a way to bring us over?" Dex asked, his fingers clutched into a fist.

Another round of coughing answered back, before he stood completely. He took one haunting look back at us and my stomach dropped.

"Reed?" Dex asked again loud enough to carry his voice across the expanse. It echoed off the walls sounding just as angry and crestfallen as I felt.

"Sorry, but you'll have to find another way over."

My mouth hung open. "Reed, wait, please. There has to be something," I called after him in desperation.

But he shook his head and turned around. I watched as he began walking away.

"Reed!" Killian and Nat called out, but he continued to shuffle away.

"Fucking bastard." Dex said, punching the wall.

My eyes began to fill with tears. What were we supposed to do now? I couldn't believe he left us like that.

"Wait, I think I see something," Nat said, pointing to a small edge that seemed to line the cavern. There was a steep drop down, but with the fire creeping closer by the second, we didn't have much choice. We either had to climb out onto the tiny ledge or be consumed by the flames.

My stomach pitched at the sight.

"I won't let you fall," Dex said squeezing my hand in his. My thumb swiped over the back of his hand, coming away bloody from when he'd hit the wall.

"Promise?"

He smiled at me then, in the midst of the chaos that threatened to consume us. It steadied me in a way that should have been concerning.

"Would I lie to you?"

I took a deep breath, knowing that he would, in fact, lie to me, but I took it as a truth anyways, stepping out onto the ledge.

My fear of heights was alive and well and clutched tightly around my middle— filling me with anxiety. Limbs shaking, I followed Nat, carefully stepping where she did. Dex followed, and Killian after, narrowly missing the roar of flames that shot out of the tunnel.

If I ever found out who selected me to be a contestant in Nocturne, I'd fucking kill them.

My back was placed firmly against the cool wall as far back as my pack would allow, with my toes hanging precariously over the edge as we shuffled sideways. I swallowed hard, trying to stuff down the overwhelming amount of fear that was coursing through my veins.

Not looking down didn't help, because with every step my body instinctively knew that I was hanging off the edge of a cliff and could fall at any moment. I should have taken my pack off and slung it around my front, but there wasn't enough time. Now, I was too afraid to anything but follow Nat's footsteps.

"Where does this even lead?" Killian asked.

"Hell, if I know," Dex muttered, holding onto my hand with a vice-like grip. It was the only indication I had that he meant what he said. He wasn't going to let me fall.

The ledge was uneven, dipping in areas, widening and narrowing with every step. It took every ounce of focus to keep my footing steady.

"Away from that fire, that's all I know," Nat said, continuing along the wall.

After a few minutes the wall began to turn and with it the ledge expanded into a full yard giving us plenty of room to maneuver. I was grateful for the space, because hanging off the edge of a wall was not my idea of a good time. As far as we could tell, no one had come down that tunnel yet. They probably assumed they'd torched anyone that was in the path of their flame.

There was no way to tell how long this abyss went on. Light filtering in from above was minimal at best, giving way to shadows and darkness. Inside, my power felt like it was thriving. Basking in the essence of its making that was all around us.

At least I wasn't in danger of plummeting straight down, I thought right before a shudder emanated from behind us.

I turned my head just in time to see a crack forming on the ground beneath Killian's feet spreading along the entire length of the ledge.

Shit.

"Run!" I cried out, pushing Nat to move and pulling on Dex's hand that was still clasped around mine.

Huge chunks of where we had just come from began falling into the chasm.

My legs were moving as fast as they could carry me. Blood rushed through my body, pulsating in my ears— muffling everything around us.

"Go faster!" Dex yelled from right behind me.

I chanced looking behind us again and saw the moment when the ground gave way under Killian's feet. One minute he was there, running, and the next he was swallowed up. Gone with nothing but his scream remaining.

"Go, go, go!" I cried, pushing Nat square in the back, hoping it would make her move faster.

"I'm going as fast as I can!" She snapped back.

The cracks were speeding up, spreading beneath my feet. I could feel the ground shaking with each step I took, wondering if I was about to fall just like Killian.

My heart was pounding so hard that I could feel it hammering against my rib cage. I could feel Dex's hand tightening in mine.

Up ahead a small alcove in the wall emerged. If we could make it there, maybe we could have a chance to survive.

The ground began to give way, and it was harder to stay ahead of the falling parts.

We had to make it, we had to—

The ground crumbled beneath me and in the next step, I felt nothing but air.

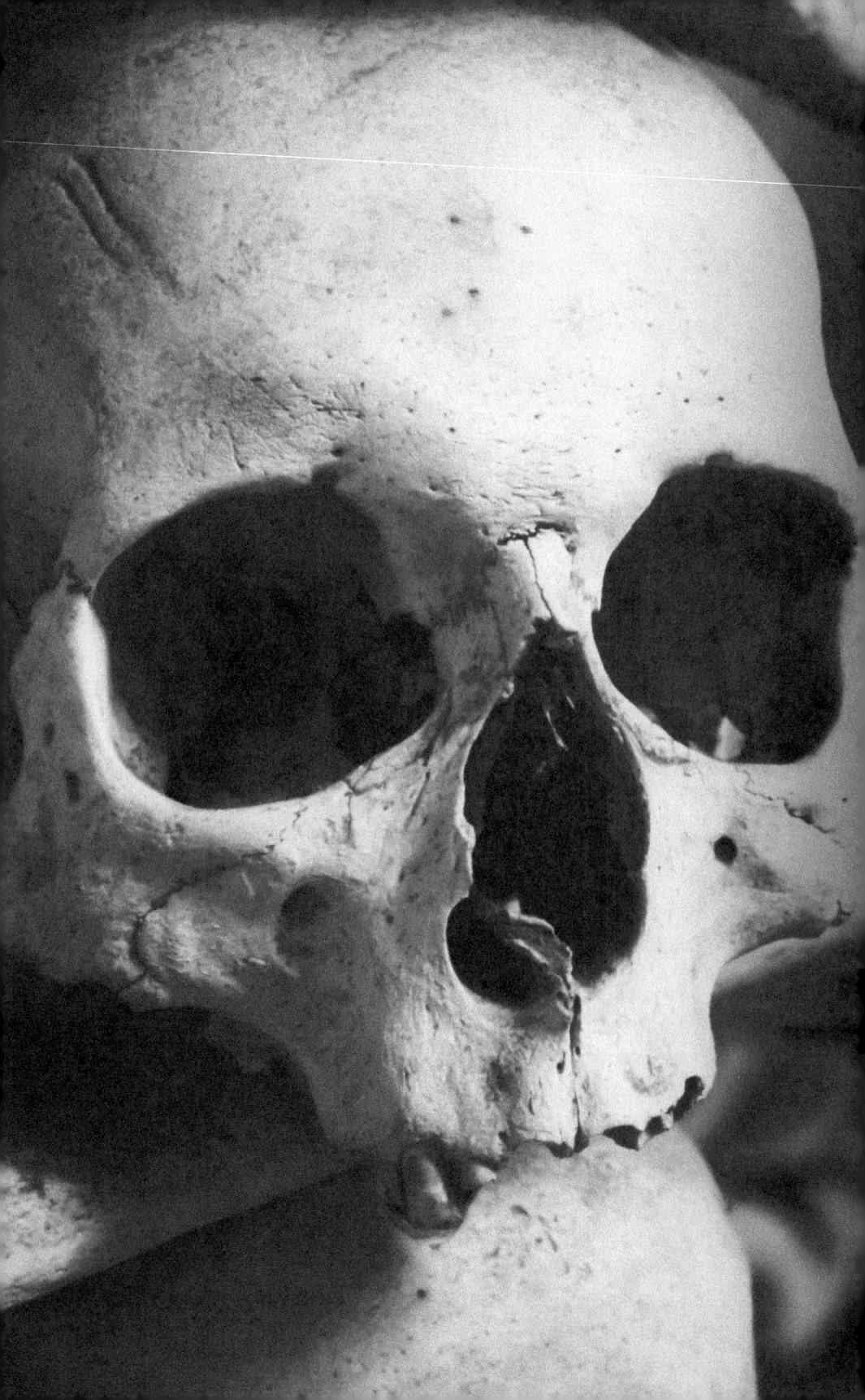

CHAPTER 21
DEX

Everything had gone to hell. From the moment the other teams descended, I'd been trying to keep Odessa safe, while still carrying out my original plan. But I was failing epically on both fronts.

Not only had two other powers slipped right through my fingers, but it seemed Odessa and I were destined to fall to an early death. The ground was cracking apart faster than we could run.

While the alcove was close, it wasn't close enough.

There were no bones nearby to manipulate into something I could use here. The light was useless, and the spider and strength powers wouldn't get me anywhere. If only I'd killed that Reed and taken his power of flight, before he fucked off leaving us to this fate.

Maybe the water could do something?

I took another step and when I did, I felt my entire body

plummet. My stomach lurched into my throat as air whipped around me.

I'd still had hold of Odessa's hand and one look at her broke me.

She was screaming, and that one haunting sound burrowed deep into my chest along with regret that I hadn't kept her safe like I promised.

Suddenly, it felt like an arm was wrapping itself around my middle, hauling me up.

Shadows, I realized.

Odessa had tapped into her power and was wielding enough magick to pull us both out of the depths. The shadows placed us into a small crack in the wall where Nat was looking at us in disbelief.

"I thought you were goners," she said.

"So did I," Odessa replied.

"Thank you. For saving me," I managed to say.

Odessa turned to me. "You lied. You said you wouldn't let me fall."

I felt a small smile pull on my lips. "Have to keep you guessing. Wouldn't want to be boring."

"Can't have that."

It took a moment for my breathing to return to a normal rhythm.

"Does this go anywhere do you think?" Odessa asked.

"It's narrow, but maybe. There's nowhere else for us to go. The ledge is gone," Nat said.

"We'll have to crawl on our bellies to fit through," I remarked, eyeing the tiny space. Fucking small spaces.

"Alright, well, why don't we get some rest here and then we

can continue on. I don't know about you, but I'm fucking wiped, "Odessa said.

"Almost dying a bunch of times can do that to you," Nat said, looking every bit as tired as I felt.

"We should take turns as lookout, don't you think?" I responded, not wanting to be caught unaware. While I knew I needed to rest, I also knew that the other teams were still out there.

"I guess," Nat said, dropping down to the ground.

There was just enough room for the three of us to sit. We'd have to sleep sitting straight up, but it would have to do.

"You both rest. I'll keep an eye out," I said, sitting on the ground and crossing my arms in front of my chest.

"Fine with me. I can't keep my eyes open for another second," Odessa said.

She must have used a significant amount of power to get us both out of there safely. She could have let me fall, but she didn't. She chose to save me.

And then she surprised the hell out of me. When she sat down next to me, Odessa laid her head against my shoulder, and it felt like she fit there, with me. It was an odd feeling to have and it made my insides squeeze with a feeling I didn't know how to name.

Sure, I'd been interested in her, and felt drawn to her. She was beautiful. No, beautiful wasn't the right word. She was breathtaking. But I'd been attracted to plenty of women in my life. I was no stranger to taking women to my bed and fucking them all night long, but I was never one for settling down. I liked the thrill of the hunt. The chase. The banter.

But somewhere along the way, Odessa had clawed her way past my defenses and settled deep into my soul.

Maybe it was this place, or maybe it was the way her small breaths felt fluttering against my neck as she slept, trusting me implicitly though she shouldn't, but I realized now that I was falling for her.

I was here to steal her power, but she'd stolen my heart instead.

Resting my head back, I kept an eye out, listening for any incoming threats, but the only sounds I could hear were of Nat and Odessa gently breathing in their sleep.

A stray strand of hair had fallen across Odessa's face, and I moved it, tucking it behind her ear, careful not to wake her.

She seemed so peaceful like this.

"Dex," she breathed out in a whisper making my heart squeeze. I loved the way she said my name— like I belonged to her.

"Go to sleep," I said, planting a small kiss to her forehead. She nuzzled against me, snaking her small arm around my middle. I pulled her against me, letting her use me like a pillow.

Nat's eyes opened briefly, looking between Odessa and me with a small knowing smile on her lips, before she closed her eyes again.

I didn't care if anyone else approved or not. And I knew that there was still that ring on Odessa's finger. She technically belonged to another man. But then how could she feel so wholly mine, despite that fact? I was determined to keep her for myself. And maybe that was selfish, but I was a selfish prick. I'd never pretended to be otherwise.

For as long as I could remember, I've always gone after what

I wanted, consequences be damned. If I wanted something, I found a way to get it. And if my plans fell through, I still found a way to make it work for me.

The way Odessa held me, let me know I at least had a chance to win her heart, like she'd won mine. I'd fight for it if I had to. I'd fight for her.

AFTER A FEW HOURS, Nat took over the watch, having me get some much-needed sleep. It claimed me quickly, though my dreams were fitful, making me feel like I was falling all over again. I jolted awake, afraid it was really happening, only to find Odessa's hand on my shoulder gently shaking me.

"We should get moving," she said.

I had no idea how long I'd been out, but I wiped the dried drool from the corners of my mouth, and dug out the canteen full of water, swishing the cool liquid around. There was a pack of gum hidden in one of the pockets that I popped in my mouth, delighting in the minty flavor on my tongue.

"You should eat something," Odessa said while nibbling on her meager rations.

"I'm good." I'd always been able to get by on little to no food. Not knowing how long we would be down here, had me wanting to save what I could for when I really needed it.

Odessa's mouth turned down as she looked at me with a hint of worry, but let it drop, finishing her food.

Having her next to me all night was something that I

wanted more of. While the situation wasn't ideal, I relished cradling her in my arms. She fit so well against me.

"You two lovebirds done eye-fucking each other so we can get the hell out of here?"

Odessa's mouth dropped open and her cheeks flushed red, but she didn't protest. Interesting. Maybe I was growing on her. A guy could hope.

To get through the slim opening, we had to drag our backpacks behind us. Honestly, I was doubtful I would be able to squeeze my broad shoulders through, but that was the only way out. Behind us, the ledge had crumpled into the cavernous abyss. So, on my stomach I went, right behind Nat and Odessa.

Nat was able to shimmy through, doing an army crawl with the pack tied around her ankle. Next, was Odessa, doing the same.

When it was my turn, I had to take several steadying breaths, reassuring myself that I'd get through this, even though I didn't know if I would.

My shoulders brushed up against both sides of the walls with each inch forward. Gravel dug into my forearms and knees as we crawled.

The further we went— I began to realize that the sides of the tunnel were changing from limestone to bones. Skulls, ribs, femurs, all began to line the walls.

"Nat. You see anything?" I asked, desperate to get out of here.

"No," she grunted back.

I pressed my forehead into the floor, feeling the mask on my face press into my skin as I worked to steady my breathing.

"You okay back there?" Odessa asked.

"Yep, just fine."

Another inch forward and the wall full of bones was pressing in tighter. My ribs were tightening as my breathing began to come in faster. I was hyperventilating and I was too far gone to get a handle on it.

Odessa turned her head as far as she could, looking back at me.

"Dex, just take a deep breath, we're okay."

I nodded, trying to get my body to listen, breathing in and shuddering, only the motion made me feel stuck as my chest expanded hitting the top and sides of the tunnel.

"Just keep moving. Follow my voice," Odessa instructed.

For her I could. For her I did.

I listened and pushed on. Following her into the dark tunnel, fighting against the instinct that was clawing inside of me to panic. To shut down.

Dark, tight places reminded me of before. And I swore I'd never go back there. Never even talk about it. Or even let myself think about it. I had to focus on the plan. No— I had to focus on my future. On Odessa.

"I think I can feel something," Nat called from ahead. "It feels like– like a button."

"Don't push it—" I said, but a moment too late.

The entire area around us began to shake and then everything collapsed.

CHAPTER 22
ODESSA

The floor slid out from underneath me, and I found myself tumbling down into a dusty tomb, entrapping me behind several large boulders and muffling the screams of Dex and Nat.

No, no, no! My fingers dug against the rough edges of the rocks, trying to claw my way out. But the bits of bone and rubble continued to slide and what little light there was snuffed out, plunging me into total darkness. My body ached from the fall, and a stinging sensation spread up my legs, letting me know that I was bleeding.

How could I get out of here?

My power surged inside me as soon as that thought crossed my mind, almost on instinct, pushing against the rockslide that threatened to bury me alive. I couldn't tell if it was doing any good, but it was better than doing nothing.

My heart pounded like a drum was shoved behind my rib

cage and sweat gathered along my brow. How long would it take for me to run out of oxygen? I'd expelled so much of my power yesterday saving myself and Dex that I didn't know how much I still had in me. With minimal sleep and a shitty breakfast, I was feeling weak and run down.

Something scurried along the ground near my feet, making me shriek in terror. Was that a rat? Gods I hoped not.

Was this how I went? Trapped beneath rock and bone, eaten by rats until my bones were a permanent fixture of this cursed place.

"Please," I pleaded, with tears gathering at the corners of my eyes as my fingers desperately scraped against the bits of loose limestone, hoping that something would give way. My power felt distant as I attempted another surge, pushing against the rock, but nothing but a whisper of magick came out.

Dammit!

The rocks stopped sliding, and I found my body wedged between a slab of limestone and what felt like hundreds of bones. There wasn't anywhere for me to move, and the weight felt unbearable. Like I was being squeezed from the waist up. I kicked and kicked, only managing to get stuck further, with the rocks pressing in against my ribs, making it hard to breathe.

Air. Air! I needed air!

Were Nat and Dex in the same predicament right now? Clawing against heavy boulders hoping that they weren't stuck forever. Or were they crushed to death by the heavy bits of tunnel that had collapsed on us? We'd already lost so many people along the way, and the thought of losing Dex too filled me with an emotion that I was too scared to put a name to.

I knew Nat shouldn't have touched that button. If the gods were watching us right now, I hoped they knew how much I hated them for this.

"Odessa?" Dex's voice penetrated through the darkness.

"I'm here!" I called back with a cough, relieved to hear his voice. He wasn't dead. "Is Nat, okay?"

"I don't know. Nat?" I listened closely for any signs she was okay but heard nothing.

"Can you see anything?" Dex asked after a moment.

"No. It's pitch-black, but I think there are rats in here."

"Okay. I'm going to try and move some of the bones."

"Okay."

I readied myself, hoping that he might be able to get me the hell out of here. The air felt thin and dusty as I waited. Then, there was a rumble of movement, and a deluge of bones fell away from me, dropping me further until I crash landed on solid ground. A moment later and another firm body crumpled next to mine with a groan.

"Nat?"

"Fuck, I shouldn't have touched that button," she said.

"No shit," Dex replied as he tumbled next to us.

"Where are we?" I asked.

"I think I have a lighter in my pack," Nat said rummaging through her bag. I'd lost mine in the rubble but still could feel the dagger that I'd hid in my boot pressing against my leg.

"Got it!" She cried, lighting it. It gave off a warm glow, illuminating the bottom of her face. We could barely make out our surroundings, but it seemed we had fallen into a room of some sort.

"Here let me see that lighter," Dex said grabbing a large bone and ripping off some of his jumper to wrap around the end.

He lit the fabric, fashioning a makeshift torch from fabric and bone. It gave off enough light that we could see far enough to take in the large room. It had a high ceiling and markings drawn all over the walls in every color imaginable. There were words and pictures painted on even the dust covered floor. It was clear no one had been in here in some time though. Maybe years. The room was filled with toppled tables and chairs covered in cobwebs, like whoever had left here, hadn't left peacefully.

My fingers dragged along the edges of the wall, outlining the words, *"Les dieux vous mentent"*. The gods are lying to you.

"Who do you think did this?" I asked in a whisper almost to myself.

"It had to be earlier contestants, right?" Nat replied.

"Right," I said, but the next words I'd found *vive la revolution*, had me doubting the truth of that.

There were rumors that when the gods first arrived, that there was an uprising of the people. War broke out amongst the citizens and gods, but without access to magick, the people were at a disadvantage and many perished in the fight for freedom.

However, the way the gods tell it was that our people were thankful for their arrival. There were parades to honor them, welcoming their new rule. The old ways were abolished, and the people celebrated the new era of the gods, erecting temples and statues in their honor. But there were some who weren't as welcoming, and they were dealt with swiftly. It's what we've been taught in school as we say our daily allegiance to their image. We honor them by pledging our loyalty to their divine rule. From the tender age of five, we were made to recite our rituals before the school day began. Even in my college courses, we remained faithful to our honoring of them. It was the way things had always been done, at least as far as I could remember. But seeing these words splattered across the walls felt like maybe there was more to what we had always been told. That maybe there was a revolution, and it had been erased from our collective history.

I already knew that the gods made sure to eradicate everything from before their rule, and any mention of it was treason. With that knowledge of what they were willing to hide from the past, there was no telling what else they might hide. Or what they still might be hiding.

My stomach soured wondering if these games were even for the reason we'd been told. They always brought out sixteen contestants. Every year like clockwork. Claiming their need for entertainment.

But if the games aren't being held for their entertainment, what are they being held for?

"Look, over here!" Nat called. She was pointing to a halfway crumbled archway. "There's a way out, I think. Shine your light over here, I want to see if this goes anywhere."

Dex brought over the flickering torch and shone the light into the opening.

"Looks like it keeps going," he said. "Why don't we break here, rest up. Take care of that cut on your head, and then we'll head down."

"But which way do we go? Left, or right?" I asked.

Dex shrugged and set his pack down, tossing me one of his rations. "Thanks." I said, opening it and breaking the hard granola in half. "Here, you have to eat too."

He sighed and then took my offering, biting off a chunk with a grimace. The food was hardly edible, but it was something.

Nat propped up one of the toppled chairs and wiped it off, sitting— or more like collapsing into it with her legs stretched out and one ankle crossed over the other. I chose to sit on the floor, not wanting to chance the rickety looking furniture that was thrown about. Who knew how long they'd been here in disarray.

"What do you think happened here?" Nat said.

"Nothing good," Dex replied, reaching down to hand me his canteen.

It was odd how quickly someone could go from annoying acquaintance and enemy to trusted support system. But I guess when you're thrown into life-or-death situations it's just human nature to seek out that comfort in another. Needing a sense of safety and normalcy that you otherwise wouldn't even engage with.

Nat might be a part of my team and Dex might make me feel safer, but there was no denying that either of them could turn on me at any time. There could only be one winner, and I wasn't sure how far either of them would go in order to win. Desperation made people do the most out of character things, and down here the air was rife with it.

We were desperate to survive. Desperate to get out of here. Desperate for the chance that we might be the ones to walk out of here with our magick intact and money flooding our bank accounts.

I may have been content with my life before, but I was here now. And no matter how much I wished it, there was no changing it.

While we were gathering our strength, I took a chance to remove my mask, just for a moment. I needed a break from having it dig against my face. Dex and Nat did the same, and it felt odd seeing them as they would normally look. I'd almost forgotten how handsome Dex was underneath his golden mask. My face felt naked now, without the mask to cover me and I massaged the skin, reveling in the feel of my own fingers. The relief was short lived, because I knew we had to keep moving.

As I stood to leave, a chilling rattle emanated from right behind me.

"Don't fucking move," Dex said eyes wide.

The hairs on the back of my neck stood on edge as a venomous black snake, slithered right between my legs. Its onyx tongue flickering as it moved.

"What do I do?" I asked watching it with wide eyes. One bite from it and I'd be dead in seconds.

"I got it," Nat said, putting her mask back on. She rose her arm and shot out her power, turning the thing into pure stone.

A breath of relief rushed out of me. "Thank you," I said.

"No sweat," she replied, shrugging.

Fuck, that was close.

We headed out, and I placed my mask back on, tying it tightly behind my head. My body felt bruised and sore with every step. Dex walked ahead of us with a new torch he'd made after the last one burned out, and we followed behind. He'd chosen to go to the right and really either way felt uncertain, so we hoped it was the correct choice.

This tunnel that we found ourselves in was wide and made of even more bones. Moisture dripped from above splashing every now and then on the stone floor. At least it wasn't acid, which I found out when it dripped right on my head, making me panic for a moment, before I realized I was fine.

"So, you and Dex seemed awfully cozy last night," Nat said, walking next to me.

She'd cleaned off the gash above her mask and now the area had dried in a jagged looking gouge. It was deep and probably could use some stitches.

"I wouldn't say cozy."

"It looked pretty cozy from where I was sitting."

"Well, tell that to the crick in my neck that I woke up with,"

Nat gave a quiet, half-hearted laugh. "I'm only asking because that ring on your finger seems pretty important."

I sighed, "It is."

"So—"

"So, I'm just trying to get through these games alive," My tone was defensive and clipped. Nat had hit a nerve because if the situation were reversed, and Theo had been the one to be summoned, I wouldn't be okay with him getting cozy with a fellow contestant. But then he hadn't even come to say goodbye to me. I would have shown up for him. And I couldn't help but remember all the times he had tried to keep me in my place. Small and obedient. Like a good little wife in training. I was tired of being what everyone else expected of me. I was tired of living small. I wanted to experience life to the fullest, especially after being threatened with my own mortality. But was that enough of an excuse for my behavior? I didn't know the answer and I was all twisted up inside about it. But down here it was a different world. Where the rules that usually applied to everyday life were thrown into a wood chipper. When the god of death's game was breathing down your neck, threatening to end your very life at a moment's notice, you learned to take stock of the things you'd always thought you'd known as fact.

"Did you end up with the power you wanted?" Nat asked changing the subject.

"No," I said with a sigh. Nat looked over at me, tilting her head. "I wanted The Healer, actually."

"No way, that one's like a death sentence."

"I know, but it was the one that I could use to save my maman. She's been sick for a long time, and we don't know how much time she has left. What about you?"

"Oh, yeah. I debated between this one and strength but turning things to stone is much cooler."

"Definitely," I agreed.

"So— up there. What were you doing before this?" Nat asked.

"Studying. I was a week away from my finals. You?"

"Baking. I was a baker."

"Really?"

"What?"

"I just wouldn't have pegged you as a baker. You seem so—formidable."

She laughed then, "And bakers can't be formidable?"

"I guess they can."

"Do you have a favorite thing you like to bake?" I asked after a minute.

"Wedding cakes. Some people come in with the most outlandish and creative ideas. Things that would seem impossible, and it's my job to make their wishes come true."

"Like a genie."

"Yeah." Her mouth quirked up in a half smile. "I guess so."

"What are you two talking about back there?" Dex asked, turning his head partly to look back at us.

"Your annoying tight ass," Nat quipped back making a smile tug at my lips.

"Oh, is that right?"

"Yep. We agree. It's annoying as hell," I said.

He hung back, waiting for us to catch up.

"We were talking about wedding cakes," Nat said.

Dex gave me a look that was conflicted, and I realized he maybe thought I was talking about mine.

"Nat's a baker. She likes designing wedding cakes," I said. "We were talking about what we were doing. You know before this," I felt like I was talking nervously, rambling. "What about you? What were you doing, before the summons?"

Dex's jaw flexed and he raised the torch a little higher as he stared off ahead. The shadows from the flame licked at his face, dancing across the gold-plated mask he wore.

"I was—"

"Wait. Do you hear that?" Nat asked in a hushed tone.

I strained my ears to hear whatever it was that had spooked Nat. At first, I didn't hear anything but our own footsteps. But then a soft crackling came from up ahead and a dim pulsating light began to grow brighter.

Flames.

Dex grabbed me by my wrist and pulled me back towards

the way we had come. The other team was fast approaching, and it seemed The Pyro was still alive, and headed right in our direction.

The tunnel quickly became hot with the flames as we ran right into three contestants that were ready and waiting for us. Trapping us between them and a wall of fire.

CHAPTER 23
ODESSA

The Healer, The Timepiece, and The Floral all stood in front of us like a formidable wall, ready to attack.

The girl with the floral powers had thick vines with thorns crawling along the ground and arching up the walls and sprouting what looked like deadly glowborn. A white tipped flower with glowing pink insides, hence the name, that was known to shoot a fatal dart of poison if you got too close. We'd walked right into a trap and there was nowhere to go. We had no choice but to fight our way out.

I pulled on my power, feeling the wisps of its tendrils grow at my command. They still felt weak, but it was all I had. Dex's hand was still wrapped around my wrist. The warmth of his skin grounded me. My power collected at the tips of my fingers, waiting.

"Can we help you?" Dex asked, his voice sounding deadly calm.

"You can give us your powers, how about that?" The one

wearing The Timepiece said with a flash of his teeth that was anything but friendly. He was of slim build and was of short stature with jet-black hair and hawk-like features and a palpable level of arrogance that let me know he thought he was walking out of here with what he wanted— us dead.

I looked at the girl wearing The Healer— Marcela. Her eyes were darting between the three of us, wide and full of fear. Maybe we could use that. People made stupid choices when they were scared.

"I don't think we'll be doing that," Dex replied, holding tight to the torch. His knuckles were blanched white from how hard he was gripping it.

"I don't think you have much of a choice. We've got you surrounded." He cracked his hands like he had all the time in the world. And with his power, I knew that to be true. He could speed up, rewind, or stop time if he wanted to. All with the snap of a finger.

"Oh, fuck this," Nat said as the flames came roaring closer. She raised her hand and within a blink of an eye her power slammed forward.

The Timepiece raised his hands, and everything seemed to slow down. But he was too late. The stone power that Nat had unleashed had already taken effect.

One minute the guy wearing The Timepiece was smirking at us, and the next his skin turned to pure stone inch by inch. He was frozen in a look of terror where he stood, and time went back to normal speed.

"You fucking bitch!" The Floral wielder screamed, sending her vines to wrap around Nat's neck. My shadows were sputtering out as I tried to use them to stop what was happening.

The thorns dug into Nat's flesh biting down hard enough that it punctures through her flesh.

Marcela took off running.

"Odessa, use your emotions!" Dex cried out as he was thrown to the ground by an invisible force. The Ghost, I realized, had been with them all along, using the power of invisibility. He looked like he was fighting against air until he grabbed the girl around her neck, making her flicker into existence.

I had to do something. Anything. My emotions were a jumble, going from utter terror to rage. How could I wield something that I couldn't even pin down?

"Let her go!" I screamed at The Floral, lunging for the vines, trying to stay far enough away from the lethal darts just waiting to be launched if I got within shooting distance.

"Odessa, look out!" Dex yelled, warning me of a sharp vine headed straight towards me. I had to duck, narrowly missing her attack.

It sliced across my cheek, and I felt the blood welling up in a sharp sting, sliding down my face. Nat's face was starting to turn blue, and her eyes were fluttering closed. The fire was nearly upon us, and Dex was scrambling to get ahold of The Ghost. She was stronger than she looked and had clawed Dex's arms up with her fingernails. He rolled her then and slammed her head into the rocky ground until she was still and no longer fighting.

Nat gripped onto the vine and slowly it turned into stone. It followed all the way back to The Floral as she began to shriek as her flesh became hardened. She tried to run but her feet were stuck to the floor. She crumpled. "No, no, please, no—" she cried out as the stone continued to turn her flesh solid.

"Nat? Nat talk to me. Are you okay?" I asked, rushing over to where she had fallen.

Her lips were cracked, and her neck was bleeding from the wounds.

"Get this fucking mask off me, please." She coughed out. Dex leaned down next to us and obliged, removing it from her face.

The gashes on her neck looked deep. And there, right in the crevice of where her neck met her shoulder, was a dart embedded deep into her flesh. "How bad is it?" She asked licking her lips.

I could feel tears welling up in my eyes as I looked at the black webs emanating from the toxic dart.

"That bad, huh?"

The black webs of poison were quickly spreading across her skin. When they reached her heart, that was it. There was no way to stop it. No known antidote to conjure or administer.

"I'm so sorry, Nat," I said clutching her hand in mine. She blinked up at me eyes wide as she struggled against the poison that was intent on claiming her body. Even if the poisonous dart hadn't lodged itself into her skin, the large gashes from the thorns would have been enough to kill her eventually. She didn't stand a chance.

"At least I got two of them, right?" She asked as blood from her wounds stained the ground.

"Right," I answered.

"You see that healer girl, with the mask you wanted?" Nat's breathing was becoming more labored and her skin looked pale.

"Yeah?"

"You get her ass for me, alright?"

"I'll try my best."

"Good." A small tear escaped the corner of her eye falling into the earth below. "You should go. The fire—"

"I'm not leaving you," I said, holding her hand tighter.

"Odessa—" Dex said gently.

"I said, I 'm not leaving her." It may have been foolish, but at least I could give her this. A hand to hold as she crossed over. Without her, we would be dead. I was sure of it.

Nat looked up at me, her eyes misting over. She began choking then, the black lines creeping up her neck before she went rigid and those eyes of hers turned dulled as she stared off into nothingness.

"We have to move," Dex said.

He was right. With the fire growing closer, we needed to move, even though I didn't want to. I didn't want to leave her there like this. But if I didn't move, The Pyro would burn us to a crisp, and then my body would be joining her.

CHAPTER 24
ODESSA

N at's blank eyes stared up into the void, unblinking and lifeless. Blood still dripped from her mouth as her body stilled.

I knew it was stupid to become attached to anyone down here, but it was human nature, after all, to form connections. To care. And I cared so fucking much.

A white-hot rage roiled in my belly at the unfairness of it all as two twin tears spilled over onto my cheeks. I wondered if the gods were watching now, reveling in our torment. We were only here for their entertainment. A spectacle of blood and betrayal. We were nothing but rats in a maze to them as they looked on, watching us struggle in vain. Did they cast bets to see who would make it to the end? Did they make a toast of nectar for the fallen, or laugh when our mortal lives were snuffed out in such brutal ways?

"I hope you're happy you fucking bastards!" I found myself screaming, my entire body shaking uncontrollably.

It was blasphemy to question the gods like I was, but I didn't care anymore. Let them smite me.

Dex closed Nat's eyes as I said the words of our people over her corpse.

"May the God of Death grant you entry past the gates of Nirvana. May your soul find the rest our world could not give you. May your memory live on in those who knew you. And may your death not be in vain," I added in that last part for myself, needing to feel a sense of justice despite everything. We'd lost so many along the way and for what? A chance at riches and power to become more like the gods that placed us here?

"Come on, we should keep moving," Dex said, gripping my hand and pulling me up. I nodded, knowing he was right.

It was just the two of us now.

Both our teams had been completely obliterated by this labyrinth full of traps. I wondered where The Healer had run off to. That cowardly bitch. If I saw her again, I'd take her power with no hesitation.

We took off running. Away from the flames and away from Nat's fallen body. The room we had come from was empty, but it wasn't far enough from the impending threat.

"Doesn't that guy's power ever give out?" I asked, feeling sour that my own power seemed to be waning.

"Yours giving you problems?" Dex asked.

How honest did I want to be? It was just the two of us now, and admitting weakness could give him the edge he needed to take me out. He was all I had left down here, and while a part of me felt inappropriately attracted to him, clinging to him for safety, another part of me felt like I had to keep my guard up. Dex could turn at any second, deciding that he wanted to win.

"Nope, no problems, just wondering if he'll ever tire out," I said finally, feeling the heavy lie upon my tongue.

Dex gave me a look that lasted a moment too long, like he was trying to figure out if I was telling the truth or not. I wasn't, but I'd rather keep my shortcomings a secret.

Exhaustion took up residence in every muscle, weighing me down with each step. The strenuous labor of having to run for my life was taking a toll, but if I stopped moving, it would give The Pyro enough time to catch up. I wanted to curl up and take a nap. I wanted to gorge myself on food and clean my body of the dust that had become like a second skin.

We had to find a way to the end, or at least, somewhere hidden that we could take refuge in. The tunnel continued on, winding into what felt like circles. We talked only when we had to alert the other of an upcoming obstacle. The deaths of my fellow contestants weighed heavy on me, but I couldn't afford to ruminate over it. They weren't coming back and nothing I did could make that a reality. They were gone for good, but I was still here, and I still had a chance to make it out. I just had to be smart.

The image of my family's faces kept my feet moving through the fatigue. Knowing they were depending on me to make it out had me pushing my body past what I knew it was capable of. I wasn't big on working out in my everyday life. I didn't have much time for it between studying and helping out at home. By the time my day was done, I usually collapsed into bed. Going from that to nonstop movement was more strenuous than I realized it would be.

The fire finally began to die out behind us, becoming less

and less until the threatening glow was extinguished completely.

"Fucking finally," Dex said.

I couldn't agree more.

"Who all is left? The Healer, The Pyro—"

"I didn't see The Gear with them."

"Do you think they killed him?"

"That or the traps got him."

"Do you think Reed is still alive?"

"If he is, I hope the bastard knows I'll kill him without a second thought for leaving us," Dex answered. I couldn't really blame him. Watching Reed walk away from our team felt like an ultimate betrayal. Especially since it led to Killian's and Nat's deaths. Had he helped us over, maybe things would have turned out differently.

"How do you think the gods watch us?" I asked, changing the subject after a moment. The question had been percolating in my mind.

He shrugged. "Hell, if I know."

I studied Dex, then. The arrogant swagger that he'd always displayed seemed to have abandoned him. It was replaced by determination and a hint of fear.

"Do you worship the gods, Dex? I feel like I don't know anything about you, but I've been acting like you're the only one I can trust down here."

He turned and looked at me, stopping for a moment. Icy colored eyes bouncing across my face in the minimal light. The way he looked at me burned hotter than if The Pyro had caught up with us. It was full of unspoken words and longing. So much longing that it hurt.

"You're taken, Odessa. I could tell you my favorite color, and how much I like to eat a scone with jelly in the mornings. I could discuss the gods and my thoughts on this fucked up game we've been playing." He gripped my arms, and I instinctively moved closer to him, feeling my breath catch in my chest as he stared down at me. "I could tell you that I know I shouldn't be drawn to you like I am, and that the fact that you have a ring on your hand marking you as someone else's kills me. I could tell you all these things, but it won't change the fact that allowing you to know me would just give me hope. And hope in a place like this, is dangerous. You shouldn't want to know me, Odessa. But if you want to know something, know that I'll do what I can to protect you."

I didn't know what to say. He was right. I shouldn't want to know him, but I did. I had so many questions. A part of me wanted to trust him. To take what he was saying as fact. But to do so could sign my own demise.

"Don't ask to know me unless you plan to stick around," Dex said.

I opened my mouth to respond, but nothing came out. He let me go then with a sigh.

"That's what I thought," he said, sounding disappointed.

It wasn't easy for me. I'd known Theo my entire life. And I loved him. At least I thought I did. Granted, I'd never felt an ounce of how I felt being around Dex. Just a small touch from Dex set my skin on fire. If I loved Theo, wouldn't I feel that way about him? Everything felt like I'd done it out of obligation. I'd never really chosen anything for myself.

Could I really choose Dex? I didn't know the answer to that.

All I knew is that we had to keep moving and find our way out of here.

CHAPTER 25
ODESSA

After what seemed like hours, I was feeling the need to rest. There'd been no sight of The Healer, Marcela, and I wondered if she'd found a secret tunnel somewhere. The Pyro too, had been quiet. Maybe too quiet.

"I don't think I can keep walking," I said, wanting to collapse into a heap where I stood.

"We have to keep moving. There isn't anywhere safe to stay yet," Dex replied.

I stuck my tongue out at him in response, which made him smile.

"Oh, well, excuse me for trying to keep us alive,"

"You're right. What time do you think it is? I'd say it was—"

"Shh. Do you hear that?" Dex asked, putting a hand up indicating that I should stop.

My ears strained to listen, and my heart began to beat fast. Was it The Pyro? Had he caught up to us? And then there it was. A soft trickle of running water.

Thirst, heavy and aching deep in my stomach roared to the surface. My mouth was bone dry from the lack of water.

"I think it's coming from over here," he said, finding a small, almost unnoticeable crack in the wall. The jagged edges were just wide enough to fit through sideways, bringing us to a large, cave-like room. The sounds of birds chirping and water rushing filled my ears.

Birds? All the way down here? I didn't think it possible.

A waterfall was cascading down from the ceiling where a faint bit of sky could be seen peeking through a small hole. Light shimmered along the surface where a pool of water sat, rippling gently along the rocks.

It was beautiful.

"Do you think it's safe?" I asked, feeling that thirst intensify with each passing second.

"Nothing is safe down here, but there's only one way to find out."

"We should flip for it. To see who drinks first. Could be poisoned."

"A taste tester? How barbaric. Fine, do you have a coin?"

"No, do you?"

"Believe it or not, I didn't really think I would be purchasing anything down here and left my wallet at home."

"Oh, why don't we use this?" I picked up a smooth stone and removed the dagger from my boot, etching an x on one side and leaving the other blank. "X, you drink, blank, I do."

"Sounds fair."

I tossed the rock and caught it in my hands x side up.

We both stared down at it for a beat before his icy blue eyes looked up at me, with that insufferable smirk pulling at his lips.

"Guess I'm the guinea pig," he said, removing his empty canteen. He dipped the metal into the shallow end of the pool.

It didn't dissolve at his touch, so that was promising. He brought it beneath his nose and sniffed.

"Interesting," he murmured.

"What, what is it?" My brow furrowed as I took a step closer.

"It smells like..." he brought the canteen to his lips and my heart beat faster, hoping that it was okay.

His tongue sneaked out and took a tentative taste of the liquid. I watched as his eyes widened, my breath caught in my chest as I waited.

"Just as I thought," he said after a moment.

"What!" My patience was snapping.

"It's nectar."

My mouth dropped as he took a swig.

Nectar was the drink of the gods. It was the most sacred and coveted of all drinks, only given to a select few mortals. People back home claimed to have tasted it only to be met with skepticism and laughter. Others still tried to peddle cheap watered-down wine or sparkling ale claiming it was authentic nectar. Only fools fell for it.

"How do you know it's nectar?" I asked feeling that surge of thirst licking along my bones.

His chin raised and his eyes gleamed. He sat back, kicking his legs out, finishing off his canteen without answering me.

"Aren't you going to have any? You must be thirsty," he said in response, avoiding my questions as usual.

I eyed him warily and finally took the canteen from him. He didn't seem to be having any kind of adverse reaction to the liquid, and I was parched. I was thirstier than I'd ever been in my life, feeling as if my tongue had been turned into sandpaper.

Damn it, I guess I didn't have much of a choice but to try it.

Bending down, I scooped up enough to refill the canteen. There was a faint flowery scent that wafted towards me as I raised the bottle to my lips. Like jasmine and lavender intertwined.

"Cheers," Dex said, fake knocking an imaginary canteen against mine with a mischievous wink.

I took a steadying breath and responded, "Cheers," with a shrug of my shoulders.

A shot of the cool liquid snaked down my throat, spreading the chilled sensation throughout my limbs. I felt instantly lighter, and my head swam. My tastebuds were alight with flavors I couldn't begin to describe because I had never tasted anything so delectable before. It was sweet and overwhelmingly addicting. My thirst was quelled immediately.

There was something in the back of my mind that I only faintly could remember about nectar. Some kind of warning or saying that was escaping me as I gulped down another canteen full before letting it slip out of my hand and topple onto the rock covered floor. It clattered and echoed off the high vaulted ceiling.

I tilted my head back and started up at the small portion of the sky that was peeking through.

"I thought I'd never see the sky again," I found myself murmuring, before tilting all the way back into a laying position. The rocks were uncomfortable and digging into my flesh, but for some reason I didn't care. I couldn't care, not when I was feeling like this. So blissful and relaxed for the first time since I got here.

My life had become chaotic and unpredictable. Danger lurked around every corner, and I should have been on high alert, but the nectar had me feeling like I was floating and untouchable. The urge to strip off my clothes was overwhelming. My entire body was covered in a mixture of dust and sweat and I needed it off me.

"Turn around. I'm going in," I said, not waiting for Dex to follow my instructions before I began unbuttoning my jumpsuit and kicking off my boots. The fabric peeled off my slick skin easily and I tossed it into a heap before I dipped my toes into the cool nectar-filled pool.

I didn't really care if he looked at me in this moment. Not when I was feeling this euphoric. The water greeted me easily, licking against my dirtied skin and washing away the grime that had built up over time. It felt better than the shower back at home.

"You can't be serious. What are you doing in there?" Dex asked, his head tilted to look at the ceiling, avoiding my naked form.

"Washing up, what does it look like I'm doing?"

"Well, I wouldn't know! You told me not to look."

I was fully emerged now in the water, tipping my head back as I floated easily in the dense liquid. It was buttery soft, sliding against my skin as I floated.

"You should come in here. It feels amazing." I was pretty sure he could see the tips of my breasts like this, but I couldn't find it in me to care. In fact, I liked it. I wanted his attention. I wanted him to see me like this.

Dex put his hands on his hips as if he was debating. I tilted my body forward so that I was no longer floating but still submerged from the chest down.

"I promise to keep my hands to myself," I said.

"It's not your hands that I'm worried about," Dex grumbled. "Fine, I'm coming in,"

"You want me to close my eyes?" I asked, covering my face.

"Nah, you can look all you want and see what you're missing."

He slowly unbuttoned his jumpsuit, kicking his shoes off to the side near where mine were. I could see my dagger laying where I'd dropped it.

I knew I shouldn't be peeking between my fingers, but he had said I could look.

"Like what you see over there?" He asked, shrugging completely out of his clothes.

He stood fully naked before me, cock hardened and bobbing in his hands. My cheeks warmed as I floundered for the right response.

I'd never seen a naked man before I'd walked in on Dex in the shower. I mean other than statues, but here, Dex was in front of me all flesh and blood. And so, so unbelievably hot. His sculpted muscles moved as he entered the pool, and I felt myself wanting to feel every ridge of his abs beneath my fingertips. My eyes couldn't stop staring at his large dick and a part of me wondered how it would feel if he were to be inside me.

He joined where I was, dipping his head back just like I had. Water droplets clung to my eyelashes as I watched him revel in the feel of the nectar. It was truly heavenly, and I understood why it was so coveted. Every fiber of my body felt like it was sparking with energy. Wisps of my power surged to my finger-tips, filling the air around me with shadows.

"Easy, you don't want to get too carried away," Dex said, placing his hands on my shoulders.

The shadows dropped, but my power, I realized had come back with a vengeance. If this was what it did to me, I wondered if it had the same effect of the gods. Giving them a sense of euphoria and limitless power.

Dex's hands were warm, and he kept them on me even after the shadows had dissipated. His thumbs made lazy circles on my wet skin, sending shivers along my nerve endings. I could feel the desire for him to keep touching me and looking at me the way he was all the way down to my toes. His hand found its way up to my cheek as he inspected my injury, thumb caressing ever so gently right beneath the cut.

"That hurt?"

"Not really," I said with a shrug. His touch was more intoxicating than the nectar I'd ingested.

I licked my lips, tasting the nectar upon them. He tracked the movement, and then I felt his hard cock graze against my leg. My eyes widened at the sudden contact, and he immediately jerked away, dropping my shoulders like they'd burned him.

"We should get out of here," he said as he hurriedly turned around, and stalked out of the pool almost angrily.

Disappointment clung deep in my belly, but I had no business being disappointed. What did I even expect anyways? For him to kiss me? Would I have let him? Would I have kissed him back?

There was no way to tell now that he was getting dressed. Damn, he had one hell of a body. His ass was on full display for me as he bent over. I found myself biting my bottom lip and tilting my head to the side, appreciating the fine form that was Dex. I bet he was good in bed, not that I had anything to compare it to, but he seemed like he would know what he was doing.

"Stop looking at me like that, Dessa, I swear to the gods I won't be able to stop myself from coming back in there and taking you if you don't." He snapped. "Now get out of that pool and get dressed. We should keep moving."

"What if I want you to take me?" I asked, beginning to step out of the water. I felt buzzed. Like my head was full of light fluffy cotton, but I also felt need. It was deep and raging in my core, wanting to be set free.

He glared at me then. A raging inferno was alight in those blue eyes of his as he saw me naked before him. His hands clenched beside him and his jaw was painfully tight. He went to say something, but then he stopped.

A low rumble vibrated the rocks underneath me.

"Mmm, that feels nice." I said with a giggle, feeling the vibrations roll through my entire body.

"We need to go. Get dressed and don't forget your mask. Right now, Odessa," Dex warned. Grabbing his backpack as he reached for my hand.

I swatted it away. When had I taken my mask off? My head felt so fuzzy, but placing my hands on my face, I found he was right. I was losing track of time and moments, that buzz rolling low in my belly with elation. It felt so good.

"You're always trying to ruin my fun," I whined.

"Odessa, we need to go. Now." His tone was forceful, but my body felt warm and happy and light. Like I could stay here forever feeling this peaceful. Maybe I should just close my eyes and fall asleep. I toppled to the ground and closed my eyes.

A sharp slap to my face jolted me, and I angrily looked at Dex.

"Ow! What gives?"

"We need to get the fuck out of here, before we become Gerataux's food."

"Gerataux...I thought those were only in fairy tales,"

"Dammit, Odessa," Dex said, pushing my underwear and jumpsuit over my wet skin. The fabric was rough and difficult to put back on now that I was soaked, but I lifted my butt up for him as he wiggled it onto me.

"Look at you getting me dressed," I said with a smile.

"Yeah, well I'd rather us both be naked and doing anything but this, but I don't want to become some monster's lunch. I need you to put your arms in here," Dex ordered, holding up the rest of my jumpsuit. I shoved my arms in and then swatted him away from my buttons.

"I can do it myself," I hiccuped, "Thank youuu very much."

"How much did you drink?" He asked, lacing my shoes up. I didn't even realize he put my shoes on.

"My knife?" I asked, looking around.

"In your sock,"

I patted my leg, and sure enough, he put it back right where I'd been carrying it this whole time.

"Come on, get up. Mask on, now," he said, pulling at my arms to get me to my feet.

"Stop babying me!" I whined.

"I'm not babying you! I'm trying to get us out of here before the monster decides to show up!"

"I could kiss you," I said swaying on my feet and stumbling forward until I was clinging to Dex's shirt looking up at him.

"You shouldn't say things you don't mean," he said with a labored breath.

"But I do mean it," I protested. Maybe it was the nectar talking, but right now all I wanted was to feel his lips on mine. Monster or no monster.

He seemed to consider it for a moment, brushing away a lock of my wet hair from my face, cupping my mask covered face with his large hand. Wait, when did my mask pop on my face? Did I get it on myself or did Dex? Had it been there this whole time?

The world seemed to tilt, and I felt myself moving in towards Dex, our mouths dangerously close to each other.

But then, a roar like no other shook the very air around us as large sharp stalactites began to fall from the ceiling, nearly crushing us where we stood and a scream wrenched free from my throat.

The thing I had forgotten, the very important piece of information that laid in the back of my mind, was that nectar could only be made in the lagoon of the deadly Gerataux. A monster so ferocious that there were hardly any stories of mortals that walked away after encountering one.

There was a reason only the gods could obtain nectar, and I was looking at it right now, in all its hideous and deadly glory.

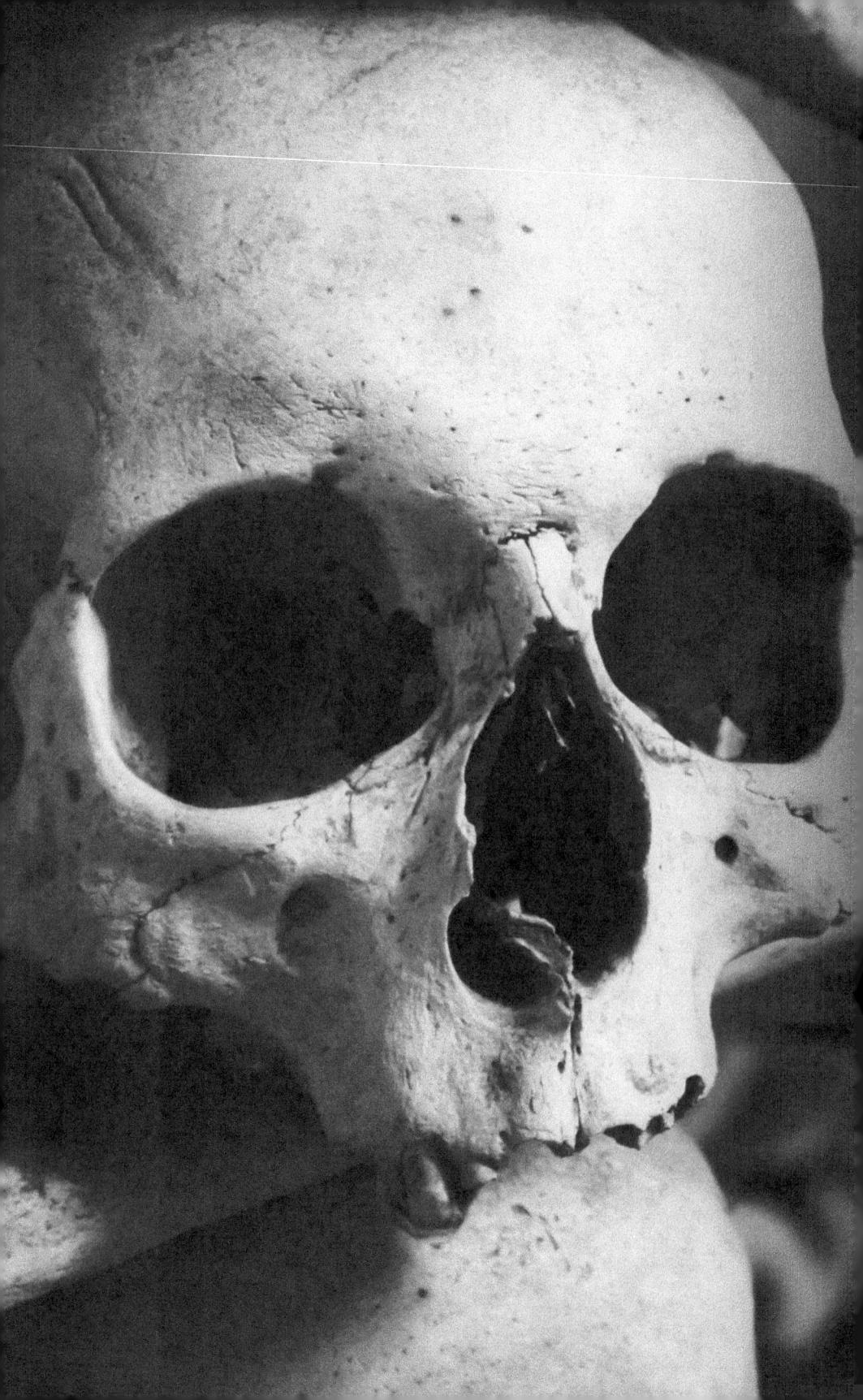

CHAPTER 26
DEX

The Gerataux. Fuck. How could I have forgotten? The creature stretched the entire height of the cave and was knocking his scaled head against the ceiling, bringing down large boulders that had managed to miss us so far. Its silver-scaled wide body and eight clawed limbs blocked the path back to the tunnel, and there was only one way out.

It towered over us, snarling and snapping its large jaw. This monster could swallow us whole if it wanted to. Often it would choose to ingest its victims and then regurgitate them later just so they could eat it all over again, only in a softer more digestible form. I shuddered not wanting that to be our fate.

Odessa gripped my forearm as she swayed. That nectar had gone right to her head, making her wobbly and a little out of it. Just great. She must have drunk more while in the pool.

I knew the legends just as well as the next person, but in my haste and nectar-filled stupor, I'd forgotten just what lurked beneath the surface of that still water. Plus, all the blood from my head had headed south the moment Odessa started taking off her clothes. Gods, her body was better than I'd even imagined. I couldn't help but sneak a peek, even though I tried to remain gentlemanly, she'd waltzed out of that pool stark naked and dripping wet, blowing every fantasy I'd had about her sky high.

Odessa stumbled into me trying to catch her bearings, her hands still firmly wrapped around my forearm. She was shivering now, and her eyes were blown wide with fear.

It was one thing to be facing fellow contestants, but facing a whole ass monster was something else entirely.

The Gerataux let out another deafening roar and more rocks began to fall. As it did, the way back became blocked right as we were about to escape. Shit.

"What are we supposed to do?" Odessa cried, her brown eyes were so unfocussed they seemed to be spinning. She drank way too much of the nectar and it had gone straight to her head.

"Over there," I pointed to behind the waterfall. If we could make it back there, maybe we'd be able to hide.

Instinct took over, and I called upon my magick, finding the right thread of power to blind him. A bolt of light erupted from me and shot directly into the creature's eyes. The monster let out an unholy screech, but it did the trick, making it cower just enough to let Odessa, and I pass.

We ran, dodging its large limbs as it blindly snapped at the air before swooping its large neck down to where we were.

"This way," I yelled, pulling at Odessa just in time to the side, avoiding the Gerataux's attempt to eat us. It crashed into the hard stone, making everything around us, including the floor we stood on, shake.

The rocks to the waterfall were slippery and narrow. One wrong step and we would fall off the edge. Knowing that it was deep enough to house the Gerataux, I didn't want to chance either of us falling. Odessa kept a death-grip on my forearm as we carefully made our way along the rocks.

"I think there's a passage back here!" I yelled so Odessa could hear me over the water.

It was loud and I didn't know how much time we had before the monster would regain its vision. We were almost there. Only a few more rocks and then we could get the hell out of this godsforsaken cave.

Odessa's foot slipped on the last rock, and I caught her before she tumbled off into the icy depths below.

"I need you to swing your legs over, okay?"

Odessa nodded her head, struggling against the pull of the nectar and the force of gravity to do what I'd asked.

"I've got you. I promise," I said.

"I've heard that before," she quipped with a grunt as she managed to barely swing herself back up to the ledge.

And just in time too. The Gerataux was looking straight at us as its monstrous body came plunging into the water, as it headed right towards us. The water rippled angrily as it swam.

"Go, go, go!" I yelled, gripping Odessa's hand and running into the passageway tucked behind the waterfall.

There were large iron sconces lining the walls here. Each filled with enough fire to light the way.

The roar of the Gerataux could be heard, but it was muffled now. Though I was sure he couldn't catch us, I still kept us at a fast pace, wanting to be as far away from the danger as possible. Even though that wasn't a reality in Nocturne.

"Stop, please," Odessa begged. "I need to catch my breath just for a second."

My eyes swept both ahead of us, then behind us, before I agreed. She collapsed against the wall and took several steadying breaths. Her eyes seemed clearer than they were back in the cave. The nectar must have been wearing off.

"Are you okay?" I asked.

Her hand was pressed firmly against her chest. Her eyes were no longer spinning. They looked deadly focused.

"I knew. I knew this would be hard, you know? But knowing and experiencing it are two different things. I mean—" she started to laugh. "That was a fucking Gerataux, Dex! I used to have nightmares as a child about them. And then my maman told me they were just a fairytale, and I fucking believed her. Oh gods, I hope I make it back to tell her she was wrong."

Her shoulders sagged then.

"What is it?" I asked, stepping closer. I knew letting my emotions and my protective feelings for this girl was a bad fucking idea, but I still kept coming back to her. Still kept treating her like she was mine to protect. Because if anything were to fucking happen to her, I wouldn't know how to live with myself.

"I don't even know if I'll make it out of here."

"You've made it this far."

"And if I make it out? I'm afraid of the things that wait for me back home. If my maman will still even be alive. She's been sick. And all I want is for her to be well again. I'd heal her with the money or new powers I got from this place if I win." She was quiet then, and her breathing steadied. "I loved my life. I love my family. I love— I love—" my chest twisted waiting for her fiancé's name to drop from her lips. "I loved knowing what was going to happen." I let out a breath and closed my eyes, grateful she hadn't said whatever his name is.

"And then, I come here. And nothing is certain. And you? Gods, you annoy the hell out of me. You're so sure of yourself, and you won't let me know you! And I shouldn't want to, Dex! I have a life. A good one. But down here? I'm different. I'm not someone's well-behaved daughter, or perfect student, or wife in training. I'm just me. And I like that too. It might be a crazy thing to even say, but I do."

I tucked a stray hair behind her ear, wishing I could do more. Gods, I wanted to. I wanted to shove her up against this wall and take her like I'd dreamed of. Now that I knew what she looked like under those clothes, I didn't know how much longer I could last without acting on that impulse. She drove me wild with her raw honesty and passion. She was transparent in all her emotions. Never hiding them from the world. That took fucking courage, to bare yourself in a way that others could see exactly how you were feeling. I'd always been taught to shove those parts of me down. That it would only make me weak. But staring at me in this dimly lit tunnel, I began to question what I thought I knew. Maybe there was a strength to be found in vulnerability.

"Wait a minute. Back there, in the cave. Did you?" She shook her head. "Did you use the power of light?" Odessa asked.

I pushed my hands into my pockets and took a half-step back.

"You did! Didn't you? That was light I saw coming from you." Her brown eyes were wide as she tried to piece everything together. "How long have you had that power?" Her voice was calm. Too calm.

In an instant, that dagger she had tucked away was at my throat.

"Who the fuck are you? And how did you get that power?"

CHAPTER 27
ODESSA

Dex raised his hands from his pockets. My arm was shaking with anger and adrenaline. I might have briefly calmed myself down from almost being eaten by a monster, but that feeling was back and in full force as I stared into the eyes of the man I'd stupidly been falling for.

"Who the hell are you?" I asked again. "You come here with an accent first of all, when it's hard as fuck to get in or out of this city. Then you act like this competition is beneath you. And now, you possess a power that you shouldn't have access to!"

"You're right," he agreed, his hair falling over his mask, and I fought the urge to brush it back. He'd seen me naked, I realized. I let him see me like that. Not even my fiancé had seen me naked, but I'd let Dex— a man I'd only known for a handful of days. What was I thinking?

"I know I am. Now are you going to tell me what the fuck is going on or not?"

Dex sighed taking a step towards me. It moved the dagger, but I stood my ground with it raised between us. My back was to the wall, pressed tight. He was standing so close to me that his breath fluttered over my face. I could flick my wrist and slice his jugular, but something held me back. I wanted to know why and how he could possess such power. His blue eyes bounced between my own brown ones. He licked his lips, and my traitorous eyes follow the motion.

"I took the masks off the mounted heads before we started the games."

"I don't understand. I thought—" The rules. The rules of the game were clear. He had to be lying.

"I know. They told us the only way to get the power was to kill another contestant, but it's not true. You only have to place a mask on your face and the power will be absorbed into your body."

"Why would they lie?" Nothing was making any sense. I glared at him and rose the dagger higher so that it was pointing straight at his Adam's apple. The tip of the blade was flush against his skin, nicking it and sending a sliver of blood trailing down his neck.

He leaned forward surprising me.

"Don't believe me?"

"I don't know what to believe anymore."

His hands gripped my hips then, pressing me flush against the tunnel wall. They felt demanding and rough but at the same time delicate, like he knew how twisted up inside I felt. That I could end him if I wanted to, but here he was touching me anyway. I couldn't think straight.

"What do you want, Dex?" I asked sounding breathless, my

thoughts spinning so much it made me dizzy. I knew I could stop him at any point, but I didn't want to. I should have, gods I should.

He sighed bringing one of his hands up to my neck. If he squeezed hard enough, he could crush my windpipe. We were at a standstill, glaring at each other with so much want it physically pained me

"I want you to kiss me like you don't plan to shove that knife right through my heart. Just this once. Then you can go ahead and stab me if you want but just let me taste those lips of yours before you do."

I didn't even think. One minute I was holding the hilt of the dagger, and the next it was falling from my grip as I pulled Dex to me by the front of his shirt. His lips were on mine in an instant, consuming me like we only had this one moment. And maybe that was true.

We'd lost both our teams along the way, but right here, after all we'd survived we still had each other. We might not make it out of here and that thought alone was enough to savor his forbidden and damning kiss.

His hands wound into my hair, deepening his access to me. I found my legs wrapping around his hips and he pushed me hard into the wall. The desperation and need was coursing through my entire body. I'd never felt this alive and exhilarated. His hard length ground up into me and I could feel every ridge of him through my jumpsuit. It made me shudder and gasp into his mouth. I needed him closer. Wanted him in ways that lit a fire within my soul. I didn't even care that he hadn't answered me. I should have. Gods knew I should have. But all I cared about was his lips on mine.

His mouth opened and his tongue licked the tip of mine, teasing me. Warmth spread throughout my entire body. Gods, I didn't want to stop. My tongue met his, tentatively at first, before I was meeting him in his desperation. All the buildup and tension between us breaking in this one thoughtless moment. There was nothing but need. The need to taste him. To feel him.

The way his hard cock ground up against me made my legs tremble and my head swim. His hands were all over me. Feeling the round fullness of my breasts and then dipping down to the curve of my ass. Never in my life had someone touched me so brazenly with so much passion and desire.

"I've dreamed of this. How you would taste. How you would feel." He confessed into my neck, sucking on my sensitive flesh and marking me with his teeth. Shivers ran over my body at the overwhelming sensation.

"I can't. I shouldn't...."

"But you want to. Tell me, does the man who gave you that ring make you feel like this?"

I tried to shove him hard in the chest, but he caught my hand in his, bringing the ring up between us. A glimmering reminder of my active betrayal.

"Does he?"

"You're an asshole," I spit out, dropping my legs.

He spun me around then, smashing my front into the wall as he pressed his hips into me. I could feel the swell of his cock on my backside.

"Tell me." His breath was hot against my neck and his hands roamed my body, feeling every curve and dip.

"No, okay. No one has ever touched me like this before."

I could feel the tug of his mouth against my skin.

"And are you wet for me?"

I was. I was so wet that I ached in places I never thought I could. The want for him was unbearable and I wanted, no— needed him to take the ache away. To fill me up and make me tremble in his arms.

"Use your words and tell me, Odessa, are you wet for me?"

"Yes." That one word damned my soul. An admission of how he made me feel, and how my body reacted to him.

"Show me." He turned me back around and I looked up at him. He was biting his bottom lip, waiting for me to comply.

I should have shoved him away once and for all. Taken that knife from off the floor and stabbed him through. But I undid my buttons one by one instead. Starting at the top of my jump-suit and ending right above my pelvic bone.

Dex slid his hand on my stomach, wrapping around my hips and moved the fabric to the side. His fingers dipped beneath my cotton underwear, sliding against my slick entrance and finding the answer to his question. He groaned at the feel, and I did too. No one had touched me there before. His fingers felt rough and warm, and my breath caught in my chest as he slid around my sensitive bud. Electricity shot through me then and my hips moved on their own accord meeting his touch, urging him on to do more.

I should feel ashamed but knowing that at any moment I could end up like my fallen teammates had me throwing all logic out the window. It was just him and me and this moment between us. That's all that mattered to me now— this feeling. How Dex made me feel. And it was so gods damn good.

"Gods, you're so wet for me." One of his fingers prodded at

my entrance and my hips bucked. He chuckled at me. "So responsive," he praised pushing all the way in.

I gasped at the welcome intrusion.

"So, fucking tight," he said in my ear, working the length of his finger in and out of me as his palm applied pressure to my throbbing clit. It felt better than I'd ever been able to do on my own beneath the covers.

He added an additional finger, stretching me wider. It felt uncomfortable at first, the pressure building and merging into a pleasurable sensation.

He dropped to his knees then.

"What— what are you doing?"

"I want to taste you. Will you let me?" The light from the fire danced across his face as he looked up at me, begging to do what no man had ever done to me before.

"Yes," I whispered.

He kissed the inside of my leg as he draped it across his shoulder, bringing my pussy closer to his face. His breath skated along my most sensitive area and my heart pounded wildly against my ribs, not knowing what to expect. No one had prepared me for this moment or what it would feel like. Marley was the only one who talked to me about this stuff, and even she wouldn't go into much detail.

His mouth pressed against my clit as his fingers curled inside of me. Shadows exploded from my hands darkening the entire tunnel as pleasure ripped through my body.

"Holy fucking shit. Please don't stop." I begged.

Dex's tongue licked around my clit.

"Aw fuck, you taste like nectar. So warm and delicious," he said sucking my skin into his mouth. I trembled, feeling my knees buckle from how overwhelmed he made me feel. I felt so aware of every little touch and tremor, ready to detonate on his tongue at any moment.

"Come for me, Odessa. Come all over my tongue," he demanded, removing his fingers and replacing them with his mouth.

I rode his face as his fingers dug into my sides. My legs quivered as I reached the pinnacle of my pleasure. He moved his hands and shoved his fingers back in and out of me, rolling his tongue over my clit again and again. Working me into a fervor of need, ready to combust.

"That's it, baby. Come for me. I need you to come."

I cried out as my orgasm washed over my entire body, shooting down my spine and erupting over every nerve. Shadows danced all around us, darkening the already dim space.

I could barely hold myself upright as my body shuddered involuntarily.

He let my leg down, and kissed up the length of my inner thighs, then to my stomach and up my neck.

"Dex," I moaned, smelling my orgasm on him. It was erotic and heady, knowing that I'd just come all over his face. "I don't want to die before I have a chance to know what it's like to be with someone who wants me. Please, I want to feel everything, and I want to feel it with you."

His head rested against the wall.

"Are you sure?" He asked. His length was pressing into my stomach, letting me know just how much he'd enjoyed getting me off.

"Yes, I'm sure. Please, Dex."

"You don't have to beg me for something that's already yours, princess."

"Princess?"

He smiled, dragging his hands up my body and cupping my breasts in his hands.

"You feel like a princess to me."

"Have you felt many princesses?"

He chuckled. "Jealous looks good on you."

"I'm not—"

"Ah, yeah. You totally were."

"Fine. Now shut up and fuck me so hard that I forget my name."

"With pleasure."

CHAPTER 28
ODESSA

With our jumpsuits discarded, I could see every inch of Dex's hard dick. I'd seen it before at the pool, and then in the shower, but I hadn't been up close. Nor in my right mind. But now that the nectar had dissipated and he was standing so close to me, I could appreciate the impressive length and shape of his manhood. Nerves clung to my stomach as I looked at him.

Deep in my mind, I knew there was no coming back from this moment. Once we crossed this line, everything would change. And if by some miracle I did make it out of here alive, I would have to confess what I'd done. It was an ending of what I thought my life would be, but the beginning of the one I chose for myself.

Too long I'd lived by everyone else's rules and expectations. Now, I would live for myself. Even if that scared me. At least it would be my choice.

Dex's hands wrapped around my hips. My hands went up

to where his mask was and undid his ties. "I want to see you fully as you enter me." I said.

He let me remove his mask, and then he did the same to mine.

"So, fucking beautiful," he murmured, caressing the side of my cheek. It was tender and reverent, like he was committing this moment to memory.

My fingers explored the wide expanse of his chest. Feeling every hard ridge beneath my skin. It was still damp from the pool, but soft, and warm, and inviting. His hard cock bobbed between us. Looking at it now, I felt a rush of embarrassment. What if I was bad at this?

"We don't have to do this if you don't want to," he said, studying my face. I must have looked uncertain, but really, I was just nervous.

"No, I do. I just— feel inexperienced. I don't know what I'm doing."

"I've watched you figure out your magick and your own inner power while surviving the unimaginable. There's no way you won't be able to figure this out too. Your body already knows what to do. I'll help you," he said bending his neck to take my lips in his. He kissed me like we might never have the chance to again. It was sweet and slow at first, but then it turned heated and full of need. His cock found its way between my legs, the tip hitting me in my most sensitive place. I was still reeling from the orgasm that Dex had wrung from my body, but I still wanted more.

"Gods your skin is softer than the sweetest nectar, Odessa," he praised as his hands roamed the length of my body, exploring. His large hands wrapped around my breasts, his fingers brushing over the nipples, pulling them between his thumb and pointer fingers with the perfect amount of pressure. It was clear he knew what he was doing, but I didn't want to think about that now. I just wanted to be immersed in this moment and how good he made me feel.

"Do you take a tonic?" I asked him. I'd taken one since I'd become engaged, thinking that now Theo might want to take that step with me. He never had.

"Yes, do you?"

I nodded and he smiled wide. "Good, then I can fill you up with my cum and make you carry it around inside you till it drips down your legs."

My mouth popped open at his words. The image he painted was dirty, but I loved it. It made me feel like I was his and he was mine.

"Now get on the ground, I want to see you laid out before me before I fuck that pretty pussy of yours."

I obeyed, putting my jumpsuit between me and the filthy floor. My elbows dug into the earth below as Dex stood above me stroking his hard cock from balls to tip in a well-practiced motion. He spat on his hand and continued to stroke himself, making his cock even larger with each pull he took.

He knelt down, knees digging into the rough ground as he put his free hand on my bent knee and pushed my legs wider.

"I dreamed about this," I confessed.

His dark furrowed eyebrows shot up, "You did?"

I nodded, "Before the games started, I dreamed you snuck into my room and looked at me just as you are now."

"I should have. Gods know how much I wanted to."

His hand moved up my inner thigh as I leaned back, feeling electricity in his soft touch.

"You're a vision, Odessa. I know I called you princess before, but your more than that. Your beauty rivals that of a divine being. A goddess that was made just for me."

I blushed at his blasphemous words. To call a mortal anything akin to a goddess was forbidden. He planted a kiss on my thigh as he lined up his cock. It pressed against my entrance, making me gasp.

"You shouldn't say such things," I said feeling that blush burn my cheeks.

"I will, and I don't care about should and shouldn't. I only care about how I feel when I'm around you."

"And how's that?"

"Like if I don't have you, I'll die. Take a deep breath in for me as I claim you for myself, Odessa."

I took a breath as he instructed and felt him press inside me with one swift thrust. It was everything and nothing like I'd imagined. The pain was more of an ache. Dull and throbbing, but also so unbelievably good.

He moved a stray piece of hair away from my face and his icy blue eyes stared deep into mine. "Are you alright?" He asked.

"Y-yes," I answered, my body shaking from what we were doing. I was overwhelmed by emotion and sensation, and the knowledge that I was no longer a virgin.

He thrust back up into me and my head tilted back. The tip of him was reaching so deep inside me that I wanted to scream. My hands reached around his body and found purchase on his back, pulling him closer to me. We were entwined in a heap of pleasure and heat. Moving together as one. His forehead rested against mine as he moved in and out me slowly. I could tell it was difficult for him by the clench in his jaw and the sweat gathering on his brow.

"It feels so good," I whispered almost reverently. My fingers dug into his back as he moved his hips, hard enough to leave marks.

He leaned down and took my mouth with his kissing me as he moved in and out of me.

"Gods, you're so fucking perfect wrapped around my cock. Taking me so well. Look at how well you're taking my cock," he says.

I looked down to where our bodies were joined and marveled at the sight. This was really happening. It wasn't just a dream or fantasy. This was real.

We moved together in a dance only our bodies knew. The rhythm was one of desperation and desire melding to make the most beautiful explosion that left tingles all along my body.

It was transcendent. Like my soul was being stitched together with his in a way that exceeded the physical sensations.

"Is it always like this?" I asked, moving my hips to meet his as he continued to fill me stroke by stroke. His cock was throbbing inside me, breaking me apart and putting me back together with each thrust.

"No," he gritted out. "It's never been this good or felt this right. I could do this for a millennium and never tire of how amazing you feel wrapped around me."

He shifted then, rolling us effortlessly so that I was on top and he was below me. My wild braid shifted, spilling down my back in a cascade of tangles and curls.

"I want to see you ride me," he said, his large hands digging into my sides, urging me on. Moving at this angle made me feel so full, but also powerful. I watched as Dex became undone. I was making him look so wild and full of need, and I loved it. I loved even more how good it felt to be on top of him. Even the smallest dip of my hips had my clit rubbing against his pelvic bone, sending jolts of pleasure along my nerves and deep into my core. My eyes fluttered and my breathing stalled as I found how to rock myself onto his impressive length.

"That's right. Just like that," he groaned watching me. The dark pupil of his eye had almost eaten up that icy blue ring of his as he took in every movement, watching my curves as if mesmerized by them. "So, fucking good. So, fucking beautiful, Odessa," he said, thrusting up into me unable to keep himself still any longer.

"Come all over my cock. I want to feel you shatter. I want to be shoved so deep inside you as you break apart for me," he said, palming my breasts in his hands. He licks my sensitive peak, then bites down. The sensation has me clamping down on him and speeding my hips up.

"Oh, you like it when I play with these beautiful, perfect breasts?"

I nod, "Uh-huh,"

"Mmmf," he groans, moving to my other breast and repeating the same motion.

"Fuck, I could let you smother me with these, and I'd die a happy man,"

"But then I wouldn't get to feel you shoot your come inside me," I whined.

He laughed and looked surprised by my words. Hell, I had surprised myself.

"Better not die then," he said, pulling my mouth down to his with a hot, impassioned kiss, making my chest rub against his. His hands tangled in my hair, deepening our kiss.

He sat up as we broke apart and changed positions.

"On your hands and knees for me, love,"

"What did I tell you about calling me love?" I asked looking over my shoulder at him as I got into position.

He smacked me right on my ass and lined up his cock from behind me.

"I'll call you whatever I like as long as I've got you wrapped around my dick,"

He shoved himself into me, making me cry out. I felt so incredibly sensitive and full, but I didn't want him to stop.

"Is- that - right?" I asked, breathless.

"You fucking know it is. You might have just wanted to see how it feels to be fucked, but this right here? What we're doing? You're *mine* now, love. So, you better get used to it, Odessa. I'm not letting you go, because we're going to make it out of here together."

His.

Why did the thought of belonging to Dex not fill me with apprehension, but elation?

His hand wove in my hair as he pulled, arching my back and making me take him deeper as he thrust into me. The feel of his balls slapping against my pussy was driving me crazy. It was so good. So intense and more than I'd ever thought it could be.

His mouth was lined up with my ear and his words hit me hot and urgent.

"You're not going back to that wet blanket of a fiancé who couldn't even be bothered to show up for you."

"Don't tell me what to do," I retorted as his hand dropped my hair and slid around to the front of my neck.

"Is that so? Is that what you want?" He pushed into me harder— faster. Like he was punishing me with every thrust. "You want to go back to being the perfect little wife in training? You want to go back to a man who wouldn't even touch you?" His hand slides down from my neck to my breast and his fingers twist around my nipple making me yell out in surprise.

Tears sprung from the corner of my eyes because deep down, I knew the answer. I knew it when I asked Dex to fuck me and take my virginity.

"No—"

"That's fucking right," he said, twisting my nipple again.

I couldn't believe that it had come to this. That we were fucking on the floor of the catacombs like two wild animals. His cock rutting against me, bringing me to the edge of pleasure, ready to jump. When I first met him, I found him arrogant and dangerous, and maybe he was still those things, but over the time we'd spent together down here, I'd come to like those things about him. I'd come to crave him and want him, and fuck, I was such a bad person for doing this. But with death lurking, now was the time to be selfish, and it felt so gods damn good to put myself first for a change.

A sizzling, all-encompassing zap of electricity built inside me, spilling over as he fucked my pussy with his hard throbbing dick. My entire body began to shake with pleasure as it took over me. It was everywhere, this feeling of elation as I came. Dex cried out and I joined him as my orgasm hit me in full force. I could feel Dex's come filling me up and spilling out as he kept pumping.

After a moment, he pulled out and sat back on his legs.

"Look at that, your pussy turned my cock all pink with your virginity," he said with a smirk.

I looked and there it was. The evidence that I'd betrayed my fiancé and given myself to another man. Given him my virginity. Something I'd been told was a sacred thing reserved for one's husband. At least that's what was taught to us. There were many that secretly didn't abide by such rules, but Theo did. I should feel ashamed of myself but seeing my blood staining him so clearly and knowing how good we were together had me feeling elated and almost giddy at the sight of it.

I laughed and kissed Dex. "Thank you, I didn't want to die a virgin."

"You're not going to die, Odessa. Not if I can help it."

I rolled my eyes. "You can't promise me something like that," I responded.

He was silent for a moment and then said, "I hope you know I'm not letting you go. Not after this."

I heard the sincerity of his words, but when we were in such high stakes with our lives, he couldn't guarantee that the God of Death wouldn't be claiming me.

"Let's just get through what we can, and then figure the rest out later," I said.

His shoulders tightened and then he was on me, his face so close to mine I didn't even have time to react.

"I think you need to be reminded of how much I want you. Did you forget already?" He asked, pressing his still hard cock back into my sensitive pussy. I gasped at the fullness of it. Succumbing to him once again and not regretting it in the least.

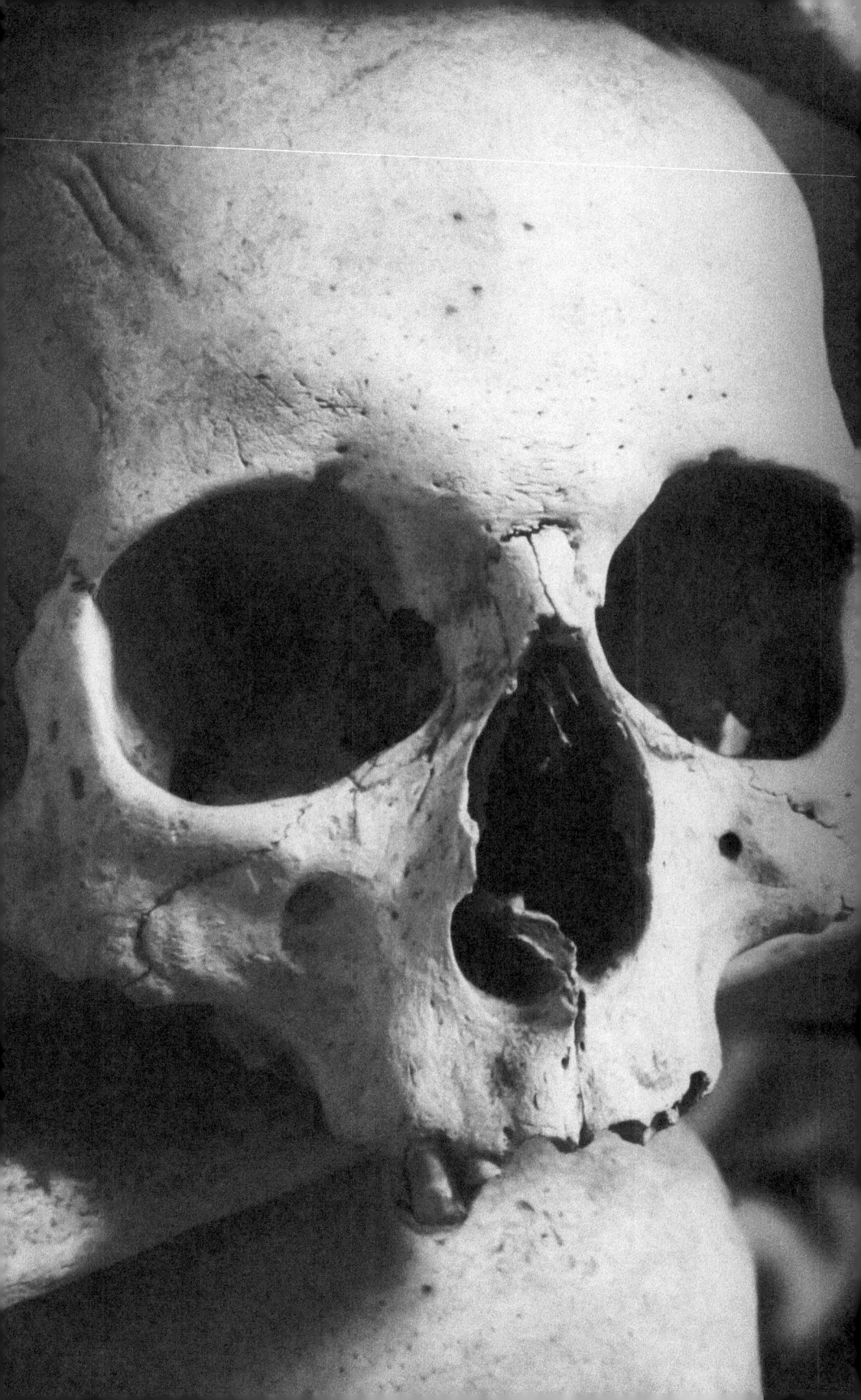

CHAPTER 29
DEX

We laid in a heap of sweat and tangled limbs. Odessa had fallen asleep in my arms. I let her get her rest. I knew eventually we would need to move on, but for this one moment. I could pretend that we weren't underground in the fight for our lives. We were just two people who were tucked away, intent on enjoying each other's company.

Her eyes fluttered open and landed on me.

"Hi," she said sounding shy.

"Hi, yourself," I said back.

She tucked her face away, hiding from me.

"Where do you think you're going?"

"My breath stinks! I don't want you changing your mind and wishing you had chosen to kill me instead."

I laughed and rummaged through my pack, digging out a wad of gum that I split in two for the both of us. She gratefully popped it into her mouth with a wide grin as I popped my half in mine.

"Better?" I asked.

"Much," she said blowing a bubble.

I liked seeing her like this. Like her walls were finally down and she was completely herself. Ideally, we'd be in a bed together instead of on the dirt filled ground, but I'd take what I could get.

She groaned, stretching her body out, "I don't want to go yet."

"So, let's stay here," I said.

She smiled and having her look at me with such unabashed glee took the very breath right out of my lungs.

"Delaying will only lessen our chances of winning," she said.

"Well then we better make it worth it," I said as I rolled her onto her back and had her legs spread for me in an instant. She looked up at me wide eyed as my already hard cock nestled between her slick folds. Odessa lifted her hips ever so slightly, giving me the encouragement I needed to take her. One thrust and I was in.

She winced as I filled her. "You alright?" I asked.

"Yeah, just sore."

"You want me to stop?"

"No, please. Keep going," she urged, wrapping her arms around to my back and pulling me tightly against her. Our skin was flush together, and I could feel every inhale and gasp she made, as I slowly rocked in and out of her.

"I'll take it slow, then," I promised, leaving a small kiss on her plush lips.

"Slow sounds good," she replied, widening her legs as I pressed in deeper. Her eyelashes fluttered as I hit that perfect, tight spot inside her.

"Oh gods, that's so good. Just like that," she said, gripping onto my back harder.

Her brown hair was spread out beneath her in a wild torrent of curls, having come undone from her braid. I buried my hands into her messy locks and tilted her head up to look at me. Her brown eyes were locked onto mine, wide and full of wonder. From this close, I could see a smattering of light freckles that dotted her nose and flushed cheeks. Her rounded chin quivered as I continued to fuck her.

"I never want to stop feeling like this, Odessa. You've ruined me. Completely ruined me for anyone else," I said.

"You don't have to lie to me."

I gripped her then around the neck, gently but with enough force that let her know I was serious. "Does it look like I'm lying? I mean it, Odessa, I haven't ever felt this way about anyone."

Her breath stuttered and she bit down on her swollen bottom lip. My hips were still moving, making my hard dick fill her over and over again.

"I mean what I say, you've ruined me. I don't want anyone else. You're it for me."

She looked at me, eyes bouncing between mine as if she wasn't sure what to do with my declaration.

"Tell me you don't feel it too? Hmm?" I lifted her legs so that they were resting on my shoulders, hitting her even deeper than before.

She cried out, tilting her head back.

"I can't, it's too much."

But her hands wouldn't let me move, she kept me firmly in place, urging me on and scratching up my back with her shortly trimmed nails.

"Yes you can. You can take it," I said with a chuckle.

"Gods, fuck, don't stop!" She cried out.

Fuck!" I cried, feeling my balls squeeze up, ready to unleash my come inside of her. "Tell me, Odessa, I need to hear you say it, even if yours is a lie."

"Fine, yes! I feel it too. I feel everything. Too much, and it scares the hell out of me, Dex. I shouldn't even be letting this happen and I did. But fuck you feel so good inside of me, I don't want to stop either."

That's all I needed to hear before I felt myself bottoming out, "Oh gods, I can't— I can't hold it. Come with me, princess, right fucking now. I need to feel you come on my dick," I demanded.

All of a sudden, she rolled us so that she was on top and I was below her. She rode my cock, taking her pleasure and making her breasts bounce with every thrust. I'd never seen anything more beautiful.

"Oh, fuck, you're so godsdamn beautiful, Odessa. So, fucking good. So, mine," I said, reaching up to hold onto those tits of hers. Her skin was glistening in the fading firelight, looking as if she'd been kissed by the stars themselves. A gift from the heavens above, just for me.

"Oh, gods. Oh, yes!" She cried, reaching that pinnacle of pleasure as she rode me.

Her hands wove into my hair and pulled as she found her release. Her walls clenched down on me, squeezing as she fell deep down into her orgasm. A burning jolt of bliss hit my spine and spilled out in one hot stream as I filled her up, watching in awe as she took every last drop.

We sat there locked together, our breathing in sync as we clutched to the other for support. Her forehead rested on mine before she stood up on shaky legs and picked up her clothes.

"We should get going," she said.

I watched as she dressed, knowing that she was right. We couldn't stay here forever, as much as I didn't want our private bubble to pop, I knew we had to move, or we'd come to regret it. We were lucky no one had found us in the night, because we'd both fallen asleep together. The other contestants could have easily ended us. Or even the creatures that roamed these tunnels. I didn't know which was worse.

Shrugging on my ripped jumpsuit, I readied myself for another unpredictable day ahead. While the gods' power was buzzing inside me, I still craved more. My boots went on next, lacing them up tight so I wouldn't twist an ankle in the uneven terrain. I'd hate to have made it this far and be taken out by a twisted ankle.

"So, are you going to elaborate on those powers you came by, or are you expecting me to forget all about that? How many do you even have now?" Odessa asked, fully dressed and plaiting her hair into submission.

I sighed. Coffee would be really good right about now. Instead, I took a bite of a crumbled granola and swig of nectar, offering Odessa the same. She took it and waited for me to answer.

"I knew that if I were to be here in Nocturne, I wanted to acquire as many powers as possible," I said.

"But why? Wouldn't winning and having riches be enough for you?"

My jaw ticked as I contemplated the right way to tell her my plans, if at all.

"Not everyone is motivated by riches," I ventured, feeling my walls go up. I couldn't help it. I'd always been a closed book, even to those closest to me in my life. I kept my cards close to my chest. It's how I knew to survive. Letting people know your plans was a sure way to end up screwed by them. As much as I wanted to let Odessa in, there was another part of me that knew she would run if she knew it all.

She raised her eyebrows at me, before sliding her mask back on.

"Maybe, I just wanted to know what it was like to have power," I said after a beat.

"Okay—"

"Okay. Should we go?"

"Yeah. Let's go." Her tone was clipped, but so was mine. The moment I felt her getting too close, I panicked and fell back into a familiar routine.

"Odessa, wait—"

"No, it's fine. We should get going. Don't want to get in the way of you collecting your powers. Should I give you mine now, or wait for you to kill me later?"

"It's not like that—" I said, but she was already walking away, down the dark corridor.

I'd fucked up and her burning silence was like a knife in my heart.

CHAPTER 30
ODESSA

This tunnel was lined with artwork the father we trekked. Statues depicting the gods were molded to the wall, all white and intricately detailed to capture their divine essence. It was reminiscent of the statues that were placed in their temple, and I wondered if they frequently used this space to gather the nectar. It had to be where their supply was located. I could still feel the hot breath of the Gerataux as it chased us down here.

Dex was right behind me, but I didn't care to slow down and walk with him. My anger at him was simmering under my skin with each step I took. He didn't want to open up to me? Fine. I shouldn't care as much as I did, but when I'd been vulnerable and fucking naked with him, hell I gave him my virginity! I felt like it was only fair.

We walked in silence, ears straining for any potential threat.

The tunnel took a sharp turn and emptied out into an all too familiar area.

I couldn't believe what I was seeing. The platform that we had started from was staring me right in the face. We were right back at the beginning. My stomach dropped.

There was a fallen body that had been badly burned splayed out on the ground. Upon closer inspection, I could see the gears on the gold-plated mask that still sat strapped to the corpse's face.

"Fuck!" I cried out, pulling at my hair.

All of that wandering through these tunnels and we weren't anywhere close to the end. How was that even possible?

"Hey, at least we know which way not to go now," Dex said, bending down to see if the mask could be removed. It came off but caused the head to crumble into dust. I felt numb to the sight, having experienced so much death already that seeing what had become of him didn't even make me flinch. What would have turned my stomach before was not even a blip on my radar at this point.

"Oh good, I feel so much better," I spat out, wanting to collapse in defeat and still feeling mad at him.

"No— none of that. I'm not having you throw a pity party for yourself. It's a setback. It sucks, but we know the way now. We just have to make a different choice."

He was right. I knew it, but I still wasn't happy about it.

Weariness made a home in my bones, making every step difficult. My boots were rubbing against my heels, and I'm pretty sure I had blisters that were forming at the tips of my toes. I wanted to bang on the platform doors and demand they let me out of here.

Keep going that deep voice from within called out to me in my subconscious. I jumped at it, forgetting that it wasn't the first time I'd heard it. It happened at the masquerade as well but had been relatively quiet since then.

I still wasn't aware of what or who it belonged to, and there'd been so much happening, I hadn't stopped to ask. I'd wanted to forget it happened and had almost succeeded.

Was I crazy if I asked the voice what I wanted to know?

You're not crazy... it responded.

Creepy. It could read my thoughts.

Well then who are you? I asked, afraid of the answer.

The voice chuckled like it found me funny.

What fun would it be if I answered that? It said finally.

"Are you good? We should head down the corridor and get to the rotunda. We could rest there," Dex said.

I could only imagine what I must have looked like. Panicked about a voice in my head, but also feeling a sense of despair that we were no farther along in the game than when we first started.

My stomach clenched remembering the way the fire roared after us, forcing us down the tunnel. We could pick a different one this time, I just hoped it was the right one.

"Yeah, I'm fine. Let's go," I said, rolling my shoulders. I could do this. I had to.

Don't be so eager to trust him. There's much you don't know...

Yeah, like who the hell you are? I retorted internally. Gods, I really had lost it. I was talking to a voice inside my head that no one else could hear. Even if they had a point. Dex had already made it clear that he had no intention of opening up to me about his plans.

He went on ahead and I followed behind him, choosing the opposite side of the platform that sat above the acid water. The dark, murky water was deathly still, reminding me that one slip of the foot would land me in its fatal clutches. The stone walls of the tunnel were charred black and still smelt of smoke.

"Gods, he really went for it, didn't he?" Dex asked, swiping his finger along the wall. When he pulled it away it was stained pitch black. He shook his head as if he couldn't believe what he was saying.

"How do you think he's able to access that much power?" I asked aloud in wonder. It really was impressive he was able to hold so much at one time and keep it going. Meanwhile, I had a hard time getting mine to do what I wanted it to.

Dex shrugged, his head tilted to the side to keep from hitting the rounded ceiling.

The voice in my mind was quiet, but its words still rang in my mind, wondering if I could trust Dex. I'd given him my body and had fought alongside him throughout the entirety of the games so far. Why would the voice find it necessary to warn me about him?

I couldn't trust some random voice either, especially since I had no idea what its agenda was.

To see you win, of course.

Get out of my head! I yelled at it. Maybe it was the magick. Could magick speak to you? I found myself wishing I had better prepared for the games. Maybe researched what to expect instead of going off what I'd been told by others throughout the years. There'd been a few cases of contestants going mad over the years, but it was always dismissed by the harrowing ordeal they had endured. Everyone knew that Nocturne was a blood-bath. But what if it was because of the masks and their powers?

Unease skirted around my middle as we walked, head lost in thoughts I was too scared to utter aloud. I resolved to not talk back to the voice, even if it showed back up again. That seemed the right course of action. Talking to it would only validate its existence, and I didn't want to have come this far to only lose myself to some chattering voice that probably wasn't anything.

You keep thinking that...

Ignore it. All I had to do was ignore it and keep walking. We had to find our way out of this hellhole sometime. The winning gong hadn't been rung yet. Meaning, we still had a chance to win.

"Let's rest here," Dex said, pulling out a squashed ration of food. I gladly inhaled the crumbs that were once a whole piece of granola. Dex's piece was no better, in fact it looked like his was mostly powder, but it was all we had.

I leaned on the wall, slipping down into a sitting position. My eyes felt heavy, and the closed on their own.

"One of us should keep lookout," I murmured, feeling sleep pull at me.

"I'll do first watch, get some sleep."

I barely had time to register his words before I was fast asleep.

"ODESSA." My shoulder was shaken, and I jolted awake, hitting my fist out in the air as if I could take whatever it was that had startled me, down by weak punches. "Woah, slow down there, killer. It's just me," Dex said catching my fist in his hand.

My eyes focused in the dark, and I saw him there, crouching just next to me holding my fist inches away from his face. He let my hand drop and I sat up straight.

"I can't keep my eyes open anymore. Mind taking over the watch?"

"Yeah. Yep," I said, wiping at my face. My mouth felt so incredibly dry. It had been far too long since I'd had a drop of water.

As if reading my thoughts, Dex said, "There's a bit of nectar that's in my canteen."

It was better than nothing. I eagerly reached for his bag as he settled on the wall, head tilted back with his eyes closed. He looked so peaceful like this.

Most of the time, Dex's face was hardened. He was constantly on the look for danger, sweeping his gaze around every corner. Never settling. But with how tired we both are, he finds the spot next to me, legs kicked out and crossed at the ankle, his head resting on the wall behind him. He shoulders slump as sleep finds him.

His breathing slowed and his long eyelashes kissed the tops of his cheeks. I'd kill for eyelashes like that.

You could kill him right now... just take out that dagger that's stowed in your boot and end it.

The voice was back and even louder after I had spent the rest of my time yesterday ignoring the beastly thing. It seemed even my sleep couldn't free me from its clutches, and a part of me wondered if it was here to stay.

I carefully undid my mask, put it down next to me, and waited.

Hello? I asked.

A few moments passed and nothing.

I tried again, this time with more force. *Hello?*

Nothing.

A frown pulled at my brows. Either whoever it was decided to hide and fuck with me, or the voice was attached to the mask like I suspected.

And if that were the case... did the voice belong to the god who'd leant me his power? The wielder of shadows himself? Kage.

I breathed in my nose and out my mouth to steady my nerves before I reached for the mask once again, tying it in the back as it automatically fixed itself to my face.

I tried one more time.

Hello?

I thought you weren't speaking to me? It asked.

So, it was the mask.

With nothing to lose, I asked the one burning question that had been gnawing at my stomach.

Are you... Kage?

Are we using first names with a god again, little shadow? His words sent a shiver down my spine as my heart rate sped up.

Dex was right next to me, snoring slightly. Did his masks talk to him as well? Did he have a whole hoard of voices in that handsome head of his, urging him to do their will? He'd collected power after power, and I'd been so focused on surviving that I hadn't stopped to question why he would do that. Sixteen of us had started this competition, but we were down to four by my count.

Dex, The Pyro, The Healer, and me.

If we were lucky enough to make it to the end, would he use

those powers on me to win? A deep, guttural knowledge roared within me at the answer. Yes. If it came down to it, no matter how much Dex had protected me, I believed he would do whatever it took to win it all. Even if that meant killing me.

If you don't kill him, you should go. You know what powers he holds. What's to stop him from turning on you?

I was on my feet with his pack in my hands before I even knew what I was doing. Kage had suggested I kill him, but I wouldn't do that. Couldn't bring myself to spill his blood, even if it meant that he would come for me later.

The noise from his zipper closing made Dex's eyelashes flutter, and I held my breath, waiting for him to fall deeper into sleep. And as he did, I turned my back on him, decision made and headed into the tunnel marked with an anatomical heart above. Leaving the one man who had been with me from the beginning of the games behind.

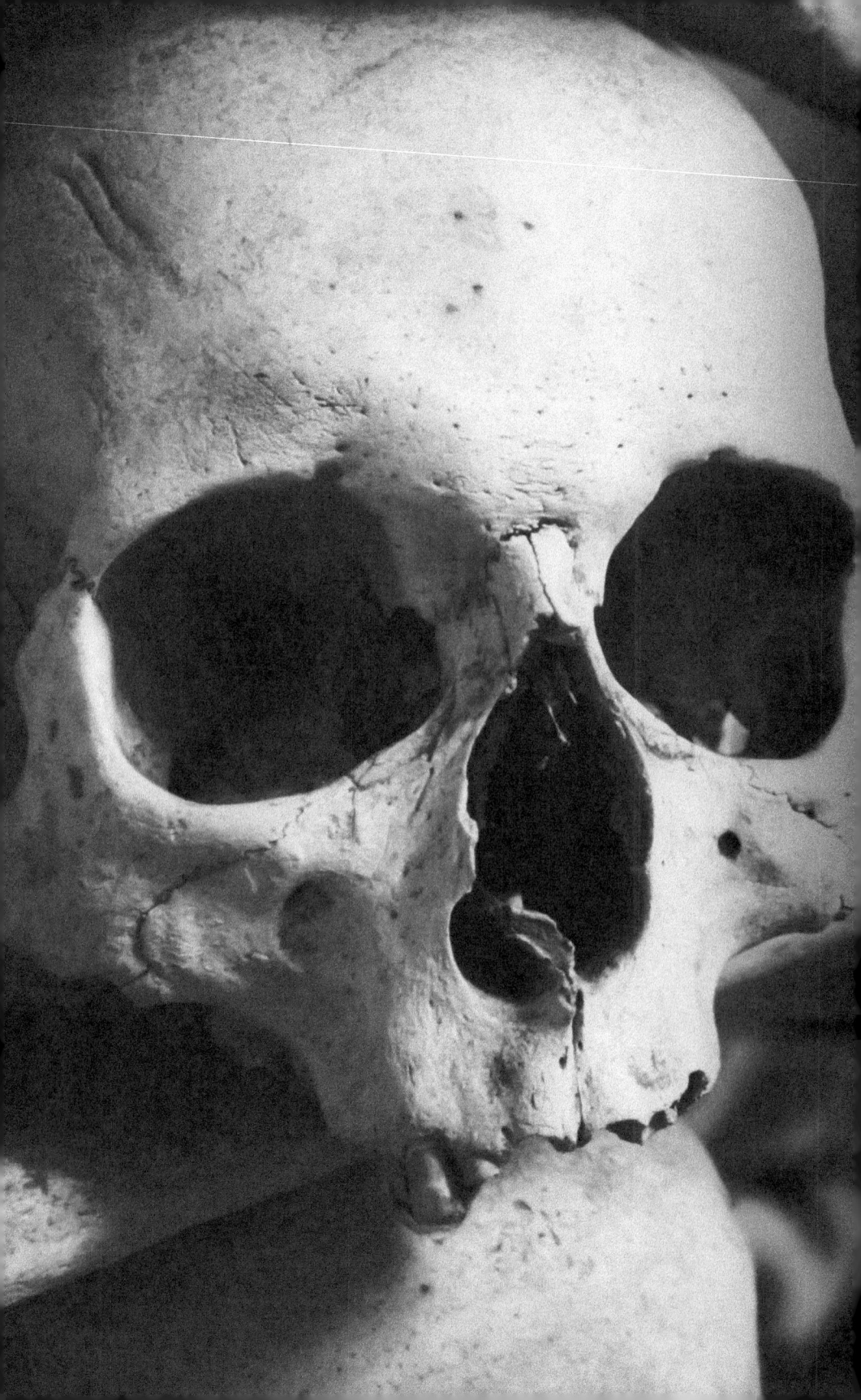

CHAPTER 31

DEX

I opened my eyes feeling well rested for the first time since we came to Nocturne. My dreams had been pleasant and filled with thoughts of Odessa. Her smiling at me without restraint and a brand-new ring replacing that ugly one she wore now, marking her as mine. We were outside the city laying in a field of wildflowers, and there was no war, no game, no death. Just us. I knew if we stuck together, there'd be no tearing us apart. That we could win this thing and get out of here.

Thinking of our future together felt like tempting fate. Something I knew better than to do, but I couldn't help doing anyways.

Without a doubt in my soul, I knew that we could make each other happy. I'd take her home and show her off to the world. A bright light like Odessa was meant to be worshipped, not hidden away like something to be ashamed of. From what I could gather, Odessa's fiancé and family relied on her to obey them. She wasn't allowed to be herself or even decide what she wanted. But she had wanted me. And that knowledge warmed me from the inside out.

The way we had fit so effortlessly together was unlike anything I'd ever known. Even with our differences, I felt like we could still make this work once we were out of here. If we could withstand the horrors that Nocturne had thrown at us, we could withstand anything. I was certain that she would break things off with what's his face, and then we would be free to do whatever we wanted.

My neck felt tight and my muscles sore, but I couldn't hide the smile on my face, that was until I looked around and noticed Odessa wasn't there. Panic clawed at my heart, and I leapt up from the ground.

"Odessa?" I called out, eyes wild and heart cracking in two.

Maybe something happened. Maybe she went to check out a noise and didn't want to wake me. I pulled at my hair trying to figure out where she went. And there, in the soot that lined the ground, were two distinct footprints that belonged to the girl that had burrowed deep into my soul.

She wasn't taken.

She'd walked away and taken the last scrap of humanity I had left in me, with her.

My hands slowly clenched into fists as the rage inside me turned into an inferno greater than the one that had burned through these tunnels.

After all I had done, she chose to leave. I protected her when I didn't have to. I'd killed for her. Granted I planned to kill anyways, but I'd did so with her safety in mind. I'd kept her secret when I could have turned her in for carrying a weapon.

And she just walked away with my pack? Like I meant nothing to her?

I cracked my neck and my knuckles, rolling my shoulders before I stalked down the tunnel Odessa had disappeared into. The fucking heart. The irony wasn't lost on me that she had taken off down that particular tunnel. Taking my heart with her.

It was dark and smelt of mold and fire, but there were dimly lit sconces on the wall that were alight with flickering flames. The shadows danced across the floor, illuminating each step her boots had left behind. Each one like a bullet to my soul.

I could tell by the pattern of her walk it was deliberately done and not done out of panic or fear of being chased. The steps were even and unhurried. I knew because I'd spent my fair share tracking in another life. I was an expert hunter, and Odessa had just become my prey.

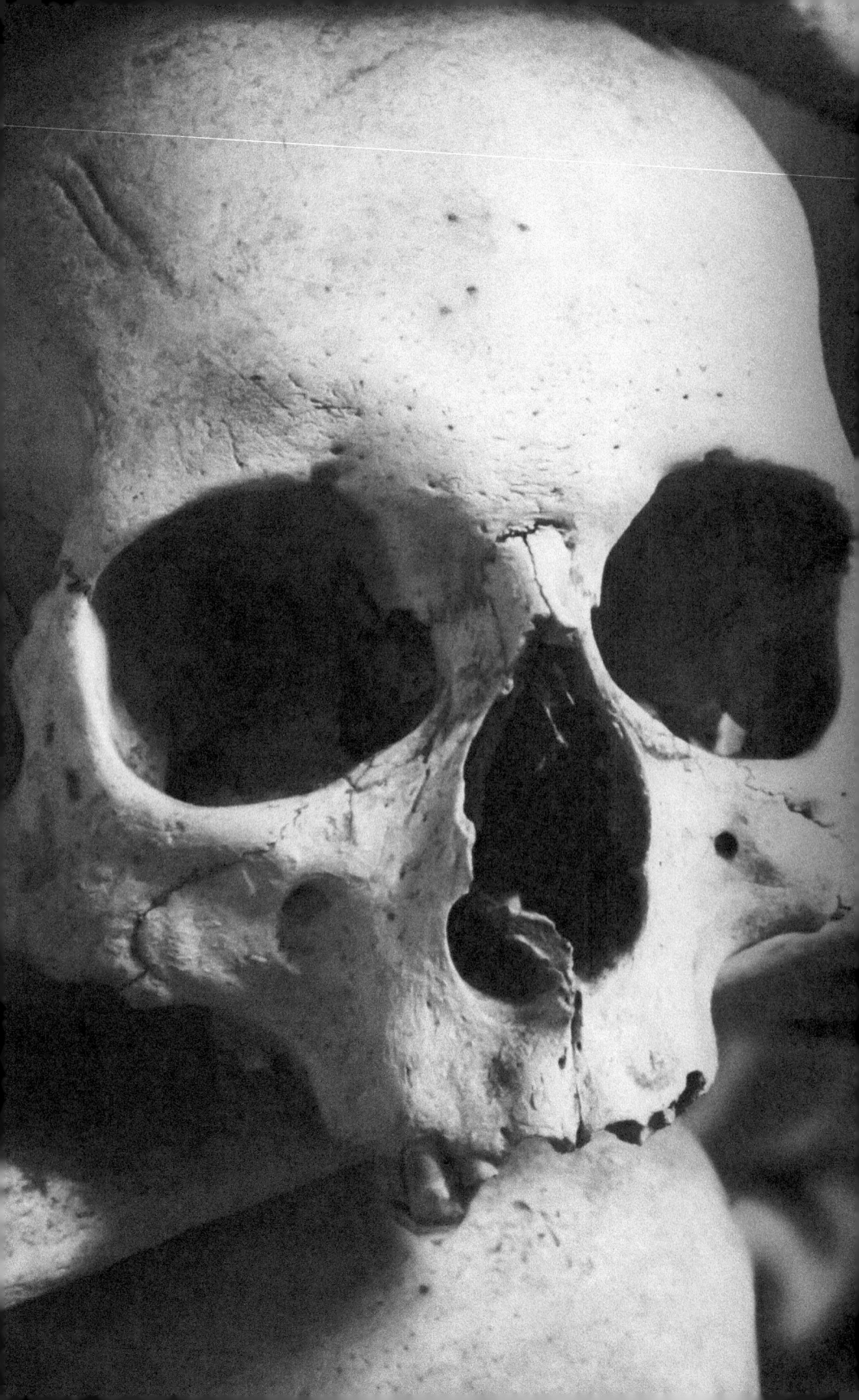

CHAPTER 32
THE PYRO

Her voice called to me. Urging my steps forward and my power to surge with just one word on her heavenly lips, *"Burn!"* She demanded of me. And burn I did. I would burn them all to a crisp to please that sweet, angelic voice that rung out in my head over and over again.

"Burn, burn, burn!"

I was an inferno. A well of endless power that connected from me to her. And I would do her will no matter what.

CHAPTER 33
ODESSA

*S*o, *this is how you watch us in the games? By using our masks?* I asked the voice as I followed the flickering flames that lined the tunnel walls.

Figured that out, did you? Kage responded with a chuckle.

I didn't know why I'd never considered the possibility that they'd be able to keep tabs on us through the masks. It was their power after all that we had access to because of it, but what else did that allow? So far, I knew that the gods could communicate through it, and they could see what we were doing through them.

Could they also control us through them? My stomach soured at that thought.

The tunnel began to narrow and become shorter as I walked on. I could still clear the ceiling, but it was a close fit.

Dex would have to duck if he were here, I thought.

That one thought of him sent a pang through my heart that I brushed away quickly. I made the right choice. Walking away when I did was the only smart option. If I let myself be around him until the end, then I'd be forced to fight against him, and I didn't have it in me to do that.

So, what are you all gathered together drinking nectar, betting on our lives, or what?

Aren't you a curious little thing?

That wasn't an answer. I quip.

Gods he was irritating.

The tunnel dipped down at an angle. I was headed deeper underground when the tunnel came to an end, opening into a large room with stone bunk beds carved into the walls. I eyed them cautiously, but there were no bodies lying in them. There were, however, initials with hearts around them painted on the sides.

D+A, C+T, J+Z, and then one that had been scratched out.

The history of these tunnels was endlessly fascinating. So much of it seemed to span the time of the games, reaching back before they began governing us as a people. I wondered if these initials were the same. People from before that had used this place. My fingers lazily traced one of the hearts.

Keep moving, there isn't time to dawdle. Kage instructed.

Jeeze, alright. I'm going. I didn't know what to make of the god that spoke inside my head. Everything I knew about the god of shadows was mere myth. He was known to be almost as elusive as the god of death, but far more approachable. While the god of death was greatly feared, Kage, was respected by many for his use of shadows. He was favored by thieves who used those dark corners to hide their wicked dealings. He was also a favorite of the rich, who reveled in nighttime pleasures that were far too sinful for the daylight.

"There you are," Dex said from behind me, startling me.

My mouth dropped open and I backed up, arms raised and ready for a fight.

I told you to keep moving, Kage said with a resigned sigh.

"Surprised to see me?"

"I guess I am," I said, jutting my chin up.

"You fucking left me," Dex said. Every word dripping in venom. I deserved his ire, but he hadn't earned my trust.

"I did."

"Why?"

"You wouldn't tell me what you planned to use those powers for, Dex."

He stalked towards me, caging me against the wall. From what I could see of his features, it looked like his face was pulled into a sneer as he looked down at me with fire in his eyes and rage in his heart.

"Haven't my actions spoken for themselves, Odessa? That I would have killed anyone that dared to harm you?"

"I don't know that," I said weakly.

"You do, but you just don't want to admit it. You thought you would leave me, win Nocturne, and go back to your shitty fiancé. Isn't that right?"

I shoved him square in the chest, but he hardly moved. "You don't know what you're talking about!"

"Don't I?" His smile was full of malice.

I'd never really considered that Dex could cause me harm. On an abstract level, I had, but in reality, I didn't think he would, until he looked at me just now. Devoid of any warmth that once lived in those blue eyes of his. Now it was pure ice like he could watch me die right here, and not even blink.

A chill ran over my skin as we stared at each other until the ground began to shake from under us.

"What the hell was that?" I asked, looking around.

Three large black bears with razor sharp teeth and enormous paws were rushing straight towards us.

"Fuck! Stay behind me!" Dex called, raising his hand and unleashing a wave of power at the beasts.

But they didn't stop.

The middle one let out a deafening roar as it led the charge.

Some kind of meat hung from its jowls, and I wondered if it was another contestant that had the misfortune of encountering the beasts. And if so, were we next?

Light burned from Dex's hands, but the bears were undeterred.

"Try something else!" I called.

"I am!"

"They're getting too close!" I screamed. Another few steps and we'd be goners.

My knees shook, but I found the courage to sidestep Dex's protection and use my own magick.

Come on, work for me, I begged.

And it did.

An onslaught of dark shadows poured from my hands like an inky black river full of power. The shadows wrapped around each bear's throat and squeezed with such force that I could hear their individual bones snap. The shadows dropped their still forms with a thud and I stood there gaping at what I had just done.

"Holy shit, Odessa," Dex said in awe.

"See, I don't need you," I spat out.

He turned on me so fast that I nearly fell over.

"You keep telling yourself that, princess. We both know the truth. You ran from me because you were scared."

"There can only be one winner, Dex. We both know that truth," I said in a flat tone as to not give away how close to the mark he had come. Maybe I was scared of him in more ways than one. Scared of how much he made me feel. Scared that if I were to make it out of here, I wouldn't return the same.

A little late for that, don't you think? A snarky Kage said into my mind.

Shut up.

"You can either admit the truth or you can keep walking away from me, but I won't follow you this time."

"Good! I didn't ask you to follow me this time!" I shouted back with my hands firmly planted on my hips. Dex took a step towards me, and I took one towards him. Our chests were nearly brushing together with a crackle of electricity running through us.

Another rumble of the ground rocked through my feet. I whipped my head to see what was causing it this time.

The fucking Pyro had found us, and a wave of fire was wrapped around his body. He tilted his head as he looked over at us and the fallen bears before he raised his arm and shot out a wall of fire right towards us.

CHAPTER 34
DEX

"Duck!" I called out to Odessa, grabbing her about the waist and pulling her down just in time. Our bodies rolled as the fire raged only a yard above us. It was so close it felt like it could burn my eyebrows off.

When the bears had been coming straight for us, I realized that my power to control bones was of no use. I had the power to control *human* bones, but seeing as the bears were clearly animal, I failed to stop them. Odessa, however had tapped into that dark power and wielded her shadows like a goddess incarnate.

But the Pyro? He was all human and with one wave of my hand, I had his form within my grasp. He stalled becoming my puppet in an instant, and the flames receded.

"What are you doing?" Odessa asked.

"Stopping him from burning us alive!" I said, sweat gathering on my brow as I began to break his bones. I started with his femurs, making him kneel on the ground in agony.

I'd lost track of time down here. There was no way to know for sure how long we'd been trapped, fighting for our lives. Days? Weeks? It was unclear. But I was fucking done having this asshole show up with his fire and try to murder us.

"It's good that you're afraid of me, Odessa," I said with a sneer as she watched me snap bone by bone. "I can be fucking deadly when I want to be."

"Stop!" He cried out. "Please, I was just following orders!"

Odessa looked at me and then him.

"Following whose orders?" She asked.

"The woman. In- my- head," he breathed out sounding labored. I cracked one of his ribs and he screamed.

Odessa's eyes went wide at his words, but I'd heard enough. Anyone who justifies hurting other by following orders isn't someone I wanted to extend my mercy to.

The last bone I broke was the one that held his head in place. I twisted it right off, and he hung in a heap of his own skin, lifeless and smelling of ash.

"What did you do that for? I wasn't done asking him questions!" Odessa stomped off, down the wide opening.

"Well, I was." I went after her, even though I said I wouldn't. She could call me a liar all she wanted to and call my bluff, I didn't care. Waking up knowing she had left, just like I'd been left before gutted something in me. She had a hold on me that I couldn't push away no matter how angry she'd made me. "You could at least give me my pack back."

"No," she said, not bothering to look at me. "I thought you weren't going to follow me."

"I changed my mind."

"Lies, again," she said narrowing her eyes at me. "That's all you have right? Lies and walls for me to climb to even get to know you? When are you going to tell me anything real about yourself, Dex?"

I stared at her and opened my mouth, only to close it again.

"That's what I thought."

She continued on, her anger at me palpable. I wasn't so thrilled with her either, but we were both going to the same place. The end of this fucking maze. Might as well follow the person who has the food.

"What do you want to know?" I asked after a few moments had passed.

She sighed, "Anything real."

"Okay."

"Okay?"

"My favorite color is green. Like a forest."

"A forest? You've actually seen a forest?"

Shit.

"Yeah, before I came to the city."

"How did you get access to the city?"

And there it was. The question I knew would inevitably pop up, and the one I had adamantly avoided. While my accent usually gave me away, I dodged it by telling them a version of the truth— that I'd been allowed to come here due to my family. Usually that was enough of an answer to satiate people's curiosity. But I knew Odessa would want to know more. She deserved to know more, but I couldn't give her that. Not yet. Not until we were at the finish line and out of here safely. Only then could I feel comfortable revealing my most inner secrets.

"It's a long story," I said hoping that would buy me some time.

"Yeah, well it looks like we have some time," she quipped.

"I don't talk about this, Odessa. It's private for a reason, and I'd hate to put you in a dangerous position."

"More dangerous than the one we're in right now?"

I was silent. If she knew the truth, it would put her in a world of trouble. And while I was angry as hell at her for walking away from me, I couldn't do that to her. The burden was mine and mine alone to carry.

"Let's just say, you're better off not knowing."

"Fine. So, your favorite color is green. Anything else?"

"I like to sing,"

That caught her by surprise. She glanced over at me with a tilt to her head that I'd come to know as her interest being piqued.

"Like what?"

"Like songs."

She gave me a heavy sigh. "Fucking hell, getting you to open up is harder than opening a pickle jar."

"Yeah, well, opening up in the past hasn't served me all that well. Especially when I entrust pieces of myself to someone who's just going to up and leave." Maybe that was cruel, but it was the truth.

She gaped at me but then schooled her features back into neutral. Like she didn't care at all. She might like calling me a liar, but she was one too. And she was lying to herself.

"Yeah, okay, Dex. I left. I walked away because you scare me on so many levels that I don't know what to do with. But I'm not like you. Everything I feel? Everything I am, is so close to the surface. My emotions and my thoughts spill out of me easily. I don't know how to stuff all that I am into a little box like you do."

"Well, then you're lucky that you've never experienced the type of pain that makes you want to hide who you are from the world. To know that as much as you might want to trust some-one, your track record shows that you'd be a fool to try again."

"You're right. I haven't experienced that. But I also know that without trust, you can't have a relationship. And this fucked up place breeds distrust. How am I supposed to trust that you won't turn on me the second we get close to the finish line?"

"I guess you can't. If my actions haven't convinced you otherwise, I don't know what else to tell you," I said feeling every bit as bitter as the words I spat out.

As we walked, the tunnel became narrower. I had to duck down just to keep from hitting the ceiling.

The tunnel curved and opened up into a large expanse. There was a narrow bridge made of rock that had several chunks missing from it. A sheer drop awaited us on either side. To go forward, we would have to jump and hope we cleared with enough space to make it to the next piece. On the opposite end there was a tunnel that was glowing with a warm amber light. A part of me hoped that maybe, just fucking maybe, that tunnel led to the end, and we could be out of here.

"Shit," Odessa said, looking out across the area.

"We can do this. We've come this far."

"Right," she said her voice shook as she looked down into the black cavernous space below. Her toe skirting the edge in trepidation.

"We'll have to take it at a run," I said, eyeing the largest gap that sat between us and the other side as I backed up.

She shook her head from side to side, swallowing hard.

"Odessa, look at me." Her eyes were fixed downwards. "Odessa," I said again, with more force. "We make it across this, and we could get out of here. Back to your family."

That got her attention. She looked at me then, with a resigned determination in her eyes, and hard set to her jaw. The parts of her face that weren't obscured by her golden mask, were covered in smudges of grime. She still had a faint mark on her cheek from the vines that had sliced into her skin. It would most likely leave a scar.

"Together?" She asked, coming over to where I stood.

I took her hand in mine. She might not trust me. She might have stomped all over my heart when she left like she did, but I'd still do what I could to get us to the end.

"Together," I agreed.

We took off at a sprint. There was just enough room for her and I to fit without falling off the edges. Our boots slapped against the rock, making the ground shake beneath us.

Please hold, I begged the bridge, hoping we would make it across in one piece.

The edge was in sight. My lungs burned as we raced towards it.

"Don't stop, and don't let go of my hand!" I called out, tightening my grip around Odessa's hand as we leapt into the air, hoping we'd make it.

CHAPTER 35
ODESSA

My stomach dropped all the way down to my toes as I felt suspended in the air for far too long. My feet narrowly grazed the edge, before I found myself dropping. Dex's grip was all that held me aloft. My free arm clawed at the rock, trying to find purchase with the tips of my fingers. He'd cleared the jump, but I hadn't

"I've got you! I won't let you go!" Dex cried, straining to pull me up.

My legs were uselessly dangling, kicking in vain to get my feet closer to the jagged wall.

"I'm slipping!" I cried out, terror gripping so tight around my chest that it was hard to breathe. "Don't drop me! Please, don't drop me!" There was nothing but an inky black void

"Odessa, I need you to stop flailing so I can pull you up. I need you to trust me. Okay?" Dex said in a firm tone. "Odessa, look at me, stop looking down. Look at me."

Black spots danced in my vision and blood whooshed in my ears as I struggled to hear what he was telling me. All I saw was my own impending death staring me right in the face.

"Odessa! Gods fucking dammit. Stop and look up at me! I've got you. You have to let me help you. Now look at me!"

Heart racing and hand slipping from Dex's grip, I looked up into his icy blue eyes feeling myself drop ever so slightly.

"I need your other hand," Dex said.

He was on his stomach reaching both hands out. One that held onto my forearm, and the other that was clawing at the rock trying to reach my free hand. With all my strength, I reached up. Our fingertips brushed together briefly before they slipped apart. I felt tears leaking from my eyes and a whimper escaped my throat.

"One more time, please, Odessa. I'm not going to let go, but I need you to try again."

I reached up and felt my hand clasp tightly into his.

"Good! Now I'm going to pull you up. Don't take your eyes off me," he said.

His jaw flexed and his muscles contracted as he pulled me back from certain death. As I went up over the edge, my hands were able to find purchase on the ground. He grabbed me by my thighs bringing the rest of me onto the narrow bridge. My heart was racing a million miles a minute, and my breathing was coming in sharp, short pants.

Sweat drenched the back of Dex's jumpsuit as he collapsed next to me.

"You believe me yet?" He asked sounding just as out of breath as I felt.

I looked over at him and saw the evidence of his actions laid out before me. If he really did want me dead before the end of these games, he could have just let me fall.

"Thank you," I said. "Really."

We stood carefully and made it the rest of the way across. There were only three more jumps that were far less distance than the first one. By the time we reached the opening of the tunnel we were dripping with sweat and breathing hard, but we'd made it. Barely.

Good job... Kage's voice chirped in my head.

I glowered at the interruption. It was just a reminder that we weren't alone. Not truly. And I still had no idea what the god's intentions were. He said it was to see me win, but what he got out of it, wasn't clear.

The tunnel sloped down and opened into a wider breadth. Up ahead, I could see where there were several other paths all colliding into this one. Only it wasn't empty. There, slumped against the wall was Reed.

I stopped in my tracks, trying to discern if he was sleeping, or if he was dead.

From how far away we were, there was no telling for sure.

Dex motioned that we stay quiet, and I nodded my agreement. My steps were deliberately taken, trying to make the least amount of noise as possible.

The closer we got, the more details I was able to take in. The light coming from the crooked sconces full of fire, illuminated just how burned Reed had gotten. It stretched the length of his arm, chest and entire face. And then he took a visible breath.

Dex's hands balled into two fists as he laid eyes on the person who'd left us for dead.

I shook my head back and forth, but that power inside me roared to life, flooding my system with the need for blood. For vengeance.

I wondered if Dex was feeling it too.

From the murderous tilt to his head and wild gleam in his eyes, I would venture to say he was.

He kicked Reed in the boot, and Reed startled awake.

"Surprised to see us?" Dex asked. Those golden horns on his mask gleamed down at Reed as he scrambled to stand.

"Fuck this," Reed said, trying to use his power to fly away.

"I don't fucking think so," Dex said, extending his hand and exerting his power all the way down to Reed's bones. It stopped him cold. It was like watching someone become paralyzed right before your eyes.

Reed's eyes looked panicked as he realized his fate had been sealed.

"Put him down," a voice called from down the tunnel.

Marcela.

She emerged from the shadows and that bloodlust that had been churning inside of my gut, sparked to a tangible, burning rage that demanded to be unleashed.

Marcela had the mask I needed, and I wouldn't be letting her get away this time.

"There's nothing you can do with that mask, but heal, Marcela," I called out.

"See that's what's so funny," she said walking towards me. The last time we had seen her, she'd run from us, too afraid of the deadly confrontation, but something had changed in her. It reminded me of how unhinged The Pyro had seemed right before he died. She had that same menacing smile and unsettling air about her that he did. Her wine-red hair looked to be standing on edge with static electricity as she moved. "I thought this mask could only heal, but it turns out it can do so much more than that."

Her arm extended and I felt a stabbing, searing pain deep in my gut. I crumpled to my knees in pure agony.

"I said drop him, or I'll yank her guts out."

Dex snapped his head in our direction and saw my writhing on the floor. My intestines felt as if they were being twisted and pulled. The pain stole my breath away. "Make it stop!" I cried out. It hurt like nothing I'd ever felt before.

One minute, Reed was frozen in place, and the next, Dex had released him.

"Get your fucking power off her now, or I swear to all the gods I'll —"

"You'll what?" Marcela's violet-colored eyes flashed as her head tilted. She still had a hold on me.

Fight back, Odessa. Kage's voice urged me.

My power surged, but the pain was unbearable. I couldn't take it.

Fight back! Come on!

With a guttural scream I sent my power slamming right into her like she did to me. It punctured her chest and began ripping her skin from her flesh.

"Fuck!!" Marcela cried. Her face twisted as blood sprayed from her open wound. It stopped her from ripping at my insides. And my power increased, making me stronger and more in control. I sent my shadows into her as I stood gripping my sore stomach. The shadows kept slicing at her skin. And then Dex, looking like death incarnate, turned all his powers at her. It started with her paralysis, then morphed into a torrent of water that he shoved down her open throat, drowning her where she stood. Her throat struggled and gurgled, but she couldn't move, couldn't fight back. And a dark little part of me was reveling in it. As my shadows wrapped around her body, her feet began to turn into stone. There was so much power flying around us that it started ripping her apart at the seams until there was nothing, but her mask left.

I dusted myself off and walked over to where her mask lay and picked it up. It felt heavy in my hands, but now I held the key to saving my mother. I just had to get out of here. I fit neatly into the backpack, joining the other masks that Dex had collected. My fingers ran along their edges, feeling the vibration of their collective power.

When I turned back around, Dex was rushing over at a sprint.

He gripped my arms, looking me over. "Are you hurt?"

I shook my head no. "I'm fine."

He brought his lips down to mine in a fierce kiss. "I thought she was going to kill you," he said, voice tight as he pressed his forehead against mine.

"I'm okay," I reassured him again. "I thought she was going to kill me too."

With everything going on, I hadn't even noticed that Reed had taken off running.

"Where did that little shit go?" Dex asked.

"I don't—"

A rumble from down the middle tunnel erupted and a

cloud of dust and smoke filled the space as chunks of ceiling came crashing down.

It seemed we had an answer.

In his haste, Reed had run right into a trap. And we were now right in its path.

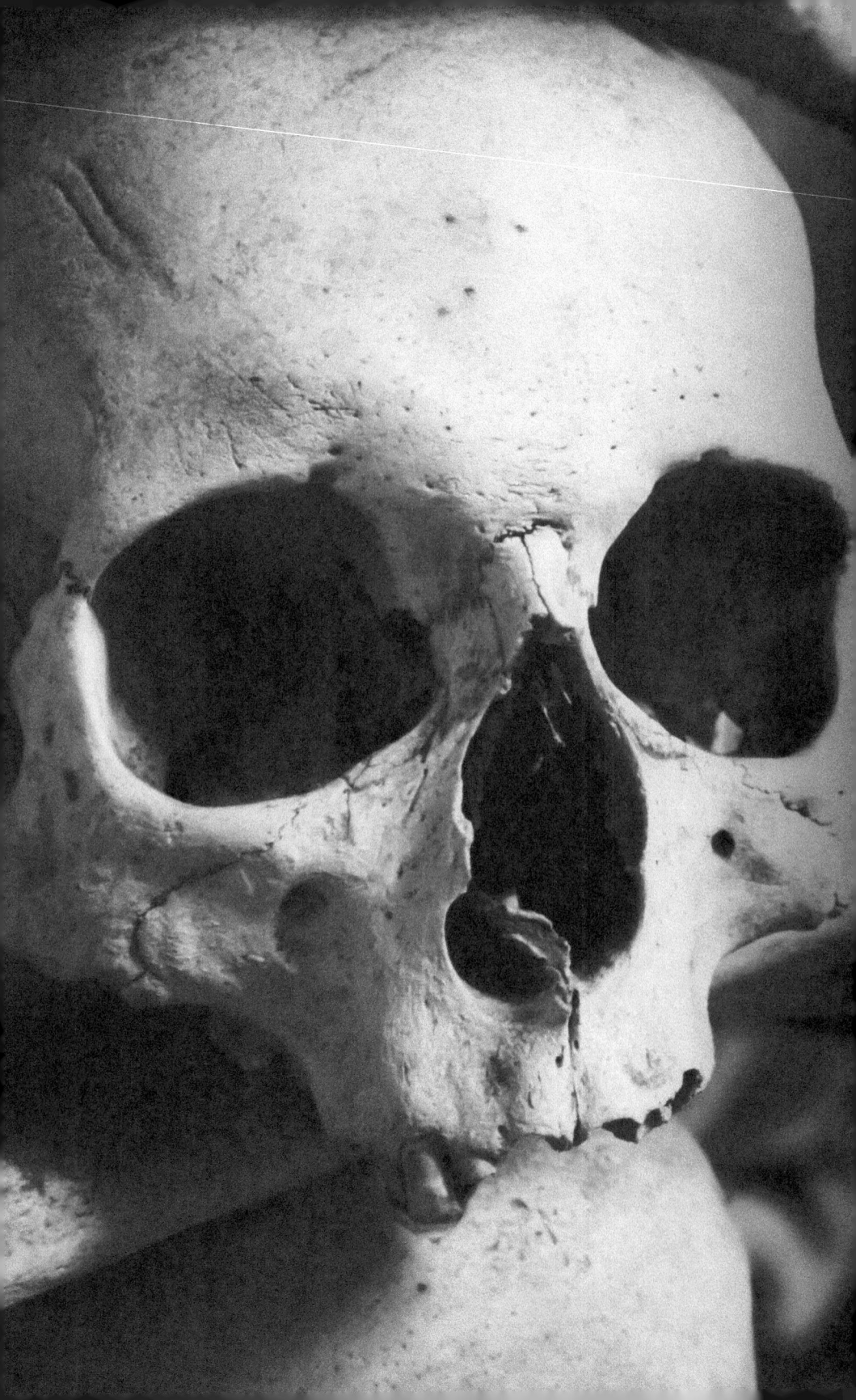

CHAPTER 36
DEX

A large boulder came careening straight at us. We broke apart just in time. My body slammed into the wall behind me as I avoided being crushed to death, but the boulder began to roll towards Odessa.

"Move!" I called out with panic in my chest.

She tucked and rolled out of the way narrowly missing being crushed to death.

The dust continued to kick up making it difficult to see as boulder after boulder fell from above. It shook the ground with each one that came careening down. Fuck Reed for tripping this motherfucking trap.

I hoped one of them crushed him until he was nothing but dust. A whisper of what he once was for putting us in danger twice.

My body moved. Legs pumping and adrenaline coursing through every nerve inside me. I couldn't see where Odessa was. Couldn't tell where the boulders were coming from.

"Odessa!" I called out, but all I heard in response was the sound of rock hitting ground. Where was she?

In the cloud of dust, a shining red light began to emanate from just ahead.

With everything in me, I knew instinctively that it was a shining beacon to the end. We were so fucking close.

A male guttural scream pierced my ears sounding like Reed had just gotten what was coming to him. I wish I could have seen it happen. Or even better, been the one to do it. But I could take the satisfaction of knowing he wouldn't be walking out of here with the grand prize.

Only a few more steps and I'd make it, but Odessa wasn't with me.

I couldn't make it to the finish line without knowing that she was okay. Turning around, I headed back. My body hit a few of the fallen boulders, knocking the wind out of me.

The dust had begun to settle and the boulders had stopped falling, but I still couldn't see where Odessa was.

It wasn't until it cleared that I found her unconscious, with blood seeping out from a wound in her head.

"Oh, fuck!" I cried, running straight to her.

She'd been hit by a smaller piece of rock, but it had knocked her out cold. Thankfully she was still breathing. I grabbed at the backpack and found the healing mask. I yanked my mask off and put on the healer, feeling its magick settle into my bones.

"Hold on, I'm going to fix you up. Good as new," I promised, finding that spark within me. It flowed into her, stitching her up and fixing the pulsating head injury she'd sustained. The healer's mask allowed me to see where exactly she needed that power, and I gladly poured what I could into her, until finally her eyelashes fluttered, and her brown eyes locked onto mine.

"What happened?" She asked, looking around.

"You got knocked out. Do you think you can stand?"

She licked her dust covered lips and nodded her head.

"Does anything still hurt?" I asked as I helped her to stand.

"No, I just feel off. Like I'm missing a chunk of time."

She wobbled a little as she got her bearings but then righted herself. I kept my hands around her waist just in case though.

"That was a close call," she said, looking down to where she'd just been laying.

"Too fucking close. You think you can stop trying to die on me?" I asked.

She gave me a half-hearted smile and then froze. "Is that—"

I looked over my shoulder to see what she was looking at. "The end? Yeah."

"And you could have gone for it?"

"I couldn't leave you here," I answered.

Her eyes shone with shimmering unshed tears as she took in my words. "You really are something, Dex."

"So, does that mean you trust me yet?" I joked.

But the look she gave me was serious. "I think I do," she said.

"You ready to finish this thing?" I asked.

"Absolutely."

I took her hand in mine, and we walked together towards that glowing beacon of hope.

"What's the first thing you're doing once we get out of here?" I asked as we sidestepped the fallen boulders.

"Taking a long hot shower. Gods, I miss running water. Oh

no! I think I changed my mind— I'm going to stuff my face with something other than fucking granola. Cake! No, cheese! Warm melted cheese and a crust of bread. If I never have to eat granola again, I'll be one happy woman."

"Agreed."

Reed's crumpled body lay crushed. All that was left were his two legs that were sticking out from underneath, reminding me of some children's story I'd heard of once.

I kicked his black boot with the toe of mine and spat on his still body as we passed by.

"Here let me help you up," I said, having Odessa go up and around a particularly difficult few pieces of rubble.

"Thank you," she said sounding giddy. "I can't believe we made it."

"I can."

"Oh yeah?"

"Yeah, there's no way it wasn't going to be you and me at the end of this thing."

"Well, I'm glad one of us knew it. You could have at least clued me in though," she teases. "What's the first thing you're going to do when we get out?"

"I think I'm going to—"

A loud crack came right from above. A stray boulder.

One second, I was holding Odessa, and the next I found myself pushing her out of the way. Feeling the moment the rock made impact with my body and darkness enveloped me.

CHAPTER 37
ODESSA

I tumbled over my own feet as Dex pushed me down. My body hit the ground hard and then I heard a sickening sound that struck fear into my very soul.

"Dex!" I cried out.

But when I sat up, I saw with sickening certainty that he had been crushed.

My hands reached out and shook his arm that was sticking out at an odd angle.

"Dex?" I didn't know why I was shaking him like he would wake up. Logically, I knew he was gone. He'd pushed me out of the way to save me, and by doing so, he'd sacrificed himself. I couldn't see. I couldn't breathe.

Tears spilled over my eyes. Snot gathered at the tip of my nose dripping down my lips and chin.

"Dex, wake up," I pleaded.

We were going to make it. The end was right fucking there.

All red and gleaming and happy. After everything we went through to get here, how could it end up like this?

I had just begun to allow myself to believe we would make it out together. I'd decided to end it with Theo. When Dex had asked me what's the first thing I wanted to do, that's what came to my mind. To run into the arms of my family, save my maman, and tell Theo that it was over. But I'd deflected, not wanting Dex to know how much I was feeling for him. And now he'd never know.

I don't know how long I sat there. It was long enough that his skin had gone cold and his muscles went rigid.

It took everything in me to pick myself off the floor.

I was the only contestant left, and it was time to go home.

Feet feeling unsteady, I dragged myself step by step until those gleaming letters were right in front of me. I'd made it, but I wasn't the same person I'd been before this game began. I felt broken and I didn't know if I'd ever feel alright again. I may have won the games, but at what cost? My hand pressed firmly against the glowing letters while Dex's lifeless body laid mere feet away from me. Tears clung to my cheeks as a large crack formed in the wall. The letters marking the end split in half and the crack continued to climb up to the ceiling before the stone wall turned to ash right in front of me.

As the debris settled, I saw a dark pair of black boots appear, staggering towards me. A guard perhaps. I blinked hard, feeling the grit of dirt against my eyes and fell to my knees at what I saw.

It was Dex.

No, he was far too resplendent to be Dex. This man resembled him but somehow was more.

More heartbreakingly handsome. More powerful. More everything. I glanced back where Dex's body lay, but there was nothing. Just a big rock where his broken body should have been.

"If I knew this was what it took to have you on your knees for me, I would have brought you here much sooner." The voice was nearly the same too, but deeper and more commanding.

This was the voice of a god.

My breath stilled in my chest. *A god.*

"Don't you recognize me, Odessa?"

I took in his tailored form. His shined boots and black pleated pants. He had a silver chain draping from his pocket to his buttons, and his black coat draped effortlessly across his broad shoulders and cascaded to his knees. He was painfully beautiful to look at, but there was no denying that I knew who he was intimately as soon as I looked into those icy blue eyes.

I told you not to trust him... Kage said inside my head.

"How is this possible?" I breathed out feeling my heart twist in confusion and anger. "I saw you die!" I yelled out, but Dex didn't even flinch at my ire. "I fucking mourned you!"

But he wasn't Dex, not really. In this moment of winning the games of Nocturne, I was now staring at The God of Death, creator of these wretched games. And my world turned on its head.

... To be continued.

ACKNOWLEDGMENTS

Thank you so much to you, the reader, for picking up this book and taking a chance on my work! Your support means everything to me, and I appreciate you so much. You're the reason I'm able to keep writing, and for that I am eternally thankful. I had a blast writing this world and these characters, and hope you enjoyed it too.

To my husband and kids, I appreciate how much you cheer me on in this crazy job of mine. Letting me drag you around to bookstores and book signings so I can live my dream of being an author. I love you so much.

I also want to thank Halla, Drea, TC, and Nika for reading this book while it was still being developed. Your feedback has been invaluable, and I appreciate the time you took to go through my words, giving me advice, and building up my self-esteem when I was at my lowest.

To Heather, Kata, Christina, and JB, who have been some of my biggest supporters. You have no idea how much your tags and shares have meant to me and helped me keep going.

And finally, to my friends for keeping me grounded and for entertaining my random ramblings and wild ideas. I'm so grateful to have you in my life.

ALSO BY DAKOTA WILDE

The Kildale Academy Series

Hell House

Hell House Halloween

Queens of Hell House

Reign of Hell House

Nightmare Acres Series

Hallows Fright

Nightmare Acres

The Nocturne Abyss Duet

The Nocturne Abyss

Standalones

My Teacher's Dirty Secret

Feed the Birds: A Dark Gothic Mary Poppins Reimagining

Truth or Dare: A Dark Stalker Romance

The Forbidden Muse

You can follow Dakota Wilde on:

Tik Tok: https://vm.tiktok.com/TTPdBkpnhS/

Instagram: www.instagram.com/DakotaWildeAuthor

Facebook: www.facebook.com/DakotaWildeAuthor

Facebook Group to Discuss Books: Dakota Wilde's Hellions

Newsletter: https://dashboard.mailerlite.com/forms/63663/56650332742092456/share

About the Author

Dakota Wilde is a best-selling author known for her captivating romance novels that delve into compelling characters and tantalizing story lines. Dakota's writing weaves together intense emotions, thrilling suspense, and steamy romance that leaves readers craving more. She loves to read, write, and shop at bookstores. She's a wife and mom to three awesome kids and she drinks way too much coffee.